To Maddi

Monkey See,
Monkey Die

Chapter 1

"Whenever you observe an animal closely, you feel as if a human being sitting inside were making fun of you."

—Elias Canetti, *The Human Province*

Jessie? I'm sorry for calling so early. I know I probably woke you. But I don't have your cell phone number, only your home number. And I wanted to make sure I got hold of you before you left for the day."

What a lot of words to be hit with at—what time was it? I forced my eyes open long enough to look at the alarm clock next to my bed.

Five-thirty. In the *morning*.

"I'm sorry, who is this?" I asked groggily.

Whoever had dragged me out of my sleep at this ridiculous hour certainly sounded as if she knew who I was. The problem was, I had no idea who *she* was. And given the fact that only seconds before I had been lost in a wonderful dream that starred both Brad Pitt *and* George Clooney, I wasn't exactly in the mood to play guessing games.

"Erin Walsh," the called replied breathlessly. "Remember me? From vet school?"

It took me a few seconds to connect the name with my years at Cornell University's veterinary college. More than a decade had passed since I'd been a student there. But slowly, through the thick wad of tissue paper still wrapped around my brain, I managed to attach a face to the name. An entire identity, in fact.

"Sure, I remember you, Erin," I finally said, though my mouth still felt as if it was coated with glue. "You and I crammed for the Neuroanatomy final together, right? I seem to remember the two of us pulling an all-nighter in the basement of the vet school library. Didn't we keep ourselves awake by eating a different candy bar from one of the vending machines every hour...?"

"That's right. Jessie, the reason I'm calling—"

"You married somebody else who was in our class, didn't you? Bill or Brad..."

"Ben Chandler," Erin corrected me. She was speaking unusually quickly. In fact, I realized that she'd sounded as if she was in a hurry ever since I'd answered the phone. "But I'm afraid I didn't call to reminisce. I need to see you. Right away. Like this morning."

The longer I talked, the more awake I became. Fortunately, I hadn't woken Nick, who was lying beside me fast asleep. The adorable man I was scheduled to marry in only four short weeks was so tangled up in the sheets, you'd have thought he'd been dreaming about alligator wrestling. Personally, I'd take the Brad Pitt–George Clooney dream any day.

By this point, my head was clear enough for me to do some calculations. I hadn't spoken to Erin Walsh in more than five years. If I remembered correctly, the last time I'd seen her was at my five-year Cornell reunion. She and Ben had both glowed like fluorescent light bulbs as they chattered away about their upcoming trip to Barbados to celebrate their wedding anniversary and their plans to open a practice together as soon as they got back.

"What's the hurry?" I asked.

"Believe me, Jessie, I wouldn't be doing this if it wasn't really important. Please say you'll meet me this morning. It's crucial that I talk to somebody like you!"

Somebody like me? What did *that* mean?

"Where are you?" I asked, still confused.

"On Long Island." She was still talking way too fast. "It's a long story, but Ben and I have been living in Bay Village for the past couple of years. I can meet you anywhere. Just name the time and place. A diner, a street corner . . . but the sooner, the better."

Mentally I ran through the calls I had scheduled for that morning. My first appointment was a cat spay surgery in Arborhurst at eight o'clock. Given the fact that it was still practically the middle of the night, that gave me plenty of time to meet Erin for breakfast.

"How about six-thirty at the Spartan Diner?" I suggested. "It's in Niamogue, right on Route 437."

"I know where it is. I'll be there. And Jess? Don't say anything about this to anybody, okay?"

"Erin," I asked, struck by the bizarreness of this entire conversation, "is everything okay?"

"That's the thing, Jessie," she replied with a nervous laugh. "I don't think it is."

"Can you at least give me an idea of what all this is—?"

She never answered my question. In fact, she'd already hung up.

With a loud sigh, I dragged myself out of bed and embarked on my morning pilgrimage to worship at the feet of Mr. Coffee. As usual, my two dogs, Max and Lou, were already running at full throttle, scampering around my feet with much more energy than any living being should exhibit before the sun has come up.

Max, my Westie, had an excuse, since he's a terrier. Terriers are like firefighters: They snap awake with ridiculous amounts of adrenaline rushing through their bodies. Then again, Max differs from firefighters in that his butt is in constant motion. It seems as if he never stops wagging his tail—even though it's little more than a stub, courtesy of the vile people who were his previous owners.

As for Lou, a Dalmatian, let's just say he's a follower by nature. Of course, the fact that he also has a heartbreaking past, one that left him with only one eye, may also be part of the reason.

My two cats, Catherine the Great and Tinkerbell, were also coming to life, stretching and yawning. Like my dogs, they were rescued from careless owners—in Tink's case, a wretch who callously left a box of kittens on the university campus where Nick attends law school.

As for Prometheus, he was already wide awake.

He's always up with the birds, mainly because he is one. A gorgeous blue and gold macaw, in fact, with feathers as bright as the jars of paint in a kindergarten classroom. My Jackson's chameleon, Leilani, was also awake, staring at me from inside her glass tank with the eye that was on the side of her head facing me.

But I was still too busy ruminating about my strange phone call from Erin to pay much attention to any of my pets.

What's with all this cloak-and-dagger nonsense? I wondered as I shuffled through the living room.

My old vet school buddy had sounded as if she was smack in the middle of a drama. And frankly, the last thing I wanted was to be recruited for a supporting role.

Yawning loudly, I opened the front door of my cottage and let Max and Lou out. I hoped this would turn out to be one of those mornings when they actually came back inside without me having to run around like a wild woman, chasing them down. Given the wake-up call I'd just gotten, I wasn't in the mood to bodily drag two unruly canines away from sniffing every molecule within fifty yards. Not that it wasn't great living in the former gardener's cottage on a huge estate. I truly appreciated the fact that the members of my menagerie had as much room to run around as they could possibly desire. It was just that sometimes, like now, I wished they'd do a little less of it.

Once my doggies and I were back inside, I took a minute to check everybody's water bowl and get Mr. Coffee perking away as energetically as if he, too, was a terrier. Then I drifted into the bathroom and confronted the bedraggled being staring back at me from the mirror.

The image before me was that of a half-asleep woman in her mid-thirties with dull green eyes. Disheveled hair in a shade I prefer to call dark blond but which would have also answered to the name dirty blond hung down to the poor unfortunate creature's shoulders.

The sight would have been frightening if it hadn't been the exact same one I encountered every morning of my life.

I did my best to breathe life into the specter standing before me with the aid of a hairbrush, a toothbrush, and a bracing splash of cold water. It was at that point I realized I had to go back into the bedroom to retrieve some clothes. Diners may have low standards when it comes to dress codes, but even the Spartan wasn't likely to serve someone wearing nothing but a faded Led Zeppelin T-shirt and a frayed pair of pink cotton underpants.

I tiptoed into the dark room as if I was imitating a burglar in a Looney Tunes cartoon—then promptly managed to exhibit the same level of wackiness by colliding with the dresser and sending Nick's cell phone clattering to the floor.

"Jess?" he mumbled as one eye appeared from beneath the sheet. The way he was peering at me reminded me of Leilani. "What's going on?"

"Nothing," I assured him, whispering even though it was obvious I'd already done the one thing I'd tried not to do: wake him up. "Go back to sleep."

Tinkerbell interpreted the fact that conversation

was going on to mean that a new day in the Popper-Burby household had officially begun. My sleek orange cat with both the looks and the self-assuredness of a tiger vaulted onto the bed, then padded up onto Nick's stomach as if she was a diva strutting onto a stage. Catherine the Great—better known as Cat—looked on enviously, as if remembering her pre-arthritic days when she, too, was capable of leaping onto a bed in a single bound.

"What time is it?" Nick asked, his question dissolving into a loud yawn.

You don't want to know. "Five-forty."

He immediately sat up, meanwhile cradling Tink in both hands. No doubt he'd spotted a glaring contradiction between the fact that I was up and around at such an obscene hour and my claim that nothing was going on.

"Are you all right?" He was doing a better job of enunciating by now, a sign that I'd not only woken him up, I'd woken him up enough that he was probably going to find it impossible to go back to sleep.

"I'm fine," I insisted. "I'm just up extra early because I'm going to meet a friend for breakfast."

I wasn't sure why I didn't mention that this friend was someone I hadn't spoken to in ages—or that she'd been strangely mysterious about her sudden need for a sunrise chat.

I guess I didn't want him to worry. Or maybe I was just feeling foolish now that the tissue paper had been removed from my brain and I realized how ridiculous this whole scenario sounded.

"Go back to sleep," I urged again, by now feeling

guilty on top of feeling silly. After all, Nick had just started a summer internship at a Long Island law firm and he was still working on making a good impression. Certainly that meant showing up without bags the size of carry-ons under one's eyes, not to mention managing to get through the entire workday without taking a nap. "I'll be out of here as soon as I throw on some clothes and grab a cup of coffee."

"Nah, I'll get up," he said.

Still cradling Tink, he threw back the sheet. As soon as he did, I realized there was no way the Spartan Diner would have been willing to serve *him*. In fact, the sight of him lying there in the snarl of sheets in nothing but his birthday suit produced in me the sudden impulse to join him. Not so I could grab a little more shut-eye either.

Dang, I thought, remembering my promise to Erin. Why on earth did I agree to rush out of the house in the dead of night for a rendezvous with someone I haven't even had an e-mail from in years?

But it was too late. I'd told her I'd meet her, and I was a woman of my word.

Even if, at the moment, I desperately wished that word had been *no*.

• • •

I did tell Erin to meet me at the Spartan Diner, didn't I? I wondered crossly as I sat alone at a corner booth, nursing the second cup of coffee the waitress had poured since I'd arrived—my third cup of the day.

Glancing at my watch, I saw it was five minutes past seven. That meant I'd already spent thirty-five minutes waiting, meanwhile consuming so much caffeine that I was probably going to set a record later that morning by performing one of the fastest spays in veterinary history.

That is, assuming I manage to get out of here in time for my eight o'clock appointment, I thought, forcing down another sip of joe. The way things are going, my mysterious meeting with my long-lost friend from vet school will have to be pretty darned short if I'm going to get to Arborhurst on time.

"Ready for a refill?" the waitress asked, hovering around me with a pot of coffee in her hand and a sympathetic look on her face. She was wearing a pink dress and a white apron that made her look like an extra in a rerun of *That '70's Show*. She even had her name, Donna Marie, embroidered on the left side of her chest.

"Thanks, I'm fine."

At that hour, only a few people were out and about, guzzling coffee at a diner in preparation for the day ahead. It appeared that even the truck drivers were still nestled all snug in their beds. That meant I'd become an object of concern, if not actual pity, in my waitress's eyes.

To demonstrate that I wasn't going to take being stood up lying down, I whipped out my cell phone to give Erin a call. It wasn't until I was scrolling through the list of received calls that I remembered she'd called me on my landline, not on my cell phone. Which meant I didn't even have her number.

Great, I thought, grimacing as I tossed my phone back into my purse. I can't even check to make sure there was no confusion about the correct time and place.

I could be in bed right now, I thought, grouchier than ever. With Nick. *Naked* Nick.

Donna Marie seemed relieved when I finally ordered some solid food, in the form of a toasted English muffin. Once she placed it in front of me, I ate it at a leisurely pace, hoping to make it last as long as I could. I also allowed her to refill my cup one more time.

As I chewed in slow motion, I kept my eyes fixed on the grimy window next to my booth, which afforded me a scenic view of the diner's nearly empty parking lot. I felt a lot like Max and Lou must whenever I leave them somewhere and they anxiously await my return, their ears pricked and their noses pulsating. At least I was able to keep my ears and nose under control.

Finally, at seven-thirty, I tucked a few bills underneath the salt shaker and mouthed *thank you* to Donna Marie, who I'd practically begun to think of as my second mother. Then I slid out of the booth and took off.

Something must have come up, I rationalized as I pushed open the glass door and headed back outside to the parking lot. But I was still cranky.

Whatever that something was, Erin should have called me to tell me she'd be a no-show. Even if she didn't have my cell phone number, she could have looked up the diner in the phone book or called Information. After all, she's the one who had dragged me out of bed at an hour so early that no one besides a bread baker should be up.

Not to mention the fact that she made it sound as if whatever she was so desperate to talk to me about was really, really important.

Oh, well, I told myself as I climbed into my van. I suppose there's nothing wrong with getting a head start on the day.

Besides, I figured that sooner or later I'd find out what was so pressing that Erin needed to dredge up an old friend who, as she'd so succinctly put it, was "someone like me."

• • •

I forgot all about the rendezvous that never happened as I threw myself into a busy morning of back-to-back appointments. Unlike most veterinarians, who treat dogs and cats and all their other patients in a normal office, the kind that's inside a building, I operate out of a clinic-on-wheels. A custom-built 26-foot white van, in fact, with blue letters stenciled on the door:

REIGNING CATS & DOGS
Mobile Veterinary Services
Large and Small Animals
631-555-PETS

Inside, I have everything I need to operate a practice that's as complete as one run by any ordinary veterinarian—meaning a vet who has the bad luck to be stuck indoors all day.

On this particular day, in addition to serving as my

office, my van played the role of corporate lunchroom once noontime rolled around. Since I don't have the option of buying a sandwich and a can of soda out of a vending machine, however, I usually plunder the refrigerator at home before running out the door. More often than not, my instant lunch consists of leftovers from a night or two before.

Case in point was the two-day-old moo shoo pork I'd brought along in its original cardboard container. I was shoveling it into my mouth with a plastic fork with only three tines, noticing that it contained a lot more moo shoo than pork, when my cell phone trilled.

The name of Long Island's newspaper, *Newsday*, flashed on the screen. Which meant only one thing: a call from Forrester Sloan.

Ordinarily, my reaction to hearing from Forrester is wariness. But after a long, busy morning, I was ready for a break—even if it did consist of talking to a man who for some inexplicable reason could not let go of the conviction that he and I were meant to go hand in hand into the sunset. That, of course, was supposed to occur as soon as I came to my senses and realized that he, not Nick, was my Mr. Right.

"Hey, Forrester," I answered glibly. "How's my favorite reporter?"

"I'm fine," he replied, sounding surprised by my cheerful greeting. "Unfortunately, I can't say the same for everybody."

I was about to respond with something along the lines of "Huh?" when he continued in an even more somber voice.

"Jessie," he asked, "do you by any chance know a veterinarian named Erin Walsh?"

It took me a second or two to answer. I was too busy marveling over the fact that her name was coming up *again*. In fact, I was about to comment on what a coincidence it was that he'd mentioned her, since that very morning she'd stood me up. But something in Forrester's tone kept me from venting.

"Yes, I know her," I replied cautiously.

"I thought you might," he said, his voice growing even more strained. "She lives here on Long Island, but that's not the only reason. She also went to vet school at Cornell, just like you. And if my calculations are correct, she might even have been there around the same time you were—"

"Forrester," I interrupted, "why are you suddenly interested in Erin Walsh?"

The long pause that followed caused my stomach to tighten. But that was nothing compared to the violent lurch my entire gut gave as he said, "Jessie, you'd better brace yourself. Early this morning, the police found Erin Walsh's body—she's been murdered."

Chapter 2

"Never monkey with the truth."

—Ben Bradlee

"N o!" I cried, unable to believe what Forrester was telling me. "That can't possibly be true! There has to be some mistake!"

"No mistake," he said somberly. "I'm really sorry that I'm the one to break the bad news."

"Erin is *dead*?" I couldn't believe it. A hundred questions swarmed around inside my head, all of them twisted up with at least as many denials. "But I just spoke to her a few hours ago!"

"Jessie, if there's anything I can do—wait a minute. You *spoke* to her? What did she—?"

"She was *murdered*?" I interrupted, still incredulous. "Are the police positive it's Erin? And...and even if it is, couldn't it have been an accident?"

"I'm afraid this was no accident," Forrester replied. "The cops found Erin's body this morning at around seven-thirty. The medical examiner hasn't done an autopsy yet, but it's pretty clear she was murdered. That's all they really know at this point—which brings me back to my original question. What did she say when you spoke to her this morning?"

I did some quick thinking, and decided I wasn't ready to come clean.

"Not much," I told him. "Actually, she sounded as if she was in a hurry."

"So she didn't say anything that might—?"

"Where was Erin found?" I demanded. There was no way I could bring myself to use the phrase *Erin's body.*

"In her car. It was parked at a weird angle in a residential area in Pohasset. One of those quiet streets without much traffic. Just big houses and big lawns."

Pohasset, located on the North Shore, was one of Long Island's wealthiest communities. It also happened to be only a couple of towns away from Bay Village, where Erin had told me she and her husband were living.

"What do you mean by a 'weird angle'?" I asked.

"Like she might have been drunk when she parked. Or maybe she was in a hurry." In a strained voice, he added, "Maybe she was even running away from somebody."

"Who found her?" I asked, my head spinning so hard I could barely focus on one question at a time.

"A man who lives on the street where her car was found," Forrester said. "He told the cops he'd just come out of his house and was about to get into his car to drive to work when he noticed the car and how strangely it was parked. When he went over to look inside, he saw that she was . . . he saw the condition she was in. He immediately dialed 911 on his cell."

My stomach gave a violent lurch as the scenario he was describing took shape in my mind. Erin had been killed not long after I'd talked to her. It was even possible that while I was sitting in the diner, doing ordinary things like stirring sugar into my coffee and buttering my English muffin, she had been . . .

"Even though the medical examiner hasn't done the autopsy yet, do the police have any idea how she was killed?" I choked out the words.

"It looks as if she was strangled. But Falcone said he's not going public with that until the M.E. files his report."

"You've already spoken with him?"

"That's right," he replied. "I gave him a call as soon as Norfolk Homicide faxed the press release over to *Newsday*."

Getting in touch with Lieutenant Anthony Falcone myself had been one of the first ideas that flashed into my mind when Forrester told me the horrible news. True, in the past, Norfolk County's chief of homicide had been anything but cooperative when it came to answering my questions about ongoing murder investigations. The fact that in some cases I'd turned out to be better at solving crimes than he was certainly didn't help.

Yet my feelings about the man aside, he was undoubtedly the best source of information. All things considered, I decided I could live with Falcone being much more inclined to update Forrester Sloan, a newspaper reporter who covered crime on Long Island, than a veterinarian he saw as meddling, bothersome, and just generally in the way.

"What else did he say?" I demanded. I needed more information, anything at all that would help me make sense of such incomprehensible news.

"That's about it. It's still too soon for the cops to know very much. Don't forget, all this just happened a few hours ago."

My head was swimming, even as I slowly began to wrap my mind around the fact that Erin was dead. That she had been *murdered*.

And then it occurred to me that I wasn't the only one who would be devastated.

Poor Ben! I thought, picturing her husband the way he had looked in vet school. I remembered a good-looking young man with a breezy air of self-confidence that made it hard not to like him. He and Erin had started dating sometime during our second year, then gotten married right after graduation.

The two of them had seemed so happy at our five-year reunion. I could still picture them at the welcoming cocktail party, both deliriously excited about their future, working side by side as they lived out their dream of working with animals. I remembered feeling a twinge of envy, not only that they were both so happy, but also that they were moving in the exact same direction.

And now...

"Look, Jess, I'm really sorry," Forrester said, interrupting my thoughts. "I'll let you know if I find out anything else, okay? In the meantime, call me if you need anything. My cell phone is always on."

"Thanks, Forrester." I hung up, blinking hard to hold back the tears that were fogging up my vision.

And then something else dawned on me.

During my early-morning telephone conversation with Erin, she'd sounded upset. She talked way too fast. She insisted she had to see me right away. And whatever it was she'd been so anxious to talk to me about, she explicitly told me not to say a word to anybody about our clandestine meeting.

Her final words echoed in my ears. In response to me asking point-blank if everything was okay, in a nervous voice she'd replied, *That's the thing, Jessie. I don't think it is.*

The violent gnawing in my stomach told me that whatever she was so anxious to talk to me about could well have had something to do with the reason she was murdered.

As I sat in my van, staring out the window, something else Erin had said during our phone call kept playing through my head over and over again.

It's crucial that I talk to somebody like you!

At the time, I'd wondered what she meant.

Now, given what had just happened, answering that question suddenly seemed of the utmost importance.

• • •

It's not often that I let my personal life get in the way of my work. But today had instantly turned into one of those days when I simply couldn't face a full afternoon of treating patients.

I knew there was no way I'd be able to make the

house calls I had scheduled. I couldn't even imagine being able to give my full attention to animals that needed my help, and just generally acting as if nothing were out of the ordinary. All I wanted to do was go home.

So as soon as I took a few deep breaths and determined that I would be able to concentrate enough to drive, that's exactly what I did. I seemed to recall that my next appointment wasn't until one o'clock, which gave me a little less than an hour to get into a frame of mind in which I could start contacting my clients and rescheduling them.

What I really need right now is to be alone, I thought as I neared my cottage.

Yet by the time I turned off Minnesauke Lane and began driving along the quarter-mile driveway that led to my front door, I knew the first thing I would do after I'd shared my bad news with Nick was sit down in front of my computer, track down Ben and Erin's address, and pay Ben a visit. Not only was I anxious to express my sympathy, I also wanted to talk to him about the strange conversation I'd had with his wife right before she was murdered.

It wasn't only because sharing what Erin had told me could prove helpful with the police department's investigation either. I also hoped that somehow it would give her husband a better understanding of what had happened.

In addition, I hoped that talking to him about what was going on in Erin's life, whatever it was, would help *me* understand how this terrible thing could have happened—and why Erin had been so anxious to have my help.

As I let myself into my cottage, I was so absorbed in the events of the day that I completely forgot to brace myself for the reaction I always get when I come home. Predictably, my dogs leaped around gleefully, acting as if I'd been away for years rather than hours. Max picked up his favorite possession, a pink plastic poodle that's just one in a line of identical toys that over the years has been loved to death. He gave it a few hopeful shakes, trying to entice me into tugging at the saliva-covered prize and then tossing it across the room so he could scramble after it.

Lou, meanwhile, grabbed the latest in an endless stream of tennis balls he'd owned, each one invariably becoming defuzzed from way too much gnawing combined with an overabundance of dog spit. From the impish look in his eye, I knew he was about to start playing the new game he'd recently invented. It seemed specifically designed to make life more difficult for his owner—who would be me.

The way it worked was that he would lie down next to the couch and poke the tennis ball with his nose until it rolled so far under that he couldn't reach it. The next step was to bark and whine and growl until said owner—again, *moi*—had no choice but to get down on her stomach and strain to reach under the couch, at times enlisting the aid of a ruler or a rolled-up veterinary journal, until she could retrieve it and return it to its grateful owner. Repeat as necessary. I must say, after about six or seven rounds, it got pretty tiring. For me anyway.

Prometheus, as much of a social being as the dogs, broke into an enthusiastic chorus of "Jingle Bells," meanwhile bobbing his head and stepping from side to side on his perch like a vaudeville dancer. Even the cats came out of hiding to say hello. Tinkerbell scampered in from the bedroom, while my older feline made a slower and considerably more dramatic entrance from the kitchen.

Unfortunately, I wasn't in the mood for Christmas carols—not to mention an invigorating game of either Slimeytoy or Make Your Owner Crawl Under the Furniture on Her Belly. For now, Prometheus had to settle for some cooing and feather-stroking, while my four-legged friends got a little ear-scratching and a few quick cuddles.

Once I'd done my part to make all my pets feel sufficiently loved and appreciated, I decided I needed a little love and appreciation myself. I plopped onto the couch and punched Nick's number into my cell phone.

"Do you have a minute?" I greeted him in a strained voice.

I guess he knows me pretty well because he immediately demanded, "What's wrong, Jess?"

I did my best not to lose it as I told him the terrible news. Amazingly, I actually succeeded.

"Do you want me to come home?" he asked anxiously. "I'm sure nobody would mind me taking the rest of the day off if I explained what happened."

"Thanks, but it's not necessary," I assured him. "I can manage. In fact, I'll probably be out most of the afternoon anyway. I'm going to try to track down

Erin's address so I can go see her husband. Ben was also in my class at Cornell."

"Okay. Just let me know if there's anything you need me to do."

"Thanks, Nick." At times like this, I wondered why I'd ever had even a moment's hesitation about marrying the man.

I'd barely gotten off the phone before it started to vibrate in my hand. I was so distracted that I answered without bothering to check caller ID.

As soon as I found out who was at the other end, I knew that being so hasty had been a big mistake.

"Jessica!" Dorothy Burby, Nick's mother, barked accusingly. From the way she sounded, I just assumed she was irritated that her future daughter-in-law had answered the phone and not her son, Crowned Prince of the Planet.

"Hello, Dorothy," I said as politely as I could. "How are you?"

"I'm perfectly fine," she shot back. "Why wouldn't I be?"

I'd been on the phone for less than ten seconds and I was already gritting my teeth. "If you're looking for Nick," I said evenly, "I'm afraid he's not home."

"Actually, it's you I wanted to speak to." Dorothy sounded as surprised as I was. "I wanted to ask you about the place cards."

"Place cards?" I repeated. Given how distracted I was, I couldn't quite remember what on earth place cards were, much less figure out why she was calling me about them.

"For your wedding? So your guests know where to sit?"

"Of course," I replied. "I don't know where my head is today."

Actually, I knew exactly where it was. And that happened to be someplace a lot more important than inside a box of place cards.

"You *have* given this issue some serious thought, haven't you?" Dorothy asked, sounding annoyed.

I hadn't even realized place cards were an "issue," much less one I was supposed to be thinking about. Seriously, no less.

"Of course I have, Dorothy. And I decided that the smartest thing to do was leave the whole thing entirely up to you." I surprised myself not only by how good I could be at thinking on my feet, but also by how diplomatic I could be. "After all, that's the kind of thing you're so good at."

Dorothy clearly decided to take that as a compliment. "That's true," she agreed, her tone softer. "But you need to make the final decision. After all, you *are* the bride."

Only Dorothy Burby could make that sound like an insult, I thought, trying to be amused instead of irritated. "Final decision about what?"

"About whether to go with a plastic flower stapled onto each one—I read that idea in a magazine—or simply to attach stickers printed with pictures of flowers."

It was definitely time for some more teeth-gritting. Still, I was hardly in a position to complain. My own mother had been killed in a car accident years before.

Both my parents, in fact. And putting together a wedding, I was learning, was practically a full-time job. Especially a wedding that was taking place in just four short weeks. And with me much too busy to put in the kind of time that was required, I'd had little choice but to leave most of the planning up to my future mother-in-law.

Which hardly put me in a position to question why we even needed place cards.

"How about attaching a real flower to each one?" I suggested. "And instead of stapling them, maybe they could be fastened with narrow satin ribbons threaded through the cardboard and tied in a tiny bow in front."

The silence at the other end of the line told me my idea wasn't exactly being received with enthusiasm.

"I suppose that might work," Dorothy finally said. Her tone was as icy as the swan-shaped sculpture that in my worst nightmare was the next topic she was going to bring up. "That is, if you don't mind those *real* flowers wilting halfway through the reception."

Frankly, I found the idea of a few scraggly flower petals a lot more acceptable than the plastic blossoms that were apparently part of Dorothy's image of a fantasy wedding.

"I can live with that," I answered cheerfully.

"Well, if that's what you really want..."

Now it was time for me to remain silent.

"Okay, then," Dorothy said, back to her efficient mode. "Let's move on to the next item on my list."

As soon as I learned that Dorothy had an actual list, a feeling very much like panic began to creep up on me. Even while discussing the heated controversy surrounding place cards, I hadn't forgotten there was something much more pressing—not to mention way more important—that I needed to deal with.

"For the ice sculpture that will go on the hors d'oeuvres table," Dorothy continued, "would you prefer two swans with their long, graceful necks intertwined or—"

I was actually relieved to hear someone knocking at my front door.

"I'm so sorry, Dorothy," I said, "but someone's knocking at my door. I'm afraid we'll have to talk about the ice sculpture some other time."

"But Jessica! The wedding is less than four weeks away! Surely even *you* recognize how vital it is that—"

Click.

I was still clutching my cell phone in my hand as I threw open the front door. I expected to find my landlady, Betty Vandervoort, standing there. Or maybe a delivery person from UPS or FedEx bearing one of the gifts well-wishers had been sending ever since Dorothy had sent out the wedding invitations.

But it wasn't Betty and it wasn't a delivery person. In fact, it took me a good five seconds to identify the person I suddenly found myself standing face-to-face with. There were things about her that looked so familiar, but at the same time it was like playing a game of What's Wrong with This Picture?

"Sunny?" I finally asked.

I wasn't sure I believed what I was seeing. After all, the Sunny McGee I knew usually wore only black garments that were preferably studded with metal, heavy black boots, a dozen gold studs along the edge of one ear, and at least as many silver rings on every one of her fingers, including her thumbs. She also had a streak of brilliant blue in her otherwise jet-black hair, which she wore cut short except for the bangs that seemed deliberately designed to hide her eyes.

I'd met that Sunny a few weeks earlier while investigating the murder of a friend of Betty's, an up-and-coming actor-playwright who'd been a member of her theater group. Sunflower McGee, so named because her parents had apparently developed their child-naming skills during the heady days of Flower Power, worked as a cleaning person at Theater One in Port Townsend while she mulled over what she wanted to do with her life, an increasingly relevant question now that she was embarking on her twenties.

Yet this version of Sunny looked as if she was about to be profiled in the *Wall Street Journal*. The petite young woman standing in front of me was dressed in a beige blazer, an off-white blouse, and a pair of dark tailored pants. The thumb rings, the studs, and all the other baubles that made her look like the lead singer in a punk rock band were gone. So was the blue streak. Even her bangs had been cut. In fact, they were short enough that I could easily see into a pair of dark brown eyes that at the moment happened to be clouded with anxiety.

Blinking, I asked, "What are you doing here?"

I'd barely gotten the words out before I realized I knew exactly what she was doing here. I'd arranged to meet her here and now so she could begin working for me as a sort of veterinary assistant. It was supposed to be a trial, the result of her enthusiasm over the idea of working with animals and my realization that maybe having a little help on the job wouldn't be such a bad idea.

Yet given all that had happened since five-thirty that morning, I'd completely forgotten about our plans. And I'd been too distracted by the news of Erin's death to look at my schedule beyond my last appointment of the morning.

"Today's supposed to be your first day working for me, isn't it?" I said, answering my own question.

"That's right!" she replied. Nervously, she added, "You haven't changed your mind, have you? About trying this arrangement for a while?"

"Not at all." I hesitated. "It's just that this has turned out to be kind of a complicated day."

As if wanting to prove my point, at that moment my two canines came shooting out of nowhere. They practically fell over each other as they made a beeline for Sunny, barking and leaping and just generally acting as if they'd both been in solitary confinement for months and were finally being let out to commune with the outside world.

"Down, Max!" I cried. "Lou, please stop slobbering all over poor Sunny!"

"No, it's great!" she insisted, laughing. "I wasn't exaggerating when I said I really love animals."

Even the ones that seem determined to make their owner look really bad, I wondered, since her profession is largely based upon being able to handle said creatures?

"Sunny, I'm sorry," I said. "But I don't think—"

"Oh, my gosh, is that a blue-and-gold macaw?" Without waiting for an answer, she dashed across the living room toward Prometheus's cage. "Hey, pretty birdy!" she cooed before I had a chance to answer her question. "Who's the pretty birdy?"

It was as if she was reading from a script—one her fellow actor had already memorized.

"*Awk!* Prometheus is the pretty birdy!" my less-than-modest bird cawed happily. "I wanna give you my love!"

I stiffened, hoping that Sunny would understand that Prometheus wasn't being fresh. He just happened to be one of the few birds on the planet that knew all the lyrics to every Led Zeppelin song, thanks to Nick's obsession with classic rock. I didn't want my brand-new employee filing a sexual harassment suit against me. Or my cheeky bird.

Fortunately, Tinkerbell chose that moment to come prancing out of the bedroom.

"You have a cat too!" Sunny cried gleefully. "*Two* cats!" she added as Catherine the Great padded out of the kitchen to see what all the hubbub was about.

Max, however, wasn't about to share the attentions of this newcomer, someone he seemed to sense might be up for a rollicking game of Slimeytoy. He scampered across the room, grabbed his favorite pink plastic poodle, and pranced back in our direction with the slimy object of his affections dangling from his mouth. As he did, he chomped on it just enough that it let out its usual ear-splitting squeals. He seemed to be saying, *Golly, who wants to hang out with a bunch of boring cats when you could be playing tug-of-war with a saliva-covered piece of rubbery plastic with its head half ripped off?*

Apparently he was right. Blazer and all, Sunny crouched down and began tugging on Max's beloved toy. When he finally released it, she showed an impressive aptitude for learning new games by hurling it across the room and watching gleefully as both he and Lou dashed after it.

It might have been charming at some other time. But not today. Not when all I wanted was to get over to Ben Chandler's house.

Suddenly I had a brainstorm. Sunny's first assignment as my brand-new assistant would be clearing my calendar for the rest of the day. In fact, as soon as I showed her how to access both my afternoon's schedule and the list of client phone numbers stored in my BlackBerry, I would be free to rush off to talk to Erin's husband. Once I took five minutes to go online and figure out where he lived, of course.

"Come to think of it," I told her, "the fact that this is such a complicated day makes it the perfect time for you to get started. How would you feel about rescheduling all my afternoon appointments?"

"I could do that," she replied earnestly. "In fact, organizing happens to be something I'm really good at."

I'd just set her up on the couch with my BlackBerry and was about to head for my computer when there was another knock at the door.

I literally threw my hands up into the air. *What now?* I thought, trying to remember if I even *knew* anybody else who was likely to be available for paying unexpected social calls in the middle of a weekday.

It turned out that I did.

"Betty!" I cried as I opened the door.

This time, it *was* my landlady. The trim, lithe woman with a smooth white pageboy and eyes the color of sapphires standing on my doorstep owned the estate I lived on. Betty Vandervoort also resided in the mansion that I always referred to as the Big House. It had originally been built by the prosperous grandson of Major Benjamin Tallmadge, a historic figure who remained a minor celebrity in the area. During the Revolutionary War, he and several other members of what was known as the Culper Spy Ring had supplied George Washington with critical information about the British military's whereabouts.

But while Betty had started out as my landlady, she quickly graduated to friend. Even though she had said good-bye to seventy long before—and for all I knew had already said hello to eighty—the difference in our ages rarely got in the way. In fact, I had developed a tremendous appreciation for both the worldliness and the wisdom she'd acquired during her long and colorful life, often calling upon both for guidance as I stumbled through my own.

Today, she wasn't alone. The furry tan clutch purse tucked under her arm was actually Frederick, a spirited wire-haired dachshund that had begun his life as Winston's pride and joy. But as soon as Betty invited the two of them to move in, she began treating him like her own pet—or, to be more accurate, like her own child.

As usual, the arrival of another canine caused my two beasts to react as if their favorite rock star had just entered the building. Max began yapping and jumping up on Betty, desperate to sniff Frederick. Lou wagged his tail so hard he looked as if he was trying to master the hokeypokey. Frederick, meanwhile, did some pretty serious barking and butt swinging of his own, even though he was suspended four feet above the ground. Once Betty put him on the floor, the three dogs sniffed and shoved and slid around with all the dignity of the Three Stooges.

"I'm afraid I'm here to ask a favor," Betty said once all the excitement died down. She peered inside my cottage, her eyes lighting on Sunny, who was camped out on the couch with the two feline members of my menagerie. "This isn't a bad time, is it?"

If only you knew, I thought. But I didn't want to delay getting over to Ben's any longer by launching into a long explanation of what had gone on so far that day. Especially when I knew there would be plenty of time later on to tell Betty all about the horrific events that had occurred since 5:30 A.M.

"I'm sorry, Betty, but I'm about to run out," I replied. "Something really important has come up." When I saw the disappointed look on her face, I added, "But I guess I can spare a couple of minutes."

I took a moment to introduce Betty and Sunny to each other and explain the role each of them played in my life. As soon as the two women had exchanged hellos, Betty turned back to me.

"Jessica," she said somberly, "I know this is probably a huge imposition, but is there any chance you and

Nick would be willing to house-sit—and, well, dog-sit—while Winston and I are on our honeymoon?"

"What? You mean you've finally decided on a destination?" The two of them had been so busy planning the wedding that had taken place outside in the garden just a few weeks earlier that they hadn't had time to make plans for a romantic getaway. Besides, Betty had done quite a bit of traveling since she'd retired as a Broadway dancer. As a result, she and Winston hadn't been able to identify a place that wasn't already chock-full of memories, thanks to all the globe-trotting in her past.

"We're going to Tuscany."

"Tuscany!" I cried. "A honeymoon in Italy sounds fabulous!"

And it absolutely did. In fact, I could hardly imagine anyplace more romantic. Which is why I was surprised when I noticed that the expression on Betty's face didn't quite match her announcement that she was about to escape to one of the world's most beautiful regions with the man of her dreams.

"That's what I thought too," she said ruefully. "At least until Chloe and James announced that they planned to join us."

I just stared. "Winston's children are crashing your honeymoon?"

"Oh, it's not just them. James is bringing his girlfriend of the moment, a French model who's on the rebound. It seems she recently broke up with a count. James is married, you may recall, but he and his wife, Grace, recently got separated. Apparently she's still living in Bristol, but he's moved to London, where he's becoming reacquainted with his hedonistic days as a swinging bachelor.

"And Chloe's bringing her husband, Rupert. She insists on bringing her daughter too. And while Fiona's as cute as a button, having a six-year-old along on our first trip as husband and wife is bound to put a damper on some of those candlelit dinners out on *il terrazzo*."

Poor Betty! I thought. Aloud, I said, "I'm sure Chloe and James will be so busy sightseeing that you'll barely notice they're around. Florence is full of fabulous museums and cathedrals, not to mention all the shops and amazing restaurants."

Betty still looked chagrined. "We won't be in Florence. We're staying out in the countryside. We found a gorgeous villa on a hillside, halfway between Florence and Pisa. It never occurred to us when we told everyone we were renting a four-bedroom place that we'd be overrun with houseguests. There's even a swimming pool, which Chloe insists is the perfect place for Fiona to spend her days."

Betty sighed. "All of which leads to the question, how would you feel about staying in the house while we're away? We're leaving on Friday, and we'll be in Italy ten days. That house is so big—and of course it has ancient wiring and even more ancient plumbing. There are so many things that could go wrong that I hate to leave it unattended the entire time we're away."

I took a few seconds to mull over her idea.

I realized that a change of scenery might help with some of the prewedding jitters I'd been experiencing, jitters that had nothing to do with Dorothy Burby. When it came to having commitment phobia, I happened to be the queen. Maybe being in a different environment would give me some emotional breathing space.

I also realized that pretending to be the grande dame of a mansion for a week and a half would give me some physical breathing space—something I'd started to need because of all those wedding presents that kept arriving on our doorstep. While I loved my cottage, it was the size of a large phone booth, which meant I was running out of storage space. In fact, I'd resorted to stashing the deep fryer, the waffle maker, and the ten-cup thermal carafe in the bathtub.

"I'd love to," I told Betty. "Of course, I'll have to check with Nick, but I can't imagine him having any objections. Especially since we don't even have to pack up all our stuff. Whenever we need something, we can just pop back to the cottage."

"That's wonderful," she replied, sounding relieved. "I'll wait for you to get a final okay from Nick, but in the meantime I'll assume it's a go. Stop by whenever you get a chance and I'll show you where everything is. Thank you so much, Jessica. You have no idea what a weight off my mind this is. At least one thing is going right.

"Now I'll leave you to get on with the rest of your day," she added, scooping Frederick up into her arms. "You, too, Sunny. It was nice meeting you."

"Nice meeting you too!" Sunny called over from the couch.

As I closed the door after Betty, I let out a deep sigh.

In the past fifteen minutes, I had made an important decision about place cards, doubled the size of the Reigning Cats & Dogs staff, and arranged to move into a gorgeous mansion and out of a one-bedroom abode that looked like the Keebler elves' weekend place.

But now it was time to get back to the important business of the day—even though the thought of confronting what I knew lay ahead caused the despondent mood that had temporarily drifted away to settle back over me.

Chapter 3

"Never hold discussions with the monkey
when the organ grinder is in the room."
—Winston Churchill

As I pulled up in front of 412 Crystal Court in my red VW half an hour later, I grabbed the handwritten note I'd tossed into my purse to make sure I'd remembered the address of Ben and Erin's house correctly. Sure enough, the house matched the street and number I'd copied off the Cornell alumni website. Yet the castle-size McMansion looming ahead of me just didn't fit with the Erin Walsh I remembered from vet school. It didn't jibe with my memories of Ben either.

The three-story structure looked as if it had been designed by an architect from the Victorian era—or at least one who secretly wished he or she was illustrating a children's book set in that period. With all the turrets, oddly shaped windows, and gingerbread trim, I half-expected Mary Poppins herself to come bouncing out the front door.

Yet despite all the old-fashioned touches, the materials that had been used in its construction were clearly modern. Instead of being shingled, the facade was covered with aluminum siding in a sickly sweet shade of baby blue. The massive front porch, lined with a glaringly white banister, was made from a synthetic type of decking I recognized from the advertising flyers the mailman routinely stuffed in my mailbox just to make sure I'd have enough unwanted paper come Recycling Day. The fact that the other homes on the cul-de-sac were all identical, aside from having facades in different pastel shades, made me feel as if I was standing in front of funhouse mirrors at a carnival.

I studied the house for a long time, trying to reconcile this showy display with the Erin Walsh I knew back in vet school. Thinking back, I pictured a remarkably pretty young woman with inquisitive brown eyes, a willowy frame, and a tangle of dark, waist-length hair streaming down her back. She'd turned heads without having any idea of the effect she was having on the male portion of the population. Or caring in the least.

That Erin didn't give a hoot about material things. She dressed in clothes from thrift stores and furnished her tiny off-campus apartment with couches and tables salvaged from curbs the night before trash pickup. I even remembered her bringing her lunch every day in a brown paper bag.

But it was more than her modest standard of living that seemed so out of kilter with the monstrosity she'd chosen as her home. Even more, it was the values I remembered her embracing that struck me as so inconsistent. Those lunches she brought from home generally consisted of organically grown fruit with tofu or yogurt—and she neatly folded up the paper bag after lunch and tucked it into her backpack so she could use it again the following day.

The wardrobe she culled from the racks of Goodwill and the Salvation Army was comprised of gauzy skirts from India, embroidered blouses from Mexico, and during Ithaca's cold winters, colorful hats and mittens knitted by the natives of Tibet. As for her eclectically decorated apartment, a forerunner of shabby chic, it had ironically been located on the third floor of a real Victorian house, one that didn't appear to have had either its paint or its plumbing updated since Queen Victoria herself ruled the British Empire.

As for Ben, I remembered him as the kind of guy who couldn't care less about where he lived. He'd been a laid-back jeans and T-shirt kind of guy, someone whose good looks and natural charm had clearly made things easy for him all his life. I recalled that he'd been a bit of a party animal, one of the few veterinary students who'd brought along his frat boy mentality from his undergraduate days.

I also seemed to remember that he'd lived in a ramshackle house a few blocks off campus, with a bunch of guys whose to-do list simply did not include tasks like scrub the mold out of the refrigerator, sweep the pretzel crumbs off the carpet, or buy toilet paper. And like Erin, Ben had outfitted his place with furniture that other people had discarded, usually for good reason. In fact, a no-frills lifestyle was something Ben and Erin had had in common.

Then again, I reasoned, maybe their modest beginnings were exactly what had prompted them to go all out once they accumulated some money in their bank account.

More than a decade has passed since those days, I reminded myself as I pushed open the door of my VW. No doubt a lot has happened in that time. People change—and so does their taste in architecture.

As I stepped onto the massive porch, I noticed that the three white wicker chairs grouped around a small round table looked brand new, as if no one had even sat in them yet. I also got a better look at the baskets of brightly colored flowers hanging from the eaves. While from afar they looked as if they were made of straw, they turned out to be plastic.

At least the flowers are real, I thought. But when I reached up and touched the petals, I discovered that they, too, were fake.

I rang the bell and listened to it echo through the house, a sign that the interior was likely to be on as large a scale as the exterior. Somehow, the sound struck me as lonely, as if there was too much room inside for too few people.

I expected a relative to answer the door, a member of either Ben's or Erin's family who had rushed over as soon as the bad news spread. Instead, Ben himself answered.

He looked pretty much the way I remembered him, with a few years tacked on. His black hair, once shaggy, was now neatly trimmed, and tiny laugh lines were carved into the tanned skin around his eyes. His build was still lean, although the barest beginnings of a potbelly protruded through his beige knit polo shirt.

He stared at me for what seemed like an awfully long time, his forehead creased and his eyes clouded with confusion. I could practically hear the wheels turning in his head.

I was about to tell him my name and remind him that we'd gone to vet school together when he gasped, "Jessie? Jessie Popper?"

"That's right, Ben. I'm surprised you recognize me after all these years."

"You've hardly changed! Boy, it is good to see a familiar face." He hesitated, then leaned forward and hugged me.

I hugged him back, expecting that we'd both let go after a second or two. Instead, he tightened his grip and buried his face in my shoulder. As his own shoulders began to shake, I realized he was sobbing.

"Oh, Ben!" I cried, letting the tears I'd been fighting to hold back fall too. "I'm so sorry!"

"God, Jessie," he wailed. "How could this happen? It doesn't make any sense! I—I just can't seem to process it."

Since I had nothing wise to say—and in fact felt exactly the same way—I simply hugged him tighter. "I'm so, so sorry," I whispered.

When he finally pulled away, he avoided looking me in the eye. "Anyway," he mumbled, "why don't you come in?"

Sniffing loudly, he rubbed his nose with the back of his hand. I was tempted to pull a tissue out of my purse and hand it to him, but I was afraid of embarrassing him even further.

I stepped inside, noting that just as I expected, everything inside the house was on as grand a scale as it was on the outside. The foyer was tremendous, with an ornate chandelier hanging from a high ceiling and a gleaming black-and-white marble floor. A sleek, narrow table made of dark, lustrous wood lined one wall, teetering on elaborately carved legs. Perched in the center was a huge bouquet of pastel-colored flowers.

Probably silk, I figured. But still fake.

Through a high, elegant archway, I could see the living room, so expansive that it dwarfed the foyer. I expected to see a crowd of relatives and friends gathered there. But there was no one occupying the pair of long snow-white couches that sat face-to-face, blending so well with the wall-to-wall carpeting that they were almost impossible to see.

In fact, there were no signs of life, making me feel as if I was touring a model house. The huge fireplace was immaculate, a sign that it had never been used. Even more surprisingly, there was absolutely no clutter—no magazines, no photographs, not even any of the veterinary journals that at my place seemed to multiply when nobody was looking.

My impression remained the same as when I'd studied the house from the outside. I saw few signs here of the Ben and Erin I'd known at school. In fact, the interior looked as if every inch had been designed by a decorator, one who didn't have a clue about who her clients really were.

I did spot one exception: a few animal-theme

touches that seemed to have been added to the room's sterile furnishings as an afterthought. Framed prints that from where I stood looked like etchings of lions and hippos and zebras hung on the wall behind the baby grand piano. A large ceramic tiger crouching next to the fireplace snarled menacingly. And the throw pillows on the couches, which at first glance appeared to be made of fabric with a leaf pattern, also had the faces of exotic animals hidden in the design.

"We can sit in here," Ben offered, leading me inside.

Frankly, I was afraid to step on the white rugs, much less park my butt on those white cushions. This didn't exactly impress me as a room made for hanging out with your feet on the couch and bowls of chips and dip on the glass-topped coffee table.

"I'm really glad you came by, Jessie," Ben said as he perched on one of the couches. Forcing a smile, he added, "Can I get you anything to drink? Or eat?"

"I'm fine," I assured him, gingerly lowering myself onto the couch opposite his. I realized I should have had the presence of mind to show up with an offering in hand, at the very least a tray of cookies or a basket of fruit. After all, that was common protocol in situations like this one. And given the fact that Ben seemed so completely alone in this big, empty house, I wished I'd done something that would make it feel more like a home.

"The members of my family are going to be descending at any minute," he said, almost as if he'd read my mind. "Erin's family too. I'm actually glad to have a chance to catch my breath before this place becomes totally chaotic. I can't begin to imagine what the next few days are going to be like."

"I'm sure it'll be reassuring to have other people around," I commented. "Where are all your relatives coming from?"

"Erin's parents live upstate, in a small town outside of Rochester," he replied, his voice strained. "A bunch of her aunts and uncles are coming too. They're all flying down this afternoon. Her sister got here about an hour ago. She lives close by, in Oyster Cove. She went out to get some food.

"And my folks are driving down," he continued. "In fact, they should be here any minute."

"It sounds as if they live pretty close," I observed.

"Westchester County. Bedford Hills, where I grew up."

I was surprised that he not only named one of the most exclusive suburban areas in the New York metropolitan area, but that he also singled out one of its wealthiest communities. I'd only driven through Bedford Hills a few times, but I remembered tremendous estates set amidst green rolling hills, barricaded with high fences designed to keep out the riffraff. I also seemed to recall that the upscale community's residents included Martha Stewart, Ralph Lauren, and Chevy Chase.

Realizing that Ben had grown up wealthy made my memories of his hang-loose persona in vet school seem even more incongruous.

Then again, he wouldn't have been the first young man to rebel against his parents' values, I thought. Nor would he be the first to embrace them once he started making some money of his own.

"This is quite a place you've got here," I said, deliberately keeping my comments about his home sweet home ambiguous. I hoped that bringing up the topic would enable me to find out more about how he and Erin had come to live in such an unlikely setting.

"Thanks," he said, smiling sincerely for the first time since I'd walked in. "I love it. I—we—just moved in a few months ago." With a little laugh, he added, "Believe it or not, I actually had to talk Erin into buying this place. She wasn't convinced it was right for us. But I figured we might as well enjoy the fact that we'd both finally started making good money. We've got a built-in swimming pool with a Jacuzzi out back. A fitness room, too, right in the basement. It even has a sauna."

I was taken aback by his sudden show of pride in his real estate holdings. But I told myself that under circumstances like these, there was no telling how someone would react.

"What have you been up to, career-wise?" I asked, figuring it wasn't a bad idea to steer the conversation toward more neutral subjects.

"I guess you didn't know that Erin and I went into practice together a few years ago. Just a few miles away in Earlington."

"I remember that at our five-year reunion you and Erin were talking about the two of you setting up a practice together," I said. "But I had no idea it was here on Long Island."

I mentally kicked myself for having been so wrapped up in my own life over the past few years that I hadn't made a greater effort to keep track of which of my friends and acquaintances from vet school had moved to the New York area. If I'd reconnected with Erin sooner, maybe she would have confided in me about whatever was bothering her long before and none of this would have happened.

"You know us Type A personalities," Ben said with a chuckle. "Doing just one thing is never enough."

Funny, I thought, I don't remember Ben being a Type A personality at all. In fact, I remember him as Type B—as in *B* for beer.

During our first year at Cornell, he'd become famous as the guy who could always be counted on to order a keg for a T.G.I.F. celebration. And more often than not, his carousing had continued into the wee hours, long after the rest of us had gone home to bed so we could get up early Saturday morning to study.

At least until he'd paired off with Erin. She had seemed to have a sobering effect on him—both literally and figuratively. While Ben had probably been attracted to her initially because of her beauty, it was almost as if the beauty of her spirit was so strong that even he had been affected by it.

Still, the relationship had changed her too. Most noticeably, instead of the hippie-style clothing she had favored, she began dressing more conservatively, trading in her quirky ethnic clothing for tailored pants and crisp blouses. Both of them seemed to move away from the extremes, toward a more central and more comfortable place.

"What else have you been up to?" I asked, genuinely curious.

"Believe it or not, I am now the part owner of a

chain of pet stores all over the New York metropolitan area," Ben announced. I couldn't tell if it was my imagination or if his chest actually puffed up.

Aha, I thought. So that explains the sudden wealth. Ben moved beyond veterinary medicine, which most people pursue out of a love of animals, into the considerably more lucrative world of business.

"Maybe you've seen them," he went on proudly. "They're called the Pet Empawrium. You know, spelled e-m-p-a-w-r-i-u-m. We sell everything from the pets to all the supplies an owner could possibly need. We have eleven stores in New York and New Jersey, including five here on Long Island."

"I've seen one," I said. "In Pine Hollow, right?"

"That's right. That was the second one we opened. The first was in Burntwood." The more he talked, the more excited he became. His eyes took on a shine, making him look more like the twenty-two-year-old I remembered from our first year of vet school than the man he was today. "It's been a ton of work, keeping up with the practice during the week and then working on the business all weekend. During the start-up phase, Don and I were busy twenty-four/seven. That's Donald Drayton, my business partner. We pretty much did everything ourselves, from putting up Sheetrock to stocking the shelves. But it's been worth it. I mean, just look at this place! There's no way I— we—would have been able to afford a house like this without the business!"

"It sounds as if it's been very . . . rewarding."

"Extremely. And I wasn't planning to tell people about this," he went on, "at least not yet, but a franchise company has approached us, asking if we'd be interested in—"

"Hello?" a female voice called.

A second or two later the front door slammed shut and a woman appeared in the doorway, lugging two grocery bags that looked ready to burst.

"Kimberly! Let me help you with those." Ben jumped up and rushed over to help. "Jessie, this is Erin's sister, Kimberly. Kimberly, this is Jessie Popper, a friend of Erin's and mine from vet school."

"Hello, Jessie," Kimberly said, nodding in my direction.

Now that Ben had identified her, I could see the resemblance. She had Erin's brown eyes, and while she wore her hair cut above her shoulders, its coarse texture and its tendency to curl gave it the same wild look as her sister's. Even though she was wearing loose-fitting khaki capris and her sleeveless pink blouse wasn't tucked in, I could see she also had Erin's slender frame, although she was considerably taller.

"I'm so sorry about Erin," I told her, once again struck by my helplessness. "I'm afraid we'd lost touch over the years." I paused before adding, "But then she called me earlier today."

"What do you mean, she called you?" Ben froze, his arms still wrapped around the bags he'd taken from his sister-in-law.

I glanced from one to the other, wondering how much to tell them.

Ben was Erin's husband, I reminded myself, and Kimberly was her sister. They both deserve to know the whole story.

I took a deep breath.

"Very early this morning," I began uneasily, "around five-thirty, the phone rang. It was Erin. I was really caught off guard since she and I hadn't talked since our last Cornell reunion, five years ago."

Ben and his sister-in-law exchanged surprised looks.

"What did she say?" Kimberly asked, her eyes clouding.

"She asked me to meet her as soon as I could. She said something was wrong and she wanted to talk to me about it." I hesitated. "She sounded really upset. And she told me not to say anything to anybody. Ben, I was hoping you'd know what it was all about."

Kimberly and I both looked at him. I don't know what I was expecting. A rush of words about something Erin had been worried about lately, perhaps, or some other explanation for the peculiar telephone call.

Instead, Ben looked at me blankly. "Jessie, I have absolutely no idea what Erin might have been referring to."

"She wasn't in any kind of trouble?" I asked.

"Not at all. As a matter of fact, things were going really well." He set the groceries down on the glass coffee table positioned between the two matching couches. "Not only has our practice been flourishing; she started doing some consulting at the New York Zoo a few months ago. She was really excited about that. She's been working for a highly respected primatologist. Maybe you've even heard of her. Her name is Dr. Annalise Zacarias."

The name didn't ring a bell. But I commented, "I had no idea she was even interested in exotics."

"The job was something she kind of fell into," Ben explained. "Someone there gave her a call this winter, and she started going there two or three afternoons a week. The timing was great, too, since I've been so busy lately with the stores, I haven't been around very much."

I couldn't help wondering what effect their busy workload had had on their relationship. Choosing my words carefully, I observed, "It sounds pretty stressful. Both of you working so hard, I mean. I would think maintaining a schedule like that would put a real strain on any marriage. I mean, my boyfriend's been in law school for the past year, and between him taking a full course load and me working crazy hours, we practically need to make an appointment to have dinner together. Not surprisingly, that's created all kinds of tension between us."

Ben looked startled. "Not us! Things between Erin and me were perfect. Which makes what happened even more—"

Before he had a chance to finish his sentence, his cell phone rang.

"Sorry," he said, grimacing. "I'd better take this.... Hello? Yes, I can hear you, Uncle Wayne. Where are you?"

As he launched into a description of the best route from the airport to the house, I picked up one of the bags of groceries. "Let's get these into the kitchen," I whispered to Kimberly.

I followed her toward the back of the house, braced

for a kitchen that looked like something out of a design magazine—one along the lines of *Ostentatious Home* or *Better Mansions and Gardens*. Yet I was still taken aback, not only by its size but also by how luxuriously it was appointed. It had a stove that looked big enough for a restaurant kitchen, three sinks, and two humongous Sub-Zero refrigerators with stainless steel doors. Granite counters that stretched on endlessly were dotted with so many small appliances that even my ever-growing collection suddenly seemed horribly inadequate.

A pair of French doors behind the built-in breakfast nook opened onto the pool Ben had mentioned. It looked large enough to host the Olympics. Dotting the edges were several pieces of wrought-iron lawn furniture, round tables with umbrellas, and lounge chairs sporting canvas cushions in splashy colors. Two blue-and-white-striped cabanas stood off to one side—the perfect place for slipping into one's two-hundred-dollar Burberry bikini.

"Is there anything I can help you with?" I asked Kimberly as I set my grocery bag down next to a machine that apparently not only brewed coffee and espresso and steamed milk for cappuccino but also ground the coffee beans.

"As a matter of fact, it would be great if you could give me a hand with putting all this food out." She cast me a sad smile, then added, "As you can imagine, I'm not exactly at my best right now."

"I'd be happy to do whatever you need."

"The hordes of relatives are going to be arriving shortly. I should probably put all these cold cuts and salads I just bought on platters and leave them out so people can help themselves."

It was only when I went over to start unpacking the groceries that I saw that Kimberly's eyes were rimmed in red and underscored by circles as dark as charcoal smudges. Still, I was surprised by how well she seemed to be holding up. She'd been amazingly organized, even remembering to pick up basics like mustard and mayonnaise in case there were none in the house.

"It's too bad you have to deal with feeding everybody," I commented as I began pulling the lids off plastic deli containers and dumping their contents into the large glass bowls I'd pulled out of a cabinet.

"Actually, I'm happy to have something to do," she said. "I have a feeling I'm still in shock. Oh, I cried for a full hour after Ben called. But through some magical process, I slipped into automatic pilot while I was driving over here." Smiling apologetically, she added, "Since then, I've been running on pure adrenaline, taking charge of everything from calling the funeral home to putting together this feast."

She glanced around the kitchen. "It's funny," she said in a strained voice, "I keep expecting my little sister to walk in and say something like 'April Fool's!' The problem is, it's not April. And deep down, I know this is no joke."

Choking on her words, she added, "I keep telling myself not to think too hard. That all I have to do is get through the next few days."

I knew more than the next few days would be difficult. But I refrained from saying so.

"So you've already made the funeral arrangements?" I asked. "I'd like to come."

"Thanks, but Ben and I decided that we'll just have a small service that's limited to members of the family," Kimberly said. "We both felt it would be best to keep things as private as possible."

"Of course," I agreed. "I understand completely."

"I'm so glad I have the next couple of months off," she continued as she began unwrapping packets of cold cuts. "I was thinking of getting a summer job, but in the end I decided I'd just do some reading and maybe some traveling. I don't know if Ben mentioned that I'm an English teacher."

"No, he didn't. High school?"

"That's right. Seaville High School. The kids are tough at that age, but they're my life. At least they have been since I got divorced. That was seven years ago. I'd been living upstate in the area where we grew up, but I moved down here after my marriage ended. I wanted to be near Erin. We've always been very close, ever since we were kids. I've always felt kind of protective toward her, too, since I'm four years older.

"Anyway," Kimberly went on brightly, "didn't Ben say you knew Erin from veterinary school? I'm sorry, but I'm not functioning at a very high level right now. Things people tell me just aren't sticking."

"That's right," I replied. "All three of us were in the same class. But we've pretty much lost touch since then. In fact, I had no idea she and Ben had settled on Long Island."

"So you two weren't close."

"Not at all. Which was why I was so surprised when I heard from her this morning."

The awkward silence that followed made me wonder for the first time if perhaps Kimberly, and not Ben, had some idea of what Erin's mysterious phone call had been all about. But I didn't know her well enough to probe. Especially since she was so clearly in a distressed state.

She broke the silence by asking, "Is your practice around here?"

"Actually, it's all over Long Island," I said. "I have a mobile services unit, a clinic-on-wheels. Even though I live in Joshua's Hollow on the North Shore, I travel all over, making house calls."

"No kidding. Do you have a card?"

"Sure. Do you have pets?"

"No. But, uh, I have a friend who might be interested."

I reached into my purse and pulled out a business card.

"Jessica Popper," Kimberly read aloud after she took it from me. "Is this your cell phone number?"

"Yes. That's the best way to get in touch."

"And when's a good time to reach you?"

"Any time. Having my own business means being on call twenty-four/seven."

"Thanks." Kimberly's eyes seemed to burn into mine as she stuck my card into the breast pocket of her shirt. "I'll tell my friend to think about whether she wants to talk to you."

Chapter 4

"We're animals. We're born like every other mammal and we live our whole lives around disguised animal thoughts."

—Barbara Kingsolver, *Animal Dreams*

As I drove away from Ben and Erin's house, I thought back to my days at vet school, struggling to reconstruct more of the past. But it wasn't Erin I was trying to remember. It was Ben.

I knew that in murder investigations, the cops always began by taking a close look at the victim's spouse.

I realized I didn't really know Ben Chandler very well. I hadn't back at school and I certainly didn't now. But one thing I did know was that there were things about the way he'd reacted to Erin's murder that sent up red flags.

He had seemed distraught, of course. Genuinely distraught. Then again, he wouldn't have been the first killer to put on a convincing act. . . .

Killer. Simply putting that word in the same sentence as the name of someone I'd gone to school with made me shudder.

Still, I couldn't ignore how animated he'd become when he'd talked about his recent success with his business venture. In fact, he almost seemed to have forgotten that only hours earlier, his wife had been murdered. He'd been too busy bragging about all the money he was making and the wonderful things he'd bought with it.

Then there was his claim that his relationship with Erin had been "perfect."

Now, *there's* a word few people can use sincerely when they're talking about their relationship, I thought wryly.

Nick and me, for example. Here we were only weeks away from getting married. Yet I couldn't deny that our relationship was—and always had been—far from perfect.

True, I was guilty of having some, shall we say, commitment issues that weren't typical of most relationships. But that aside, the fact that we were both busy with our own careers caused all kinds of difficulties. Working long hours, usually under a great deal of stress, often made us tired, cranky, and hard to live with. That was bound to be a common syndrome with any couple in a similar situation.

Then there were the differences in our personalities. Again, I didn't think we were that unusual in that we had slightly different approaches to life. I tend to be intense and at times overly emotional, while Nick generally adopts a more logical approach. So it's only natural that we butt heads from time to time.

Not even close to perfect.

Even Betty and Winston, two moonstruck lovers with stars in their eyes, had had their ups and downs. And as far as I was concerned, those two were pretty much the poster children for living happily ever after.

I wished I had a better sense of who Ben was and what his relationship with Erin had really been like. I tried picturing him back when I knew him at Cornell. As I did, I realized that it was hard to think of Ben Chandler without imagining his best friend hovering nearby.

What was his name? I thought, frowning as I veered into the right lane so I could get onto the Long Island Expressway. John, Jake...

Jack! Jack Krieger! I would have snapped my fingers if I weren't curving around an especially hazardous entrance ramp to the road commonly known as the Long Island Distressway.

The two of them had been inseparable, I now recalled. Jack and Ben became buddies early on in our first semester. Maybe even during orientation. They'd chosen each other as lab partners, studied together, and even opted to become roommates after the first couple of semesters.

But I frowned again as I plunged deeper into my hippocampus and dusted off another memory that had been stashed away for more than a decade. It wasn't a particularly pleasant one either.

Toward the end of our fourth and final year, just before graduation, there had been a rift between them. Rumors had flown about the close friendship that had dissolved very suddenly. Theories ranged from Jack and Ben vying for the same job after graduation to a relationship with overtones of homosexuality going awry.

Maybe I didn't get a chance to know Ben Chandler well, I thought, pressing down on the accelerator until my speed matched that of the crazed cars around me. But Jack Krieger did.

Which meant one thing was for sure. As soon as I got home, I'd be scrolling through the alumni listings on the Cornell website for the second time that day.

• • •

My plans to track down Jack Krieger immediately went on hold when I opened the front door and found Sunny sitting on the couch with Cat in her lap and Tink at her side. I'd been so engrossed in Erin's murder that I'd forgotten all about the fact that a few hours earlier I'd set Sunny up with her very first task in her new job as assistant to Jessica Popper, D.V.M.

"How did rescheduling my appointments go?" I asked. I crouched down to give my two dogs the attention and reassurance they so desperately craved after having been separated from me for the unconscionably long period of almost three hours.

"Fine," she replied. "Great, in fact."

Yet when I glanced up, I saw she was frowning.

"Actually," she went on, biting her lower lip, "I ran out of things to keep me busy. It only took me about half an hour to reschedule all your appointments. They're all in your BlackBerry. I also have them written out on a piece of paper."

"Thank you." I glanced at the handwritten schedule,

surprised that she'd been even more thorough than I'd expected. "Great job, Sunny."

"Thanks. But like I said, I got kind of bored after I was done. I hope you don't mind, but I walked around the house and found some things to do."

"Like what?" I asked nervously.

"I really hope you don't think I'm intruding . . . but I started out by sorting through a pile of junk mail I found," Sunny explained. "I separated the envelopes by category and put rubber bands around each group. See? They're all laid out here on the coffee table. This pile is credit card offers, this one is coupons that are still good, this one is coupons that have expired, this one is solicitations for contributions . . . I even found a few bills in there. I put those in this pile. And here are all the catalogs. I stacked them together so you could leaf through them and decide which ones to keep."

"Wow." I didn't try to hide how impressed I was. How grateful I was for all the time she'd saved me either.

"I also did a couple of things in the kitchen." Anxiously she added, "I hope that's okay."

"What kinds of things?" It wasn't that I was irritated. It was more like I was embarrassed. When it comes to maintaining order in the kitchen, I seem to be missing the Martha Stewart gene. Not the worst offense in the world, I realized, but that didn't mean I wanted my lack of home economics skills exposed to someone I barely knew.

"I threw out some stuff that was in the back of the fridge," she said, sounding almost apologetic. "Rotting fruit, some yogurt that expired a couple of months ago.... I organized your pots and pans too. I put all the baking pans together, under the sink, and I moved all the drinking glasses to one shelf. I also unpacked some nice new ones that were still in the box."

"Ri-i-ight," I said, sounding as awed as I felt. "Wedding presents."

"There's one more thing." She paused to take a deep breath. "I alphabetized your spices."

"Seriously?" I'd heard of such things, of course. I knew, somewhere in the back of my mind, that there were people in this world who were organized enough to keep their spices in alphabetical order. It just never occurred to me that I would ever have the time, energy, or focus required to become one of them.

I hadn't realized I owned that many spices either.

"I also organized your closets," Sunny went on. "Nothing fancy. I just grouped the different garments together. Short-sleeved shirts, then long-sleeved shirts, then pants, then skirts..." She bit her lip. "I hope you don't mind. I'm afraid I get a little carried away sometimes. I like things to be in order."

I do, too, I thought. I just never get around to *putting* them in order.

"Sunny, it all sounds fabulous," I told her sincerely. "Thank you so much. And I promise that on most days, you'll be coming with me in my van to help me with my work. That was our agreement after all."

She shrugged. "I'm supposed to be your assistant, right? So I'm happy to assist you in whatever you need."

As I was mentally thanking whatever force it was that brought Sunny McGee into my life, she added,

"Uh, Jessie? There's something else I want to talk to you about. Ask you about, actually. An idea I had."

"What is it?"

"It's not really an idea. It's more like a favor."

"Okay. Shoot."

"Actually," she said, grimacing, "it's such a big favor that you'll probably say no."

"Sunny, why don't you just go ahead and ask—"

"No, it's too big a favor to ask. I should just forget all about it. Pretend I never even brought it up."

"Sunny!" I shrieked. "Tell me!"

She took a deep breath. "I overheard your landlady asking you if you'd be willing to house-sit while she and her new husband go on their honeymoon."

"That's right."

"Which means your cottage is going to be empty for the next week or so while you're living in her house."

"True."

"So . . . I was wondering if maybe I could house-sit your cottage while you're house-sitting Betty's place."

Before I had a chance to ask why she'd even be interested in such an arrangement, she went on, "See, right now I'm living with my parents. Don't get me wrong—they're great. It's just that I'm twenty years old and I still haven't had a chance to live on my own. I mean, I've never actually had my own place. So I was thinking that since your cottage is going to be empty anyway . . . You hate the idea, right? You think it's the dumbest thing you ever heard."

"As a matter of fact," I replied, "it's not a bad idea at all."

Sunny's face lit up. "Really?"

"Sure. In fact, ever since I talked to Betty, I've been assuming I'd bring the dogs and cats with me to the Big House. But I'd much rather leave Prometheus and Leilani here. I figured I'd come by a couple of times a day to check on them and to keep Prometheus company. He's really a people person. Uh, people *bird*. But if you're here, I don't have to worry about him getting lonely."

"Wow! That would be so great!" Sunny cried. "I mean, I didn't really think you'd ... Wow. Thanks, Jessie!"

"I still have to check with Nick about this whole house-sitting arrangement," I reminded her, "but I can't imagine that he'd have any objections. I think it's going to work out for all of us."

In fact, I was already picturing Nick and me snuggling up in the king-size bed with the luxurious Italian sheets and fluffy down pillows—and lingering over leisurely breakfasts on the sunny patio and romantic candlelight dinners in the palatial dining room. Maybe we didn't have the time or the money for a vacation in Italy, but playing house in Betty's mansion sounded like the next best thing.

• • •

As soon as Sunny left, no doubt rushing to her parents' house to start packing, I took a tour of my cottage, anxious to see what she'd accomplished.

She really did an impressive job, I marveled as I checked my bedroom closet, my baking pan collection, and my vast collection of spices that went all the way from allspice to turmeric.

I only wished every aspect of my life could be so orderly.

With that thought in mind, I headed for my laptop and for the second time that day clicked onto the Cornell website. A few more clicks and I located Jack Krieger's current address and phone number.

He was living in a small town upstate. I wasn't surprised, since I seemed to recall that he'd grown up on a farm. In fact, when he first came to Cornell, he'd intended to specialize in dairy animals.

I sank onto the couch and dialed his number on my cell phone. As I listened to it ring, I remembered that Jack had been the only student in our class who'd shown up the first day dressed in a pair of overalls. He'd quickly switched to jeans and eventually khakis, but that didn't change his image as a wholesome small town boy who planned to return to the quiet life he knew best. He never stopped seeming like someone who was capable of saying "Aw, shucks" at any moment.

I was disappointed when a machine picked up.

"Hi, Jack," I said after dutifully waiting for the tone. "This is Jessica Popper. I don't know if you remember me, but we went to vet school together. There's, uh, something I need to talk to you about. It's pretty important, so I hope you'll call me back as soon as you get this message. I'll leave both my home and cell numbers...."

I didn't mean to sound so mysterious. It was just

that I didn't know if he'd already heard about Erin—
or if I'd be the one to break the terrible news.

After I'd hung up, I remained half-sitting, half-lying
on the couch, so devoid of energy that I couldn't
move. Cat was curled up comfortably on my stomach,
Tinkerbell was happily swatting at the fringe on the
throw rug, Lou was dozing with his chin on my foot,
and Max was chomping on a rawhide. Prometheus
was making more noise than anybody, loudly crunching on seeds. It would have been a homey scene if it
wasn't for the fact that a heavy cloud hung over the
room—at least, one that I was aware of.

I was still camped out on the couch when I heard
Nick's Maxima pull into the driveway. The dogs
heard him, too, and within a fraction of a second
they'd positioned themselves at the front door. Their
toenails skittered across the wooden floor and their
bodies slammed against each other as they vied for the
best spot, both of them snorting and whimpering as
they tried to plant their noses as close as possible to
the slit between the door and the frame.

Nick walking in the door was a welcome sight.

"How did it go today?" he asked anxiously as he
crouched down to allow the dogs to welcome him
with their usual fanfare. "Did you get in touch with
your friend's husband?"

"Yes. I went over to the house."

"How's he holding up?"

"Pretty well, all things considered." I decided not
to mention my suspicions about why that might be.

"How about you, Jess?" Nick sat down next to me
and took my hand. "How are *you* holding up?"

I let out a deep sigh. "Most of the time, I'm still having trouble believing it could possibly be true," I replied. "But during the moments when I do manage to comprehend the fact that it really happened, I just feel totally confused. And powerless. And angry and...and overwhelmed and horribly sad."

We sat in silence for a while, just holding hands.

Nick finally broke the silence. "It's kind of dark in here," he said softly. "Mind if I turn on a light?"

In response, I reached up and snapped on the pole lamp next to me. The glaring brightness helped bring me out of my stupor.

"How about you?" I asked. "How was your day?"

"It was fine. I'm starting to feel less like the new kid on the block and more like I really belong there."

"Your mother called earlier," I told him. "She wanted my opinion on place cards. And ice sculpture."

Nick rolled his eyes. "I hope she's not driving you totally crazy."

Only partly crazy, I thought. All the other things going on in my life right now are doing the rest of the job. "She's actually turning out to be a big help. Planning a wedding is a huge job."

At least if you expect it to be on par with Prince Charles and Lady Di's, I thought. And look how well *that* marriage turned out.

Nick leaned over and planted a kiss on my cheek.

"What was that for?" I asked, surprised.

"For being a good sport," he replied. "Actually, you deserve a medal for putting up with my mother. I know she's not the easiest person in the world. And that you two have had your differences in the past."

He was referring to his parents' visit a few weeks earlier. Dorothy and Henry Burby had insisted on staying with us, which made our tiny cottage feel like the shoe that housed the Old Woman and all those children she didn't know what to do with. And finding enough space to set down a coffee mug was the least of it.

"Speaking of being a good sport," I said, "Betty came by this morning to ask a favor."

"You know I'd do anything for her."

"She and Winston are finally going on their honeymoon. They've rented a villa in Tuscany. She wants us to house-sit while they're away. She needs us to look after Frederick too."

Nick thought for a couple of seconds, then nodded. "I could get used to living in the lap of luxury."

I laughed. "I thought you'd feel that way. And while Betty and Winston are feeding each other grapes in Tuscany and you and I are pretending to be Jay Gatsby and Daisy Buchanan, Sunny wants to stay here in the cottage."

"Sunny's your new assistant, right?"

"That's right. She can keep Prometheus company." And probably sort our socks by color, length, and fiber content.

"Sounds like a plan," Nick replied with a little shrug.

"Great. Then I'll tell Betty and Sunny it's—"

"There's one important thing I have to know before I say yes."

"Which is?"

"Can we go joy-riding in Winston's Rolls-Royce while they're away?"

Before I could come up with a snappy answer, my cell phone started to hum.

"Excuse me, Michael Schumacher," I said wryly, "but I'd better get this."

I figured the unfamiliar number on the caller ID screen belonged to a frantic pet owner, so I answered. "Hello, this is Jessica Popper."

"Jessie?"

"Yes . . ." Even though I have scores of clients, I can usually attach a name and a face to a caller. Yet while this voice sounded vaguely familiar, I couldn't place it.

"This is Kimberly. Erin's sister? We met this afternoon."

"Of course." As if I could forget, I thought. "How are you, Kimberly?"

"Holding up. Thanks for asking. But there's a reason I called." At the other end of the line, I heard her draw in a deep breath. "I was wondering if you and I could talk. The sooner, the better."

•   •   •

As I drove to my meeting with Kimberly early the next morning, I was enveloped by a strong sense of déjà vu.

The second mysterious rendezvous in two days, I thought uneasily.

True, this one was scheduled to take place at a much more reasonable time than the other one: eight o'clock in the morning, rather than six-thirty. And this time we'd agreed to talk at Starbucks, where the coffee was light years better than it was at the Spartan Diner.

But there was one major thing both meetings had in common: an air of urgency.

After parking my van, I headed inside and immediately spotted Kimberly sitting alone at a table for two. Even though three or four other tables were available, I noticed that she'd picked the one that was separated from all the others by a display of coffee beans and mugs.

She was sipping from a paper cup big enough to hold popcorn. "Venti" it was called in Starbucks' lingo, meaning the largest amount of coffee customers could ingest without placing their mouths at the end of the spigot. Her eyes were glazed, as if she was lost in thought.

"Kimberly?" I said softly as I approached, not wanting to startle her.

She jerked her head toward me. I wondered if her nervousness was due to ODing on caffeine or if something else was responsible. "Hi, Jessica. Thanks for coming." Gesturing toward the Papa Bear–size cup in front of her, she said, "I hope you don't mind, but I went ahead and got my coffee."

"No problem," I assured her. "I'll be back as soon as I get mine."

A few minutes later, I sat down opposite her with my own cup of liquid energy. "That's a lot of coffee," I commented, gesturing toward her cup. My twelve-ounce latte, a "tall," was making me look like a real lightweight by Starbucks' standards.

"I didn't get much sleep last night," she explained.

"I was hoping this would help me get through the day. Especially since it's going to be another tough one."

I just nodded, then sipped some of the foamy milk that sat on top of my cup like a small cumulus cloud.

"How about Ben?" I asked gently. "How is he doing?"

I expected her to shake her head sympathetically and tell me that Erin's poor, bereaved husband was managing just fine, considering the terrible thing that had happened and how deeply he was grieving. Instead, she let out a contemptuous snort.

"Like I care," she muttered.

I did my best to keep my eyebrows from jumping above my hairline. "I take it you two don't get along?"

"Oh, we get along just fine," she replied, her voice bitter. "At least on the surface. It's just that I don't trust him as far as I can throw him. In fact, I wouldn't be surprised if he had something to do with Erin's murder."

It took me a few seconds to recover from the shock of what she'd just said. Not that I hadn't had the exact same thought myself. It was just that I hadn't expected Erin's sister to openly voice the same opinion. Especially to me.

Kimberly glanced around as if wanting to make sure no one was listening. I automatically did the same, noting that not only were we sitting far away from any caffeineophiles, the other early birds fueling up for the day were absorbed in either books, laptops, or their own conversations.

"You know how Ben said things between him and

Erin were perfect?" she said, her tone still harsh. "That was total bull."

Her choice of words surprised me. After all, this was a woman who taught high school.

All the more reason to be in the habit of speaking directly, I decided. Especially since the state of Erin and Ben's marriage was clearly something she felt strongly about.

"Erin had been unhappy for months," she went on. "Maybe even longer. But I found out just how bad things were between them a few weeks ago when they were over at my house for dinner. I walked into the kitchen, expecting to find her whipping cream for the peach pie she'd brought. Instead, I found her crying her eyes out."

She paused to sip her coffee. "I think I mentioned yesterday that I've always felt protective toward Erin. After all, she's my kid sister—and my only sibling. So naturally I put my arms around her and begged her to tell me what was wrong. And what was wrong was Ben. She told me he'd changed. That starting this new business of his—all those pet stores—was ruining their marriage."

"It sounds as if he's been working crazy hours," I observed.

"But that's the thing. I don't think it was his work schedule that was the problem. I mean, Erin worked hard too. She wasn't home any more than he was."

"In that case, what *was* the problem?"

"I'm not sure." Kimberly let out a frustrated sigh. "I couldn't get her to tell me much. All she would say was that they had some serious issues."

"I'm sorry to hear that," I said sincerely. "But I have to ask you, Kimberly: Why are you telling *me* this?"

"Because of our conversation yesterday," she replied quietly. "Or, to be more accurate, the conversation you had with my sister yesterday morning."

She studied me for what seemed like a long time before adding, "Jessica, I believe that you're someone I can trust. And that's because Erin clearly trusted you. After all, you're the person she called right before she was ... right before. She obviously sensed that something bad was about to happen, and you were the one she was looking to for help."

Leaning forward, she added in an even softer voice, "Like you, I believe she was in some sort of trouble. Or that somehow she'd gotten in over her head."

"In what?" I asked without thinking.

Kimberly's eyes clouded. "I was hoping maybe you'd be able to figure it out."

I held out my hands in a gesture of helplessness. "Kimberly, I have no idea what was going on in Erin's life. That's what I was trying to explain at the house yesterday. I haven't spoken to her in years. I didn't even know she was living on Long Island or ... or that she was working at the New York Zoo. There's no way I'd able to figure out what's been happening with her."

For a few seconds, Kimberly simply stared at me in silence. "There's something I want to show you," she finally said.

She reached into her purse and pulled out a Ziploc

bag with a white square inside. I noticed that her hands trembled slightly as she handed it to me.

I smoothed it out on the table, halfway between us. Inside the clear plastic bag was a small paper napkin, the kind that's used at any social gathering that demands something better than the scratchy supermarket variety that's sold in packages of two hundred. Sometime in the past, probably during the days of pillbox hats and white gloves, it had become known as a cocktail napkin.

But instead of being covered with martini stains, this one had writing on it. With a blue ballpoint pen, someone had scribbled:

100 Brown BB +
NGIPPL IFAWCI
A2RX X ☺

The letters were nothing but jibberish to me. As for the hastily sketched drawing, it looked like a wobbly smiley face with an X drawn through it.

"Where did this come from?" I asked, not even trying to hide my confusion.

Kimberly took a deep breath. "A few weeks ago, Erin had to go to some fancy fund-raising dinner for the New York Zoo. She was complaining she didn't have anything dressy enough to wear, so I offered to lend her a black velvet jacket with gold embroidery I'd just bought. I hadn't even worn it yet. Erin and I have never been the same size, since I'm quite a bit taller and my shoulders are broader. But it was cut loose and I figured it would fit her just fine.

"Anyway, she borrowed the jacket for the party and then returned it a few days later. When I went to put it back in the closet, I found this in the pocket." She gestured toward the paper napkin. "I didn't know if it was important, so I called Erin and said I'd found a napkin with some notes she'd made and asked her if she needed it back. Her reaction really surprised me. She said, 'Oh, don't worry. I remember *exactly* what I wrote.' But she said it in a strange voice. Bitter, somehow. She didn't sound at all like her usual self."

Kimberly paused for a moment, as if she was trying to regain control. "Something about the way she responded prompted me to stick it in a drawer instead of throwing it away. Then I pretty much forgot all about it. At least, until yesterday.

"As you can see," she pointed out as I studied it, "the handwriting's a little sloppy, and there's a tear over here. Writing on a paper napkin with a ballpoint isn't exactly the best way to take notes. In fact, I'm not even sure I can read the letters correctly."

I scrutinized the writing more carefully. She was right; it was hard to be one hundred percent certain what some of the letters were.

"This is Erin's handwriting?" I asked.

"I think so," Kimberly replied. "In fact, I'm nearly positive. Besides, when I described it to her over the phone, she didn't correct me when I said it had some notes on it that she'd written."

"Do these notes mean anything at all to you?" I asked. "Did she ever mention someone or something named Brown or . . . or anything else that could possibly resemble any of these strange words she wrote?"

"Not to me."

"What about while she was speaking to somebody else?" I persisted. "Did you ever hear her say something that sounded like 'naggipple' to Ben? Or maybe while she was talking to somebody else on the phone?"

Kimberly shook her head.

"What about the police? Did you show this to them?"

Smiling coldly, she said, "There's kind of a story there. Yesterday, right after you left, the county's chief of homicide came by."

"You must mean Lieutenant Anthony Falcone."

Kimberly's surprise registered on her face. "You know him?"

Dryly, I replied, "We've met."

"He asked me a bunch of questions, and then at the end asked if there was anything else I wanted to tell him. I mentioned a few things, but..." She frowned. "I don't know how well you know this guy, but he has, shall we say, a bit of an attitude."

Oh, yeah, I thought. "I'd say that's a pretty accurate statement."

"I started to tell him about the jacket and what I found in the pocket," she continued, "but I'd barely begun before he got really impatient. He made a nasty comment about how he was only interested in relevant information, not fashion advice. So I never did tell him about this."

That's my boy, I thought.

"So what do you think?" Kimberly asked hopefully. "Does what Erin wrote mean anything at all to you?"

"I'm sorry, but I'm afraid it doesn't," I replied with a helpless shrug.

I started to hand the napkin back to her. But she held up both hands. "No, I want you to keep it."

"What for?" I asked, surprised.

"I have this crazy idea that somehow these scribbles might have something to do with the reason Erin was murdered. I know it's a long shot, but I'm willing to try anything that might help us find out what happened." She paused. "Since you were somebody she trusted—and you're a veterinarian, like Erin was—I thought you might be able to help me figure it out. I mean, you did have a common bond. And you've traveled in the same circles as Erin."

Her eyes moistening, she added, "You also care about animals as much as she did."

A hundred different reasons to refuse to get involved in Erin's murder raced through my head. I had a wedding to plan. I had a career to run. On top of that, I had my own grief to deal with.

I also had a boyfriend—no, make that a fiancé—who had never exactly been crazy about my penchant for investigating murder.

"Kimberly," I said gently, "I appreciate the fact that you trust me. And I understand completely that you want everything possible to be done to find out who killed your sister. But I don't think I—"

"Will you at least think about it?" she interrupted. She pulled a pen and a scrap of paper out of her purse. "Look, I'll give you my phone number. And I really hope to hear from you soon."

As she handed me her number, she fixed her eyes on

mine and said, "Jessie, you may have been the last person who talked to my sister before she was killed. She called you explicitly to ask for your help."

Her eyes were pleading as she added, "If she wanted you to help her while she was still alive, don't you feel you owe it to her to help her now that she's been murdered?"

Chapter 5

"Monkeys are superior to men in this: when a monkey looks into a mirror, he sees a monkey."

—Malcolm de Chazal

Kimberly's words reverberated inside my head as I pulled out of Starbucks' parking lot—so loudly, in fact, my temples throbbed. She was right. Like it or not, I was involved in Erin's murder. In her final moments, when she had known something bad was happening, I was the one she'd reached out to.

And I hadn't been able to help her when she needed me most. Which meant I did owe her. Big-time.

When I stopped at a red light, I glanced over at the paper napkin lying on the seat beside me, still safely sealed up inside the Ziploc bag. Kimberly believed that deciphering the words or initials or whatever it was Erin had scrawled could provide a link to her killer. Yet the strange scribbling was as puzzling to me as Egyptian hieroglyphics.

Is it code? I wondered. Or some kind of shorthand?

Whatever it was, it could turn out to be an important piece of evidence. I made a note to make a few Xerox copies the first chance I got, then store the original safely away in the same place I kept all my valuables: the top drawer of my dresser.

But as the light turned green and I stepped on the gas, another question gnawed at me, one that was much more fundamental. Was it even possible that Erin's jottings had something to do with her murder, or was Kimberly's fixation nothing more than a grieving sister's desperate attempt to make sense of a horrible tragedy?

Even though I knew that the latter was much more likely, the depth of Kimberly's anguish made me yearn to help her. If figuring out this one thing would give her some comfort, that alone made it worth doing.

I ran through the list of things I had to get done in the next few weeks, meanwhile massaging the taut muscles in my forehead with two fingers. In addition to making house calls all over Long Island, doing my weekly TV spot, and keeping my day-to-day life from disintegrating into chaos, I had to schedule fittings at the dressmaker, write thank-you notes for the steady stream of gifts that kept arriving, and indulge my future mother-in-law by agonizing over silly details like place cards and ice sculpture.

And of course there was the fact that Nick, my betrothed, had never been crazy about me poking around murder investigations. Something about me squandering my all-too-precious time, not to mention nearly getting killed myself on a few occasions.

Still.

What's that old saying? I thought. If you want something done, give it to a busy person? I suppose I can squeeze in a few phone calls and find a couple of spare minutes to play around on the Internet. And I haven't been to the New York Zoo in ages.

You *have* to do something, I thought. You owe her.

And given how tormented I was by the memory of Erin's frantic early-morning phone call and the horror of what had happened next, I knew I owed it to myself.

• • •

After yesterday's devastating events, it was a relief to throw myself into my veterinary practice once again. Yet today was the first time Sunny would be accompanying me on my house calls, and I was a little nervous about how things would go.

I was relieved that my first appointment of the day was with one of my favorite patients. Toby, a black toy poodle, was the sole housemate of a single woman in her mid-forties named Meryl Lytle. She was completely devoted to him, and I couldn't blame her. Toby certainly managed to put a smile on my face every time I saw him.

Even pulling out his folder made me chuckle. On those that contain the records of dogs that tend to bite, I put a red dot on the outside as a warning. But on Toby's, I'd written the word *Houdini*. I didn't want to forget that this six-pound imp was an accomplished escape artist. On more than one occasion, he'd managed to wriggle out of Meryl's arms and disappear somewhere inside my van. He also had a way of helping himself to anything he could fit in his mouth, then slipping out the door without anyone noticing that he'd filched a souvenir.

"Toby's a real cutie-pie," I told Sunny as I pulled up my van in front of his owner's house. "But make sure you keep an eye on him. The little scamp is always getting into something."

"I'm on it," Sunny assured me cheerfully.

As Meryl carried him into my van, Toby was chomping on a plastic toy in the shape of a yellow-and-red flower. That didn't stop him from wagging his tail with alarming enthusiasm as he desperately tried to squirm out of her arms. He acted so excited you'd have thought he'd just come upon a couple of long-lost friends.

"Hey, Toby," I greeted him, unable to resist giving him a quick cuddle. "How's my special pal doing?"

"He's great, except for his foot," Meryl replied anxiously. She was wearing a yellow T-shirt with a picture of a black poodle that was almost as cute as Toby. "It's like I told you on the phone. He seems really reluctant to put any weight on it."

"Let's get him up on the examining table," I said. As his tiny feet skittered across the smooth stainless steel surface, Sunny helped steady him. "Which foot is it?"

"The left rear," Meryl said. "I guess I should also mention that lately he's seemed kind of subdued."

Sunny laughed. "If this is Toby when he's subdued, I can't imagine what he's like when he's feeling one hundred percent!"

After checking the poodle's eyes, teeth, and ears,

then palpating his organs, I said, "I'm going to see what's going on with that foot—and he's not going to like it. Sunny, would you mind holding Toby's head so he can't bite?"

"He never bites!" Meryl insisted.

"It's just a precaution." I knew that even a dog with the sweetest temperament could react badly when someone caused him pain, even with the best intentions.

"Hey, Toby," Sunny cooed, holding the dog's head with one hand and wrapping the other around his compact body to keep him from sliding off the examining table. "I'm not going to hurt you, sweetie. I promise."

Once I knew that Toby was under Sunny's control, I gently ran my finger along his ailing foot. "So far, this is what a normal leg feels like...."

But when I touched the foot pad, Toby let out a yelp.

"Steady, boy," Sunny said softly. "You're okay."

I turned to Meryl. "He's extremely sensitive to that area, which might indicate a broken toe. I could try to get an X-ray, but it's really difficult to get a good one. We usually just leave it alone and recommend a strict rest period. We could also splint him for four to six weeks, checking him after a week or so.

"In addition, I recommend a nonsteroid anti-inflammatory. The only downside is that it can feel so much better that he'll want to walk on it, so you'll have to keep him from going up or down any stairs."

"I'm up for trying the splint and the anti-inflammatory," Meryl said, her face tense with worry. "I want to do everything I can to help my little guy."

I set Toby up with a plastic splint, then gave his owner a bottle of Rimadyl tablets.

"Give him one a day with food," I instructed. "And I think it's smart to go with the splint. The benefit is that there's no pressure on the bone, which will help it heal faster."

Once we'd finished our paperwork, Toby seemed happy to be on his way out. As for me, I was also pleased, mainly because of the way my new assistant had performed.

"Thanks, Sunny," I said. "You really did a good job."

She beamed as if I'd just paid her the best compliment she'd ever received in her life.

• • •

By the end of the day, I felt like my old self again. There's something about concentrating on nothing but the four-legged creatures that have come to me for help that always makes me feel calm, collected, and in control.

Those feelings vanished the moment Sunny and I walked into my cottage and I was suddenly confronted with the chaos I'd left behind.

Early that morning, before leaving for my meeting with Kimberly, I'd started piling up the things I planned to bring over to the Big House on Friday. Clothes, mostly, which at the moment were strewn across the back of a chair, but also some work-related possessions.

As I'd opened drawers and closets, I also came across a few things I'd shoved out of the way ages ago, planning to attend to them one of these days. But somehow, "one of these days" never seemed to roll around. Once I'd pulled them out to see what they were, I didn't have time to put them away.

"Sorry about the mess," I said, halfheartedly shoving aside a box of old cards, letters, and other mementos I'd left in the middle of the living room.

"No problem," Sunny assured me. "Hey, what's this?" She peered inside the cardboard carton taking up half the couch. It contained my collection of antique bank statements, invoices printed off my computer, and handwritten notes jotted down on pages ripped out of notebooks and in some cases the backs of envelopes.

Busted, I thought.

"Uh, just some papers," I replied. I wasn't exactly airing my dirty laundry in public. It was more like I was airing my aversion to careful record-keeping. "Nothing important. If it's in the way, just stick it wherever you can find a place."

But Sunny was already pawing through the box. "These are your financial records, aren't they?"

"No, they're..." I decided to come clean. "Yes. That's exactly what they are."

"I could straighten out them out for you, if you'd like," Sunny offered cheerfully. "Put all these loose pieces of paper in order, tally up the figures, that kind of thing."

I blinked, thinking, Why didn't I think of that?

"Isn't it time for you to go home?" I asked, not quite willing to believe this was really happening.

"Yeah, but that's okay. I'd much rather learn more about running a business. Besides," she added, grimacing, "it's my dad's turn to cook dinner. That means veggie burgers."

I couldn't believe how much I was enjoying having an assistant. This was only the second day and she'd already proven that she was worth her weight in gold. More, since Sunny looked as if she didn't weigh much more than Max and Lou combined.

Aside from having just been freed from a hateful chore I probably would never have gotten around to anyway, I now had a chance to give some serious thought to what might have been going on in Erin's life. I decided to start by learning a bit more about zoos.

I sat down at the dining room table that doubles as a desk, turned on my laptop, and Googled "history of zoos." I clicked the various websites that came up and began piecing together the story they told.

I learned that Egyptian Queen Hatshepsut built the first zoo around 1500 B.C. Five hundred years later, Wen Wang, the emperor of China, constructed a huge zoo called the Garden of Intelligence. Other zoos sprang up in China, as well as in India and northern Africa. But as was the case with the earliest collections of animals, they were built by wealthy individuals whose main purpose was showing off. The one exception was the ancient Greeks, who created zoos to promote the study of animals. They were also open to the public.

In Europe, zoos began gaining popularity when explorers who traveled to the New World brought back animals that no one had ever seen before. The oldest one still in existence is the Vienna Zoo in Austria, which the royal family, the Hapsburgs, created in 1753. In 1794, Europe's first public zoo opened in Paris, the Ménagerie du Jardin des Plantes. In 1828, the London Zoological Gardens was established so scientists could study animals. In 1847, it opened to the public and was the first facility that was called a zoo. In 1860, Australia's first zoo opened in Melbourne.

The first zoo in the United States, the Central Park Zoo, also opened around then. It was believed to have started when workers at the park were given a few animals, including a bear, as a gift. It quickly became a popular attraction.

In 1899, New York got its second zoo, the Bronx Zoo. Then called the New York Zoological Park, it was created by the Wildlife Conservation Society, an organization that was founded by such movers and shakers as Teddy Roosevelt and Henry Fairfield Osborn, then curator of the city's natural history museum. The WCS was one of the first conservation organizations in the country, meaning that conserving wildlife was one of its top priorities.

I was about to hunt down the website of Long Island's own New York Zoo when a knock at the door interrupted my concentration.

"Want me to get that?" Sunny offered.

"That's okay," I replied, figuring I was going to have to deal with whoever it was myself anyway.

I opened the door and found Marcus Scruggs grinning at me. Or maybe *leering* is a better word, since the man can't seem to stand within fifty feet of any female without looking as if he's imagining her naked.

I'd first met Marcus when I was applying to vet school. Since he was a Cornell alum who lived nearby, I'd looked him up, hoping he'd be a mentor. Instead, he turned out to have way too much testosterone and too large an ego to see past the fact that I possessed only X chromosomes.

Even his car was a phallic symbol. Behind him, his sleek red Corvette was smack in the middle of my driveway. He'd parked it at such an odd angle that it blocked me from getting out and anyone else from getting in.

"Hey, Marcus," I said halfheartedly, doing my best to obstruct the doorway. I hoped he'd realize it was a sign that I wasn't exactly happy to see him.

As usual, subtlety was wasted on him.

"Hey yourself, Popper," he said jovially, somehow managing to wriggle his way into the cottage through the three-inch space between my ribs and the door frame. And the man is over six feet tall. "Long time no see. Sorry I've been making myself scarce lately. But that's the Marc Man for you. When you're as much in demand as I am, somebody's bound to suffer."

"I'm kind of busy at the moment," I said. "Exactly what brings you—?"

"Well, well, well," he interrupted, focusing on Sunny as if he'd come to take an eye test and she was the chart. "What have we here?"

"Forget it, Marcus," I grumbled. "She's much too young for you." Much too smart, too, I thought.

"I think I should be the judge of that." He ran his fingers through his blond hair as if he was filming a hair gel commercial. "Me, and the startlingly attractive young woman in question. And this one happens to be named . . . ?"

"Sunflower," Sunny muttered, barely glancing up from my box of records.

There were two things about her response that told me that even though he'd barely walked in the door, she was already on to him. The first was her sullen tone of voice. The second was the fact that she gave Marcus her full name, which she rarely used because she found it so embarrassing. I sensed that she was trying to turn him off before he got any more turned on.

"Sunflower, huh? Pretty. And, uh, different. Tell me, Sunflower, what brings you to Jessie's cozy little hideaway?" He leaned against the door frame and folded his arms across his chest. I half-expected his next line to be: *The name is Scruggs. Marcus Scruggs.*

"Work," Sunny replied dully, appearing to be as enthralled with my last cell phone bill as she'd be if she'd just stumbled upon one of Shakespeare's original manuscripts.

"Ah. I see you're a woman of few words. That tells me that you're the kind of woman who—"

"I think it tells you she's the kind of woman who's very busy," I said. And not the least bit interested in dirty old men.

"In that case," Marcus said breezily, "I'll catch up with *you* later." And he actually formed a gun with his thumb and forefinger and pretended to shoot her.

"Jessie," Sunny said, finally looking up, pointedly

only at me, "would you like me to take over doing that computer research while you finish up with your ... *guest*? I know you don't have a lot of time."

From her overt references to both finishing up and me not having a lot of time, I could tell she hoped Marcus would take the hint and keep his visit short. I knew better.

"That'd be great," I told her. "Let me show you what I've already found ..."

Once I'd set her up with my laptop, I had no choice but to turn my attention back to my uninvited guest.

"What can I do for you, Marcus?" I asked, hoping he'd be able to tell me in twenty-five words or less.

Instead, he plopped his lanky frame down on my upholstered chair, in the process knocking my good white silk Liz Claiborne blouse on the floor. Then he stretched out his long legs, bumping against the coffee table and nearly knocking over the neat stack of gas station receipts Sunny had piled up.

"I've got important news, Popper," he said, rubbing his hands together.

Somehow, I had a feeling I wasn't going to be the least bit interested in his important news. And that I wouldn't consider it even minimally important.

"I've gotten into something big," he continued. "Really big. I decided that practicing on my own is small potatoes. Instead, I've gone into business with three other vets. And I'm not exaggerating an iota when I tell you that our clinic in Woodview is breaking new ground in the veterinary business."

Personally, I've always hated thinking of taking

care of animals' health as a business. I much prefer thinking of it as a calling.

"The clinic is called Innovative Pet Care," he went on, practically bursting with pride. "It's state of the art, Popper. Completely outside the box. We're offering services that have never been offered to pet owners before."

"Like free nail clipping and complimentary flea collars?" I asked, doing my best to sound enthusiastic.

He smiled smugly. "How about a wine bar to help clients relax before and after their pets' appointments?"

"I think I get it. You mean the clients get drunk and the dogs and cats are the designated drivers?"

Sunny, I noticed, was trying to hide a smile.

"How about hotel rooms right on the premises?" Marcus continued, barreling ahead. "Clients can stay with their pets overnight in the same room if the animal is too sick to go home."

I had to admit that idea actually had some appeal. It was certainly an effective way of lowering an animal's level of stress. An owner's too.

"The most discriminating clients will probably choose the French Poodle Suite," he explained. "That one comes with champagne, chocolate truffles, and an authentic reproduction of a Louis Quatorze bed. Or they may prefer the English Bulldog Suite, which comes with tea and scones and Monty Python DVDs."

"Is there a Siberian Husky Suite with free ice cream and really good air-conditioning?" I asked, trying to demonstrate my appreciation for the concept.

Sunny let out a snort. "Sorry," she mumbled. "Allergies."

As for Marcus, he chose to ignore my cleverness. "The rates are surprisingly reasonable," he went on. "They start at four hundred a night."

"Four hundred *dollars*?" I hoped he meant four hundred Milk-Bones.

"I know!" he replied, grinning. "Hard to believe we can offer our clients such a great deal, isn't it? But wait. There's more. Check this out."

He whipped a glitzy dog collar out of his jacket pocket, a pink suede jobbie studded with large gleaming gems.

"Nice," I said dryly. "Exactly what the world needs: a rhinestone dog collar."

"Rhinestones?" Marcus looked as offended as if I'd just maligned his mother. "These aren't rhinestones, Popper. These are diamonds. The real thing."

"Diamonds?" I repeated. Surely I'd heard him wrong.

"The height of luxury," he said proudly.

"The height of decadence," I shot back. "Marcus, there are children in this country who go to bed hungry every night, and you mean to tell me that—"

"Wait. I'm just getting started." He clearly wasn't the least bit interested in my diatribe about the current condition of the world. He was too busy reaching into the bag he'd dragged in with him. He unfolded the small, oddly shaped garment he pulled out as carefully as if it was the Shroud of Turin.

When he held it up, I saw that it was actually a khaki-colored jacket. For dogs. But the designer clearly hadn't been concerned in the least that our canine friends aren't exactly famous for their manual dexterity. It was covered with pockets, each with a decorative flap held closed by a button.

"Pretty classy, huh?" Marcus asked.

"Extremely," I replied, my voice dripping with so much sarcasm I should have been sitting on a drop cloth.

"You know what this is, don't you?"

"Sure. It's a safari jacket for cocker spaniels with dreams of becoming movie directors."

"Better." Marcus's eyes gleamed as he said, "It's a sun-proof jacket."

"Excuse me?"

"It's a jacket for dogs, all right, but it's made of special fabric that's SPF 30."

"To keep dogs from getting sunburned?" I asked, thinking that maybe this wasn't such a bad idea after all.

A look of confusion crossed his face. "Oh. Yeah, I guess that too. But it's mainly meant to keep dogs and cats from becoming prematurely wrinkled. See? It even has this hood to keep the sun off their faces."

Before I could find the words to express my utter disdain, he pulled out one more item and held it up.

"Guess what this is."

"Marcus, I really don't—"

"Go ahead, guess!"

"Uh, a can of cat food?"

"Close, but no cigar." Beaming, he explained, "It's a can of gourmet cat food...with truffles in it! Truffles, Popper!"

"I didn't know cats were mushroom connoisseurs," I replied cynically.

"Of course, this is just a sampling."

"A sampling of what?" Stupid pet products for a new segment on the Letterman show?

"Of the unique products for the pampered pet we're going to be selling at the clinic's gift shop!"

And here I'd thought nothing the man could say would shock me. "Marcus, tell me you're not serious," I pleaded.

"Oh, I'm very serious. Hear me out, Popper. Today's pet owners are busier than ever. They barely have time to take their animals to the vet, much less the time they need to find just the right products for them. At Innovative Pet Care, we've solved that problem!"

"I get it," I replied. "One-stop shopping, right? A client can bring in a dog or cat and spend fifty dollars on health services and another five hundred on a diamond collar."

"Five hundred?" Marcus cast me a scathing look. "Try five thousand. These stones are the real deal."

"Gee," I muttered. "Looks like I'd better withdraw my application for *The Price is Right*."

"Did I mention that we have a party room for dogs and cats?" he went on. "Well, maybe not cats. But we provide everything for the perfect puppy party: decorations, paper hats, even birthday cakes—made of USDA prime beef, of course. Oh, and let's not forget the goodie bags filled with special treats for the guests to bring home."

Don't tell me, I thought. They're called doggie bags.

"So tell me what you think," Marcus insisted. "Honestly, don't hold back." Before I had a chance to answer, he said, "It's all too fabulous, right? And if you're not already totally impressed, check out the shopping section on our website."

I blinked. "You're joking, right?"

"Hey, these days everybody has a website! But that's only one part of the package. Believe me, veterinary medicine isn't what it used to be. Look at me and you're looking at the future, Popper! I'm at the cutting edge!"

If only he'd fall off, I thought.

"Very nice, Marcus," I said, hoping I'd get rid of him now that his dog-and-pony show was over.

I handed him back his collection of designer disasters. But he held out his hands to stop me.

"Keep those," he insisted. "Not the diamond dog collar, of course. But hang on to the other things. Maybe you'll decide to show them to your clients. And don't forget that they can order these fabulous items and hundreds of others online. Not only is shopping on our website fast and easy; it also entitles them to a ten percent discount."

Terrific. All of a sudden, I'd found myself living in an infomercial.

"You know, I just had an idea," he said, snapping his fingers. "All this talk about embarking on new ventures made me think of it. Maybe I could go on your TV show sometime."

"Marcus, I'm not about to—"

"Not to talk about my new practice," he insisted. "Just to provide a little variety. You know, give your viewers a different perspective on the vet biz while giving the Marc Man a little well-deserved exposure."

I eyed him warily. Personality flaws aside, the Marc Man happened to be a terrific veterinarian. "Maybe," I said.

"Great!" he replied. "Just tell me when. I'll be there. And I can talk about any topic you want. You know there's no better vet in the entire universe!"

When I finally closed the door after him, Sunny turned to me and asked, "If you don't mind me asking, what was *that*?"

I let out a long, deep sigh. "That," I replied, "is a classic example of the male ego gone out of control."

She grimaced. "The next time he comes around, let's shut off the lights and pretend we're not home. Now back to more important things—like what I found out about zoos while you were impressing the heck out of me with how polite you can be."

"I'm all ears," I said, peering over her shoulder at the computer screen.

"Zoos started out as fairly horrible places," she began. "The animals were pretty much kept in cages with concrete floors. But these days, most zoos are committed to animal conservation. About twenty percent of the zoos all over the world are actively working on ways to protect endangered species.

"There's an organization called the World Association of Zoos and Aquariums—its acronym is WAZA—that's the umbrella organization for zoos and aquariums all over the world. It strives to ensure high standards at zoos and promote wildlife conservation all over the world. It's also fighting the importation of wild animals and working to ensure that animals can continue to live in their natural habitat.

"Here in the United States, we have the Association of Zoos and Aquariums, which was founded in 1924. Just like WAZA, it's dedicated to advancing both animal care at zoos and wildlife conservation. Both organizations also develop conservation programs that focus on exploited wild species." Glancing at me, she asked, "What does 'exploited wild species' mean, exactly?"

"It means wild animals, including endangered species, that are hunted for illegal use as pets or souvenirs or even for food," I explained. "One of the best examples is killing elephants to get the ivory from their tusks. Some wild animals are even killed to feed people's superstitions, like grinding up rhinoceros horns to make a powder that some people falsely believe is an aphrodisiac. The tragedy is that so many rhinos have been killed and left to rot just to get their horns that they're now endangered."

I sighed. "It's a real threat, not only to the animals themselves but also to maintaining the biodiversity that's crucial to keeping the whole planet going."

I knew I'd barely scratched the surface of all there was to learn. But having discovered that zoos all over the world were now working to ensure both the welfare of animals and that of the entire planet, I understood why Erin had been drawn to working at one. Despite her showy new house—and despite the way her husband had changed—she was starting to sound like the same old Erin I'd known back in vet school.

I finally felt as if I was reconnecting with her. True, I was saddened by the fact that I'd never have the chance to talk to my friend again. But I was also hopeful that having a strong sense of who she was might help me track down her killer. And paying a visit to her boss at the New York Zoo, the venerable Dr. Annalise Zacarias, seemed like the ideal way to start.

Chapter 6

"Zoo: an excellent place to study the habits of
human beings."

—Evan Esar

The New York Zoo was located in Riverton, the
point at which fish-shaped Long Island diverges
into two "tails," the North Fork and the South
Fork. It was also the end of the Long Island Expressway.

For a long time, Riverton had been the end of the
road in the figurative sense as well. But over the past
couple of decades the area had become a haven for
both tourists and locals. In addition to the zoo, the island's largest outlet mall had sprung up there, as well
as an aquarium, a water park, and a branch of just
about every big box store in existence.

I wasn't the only person who'd decided to take advantage of a beautiful June day like this one by com-
muning with some of the most fascinating creatures
that share our planet. As I wandered along the zoo's

meandering walkways, grateful for the shade provided by the tall trees, I was accompanied by mothers with strollers, groups of rambunctious kids cutting loose on an end-of-the-school-year trip, and a few intense-looking student types bearing sketch pads and boxes of charcoal.

The place was so congenial, in fact, that I had to remind myself that I'd come here on a mission. I decided to head directly for the Animal Health and Research Center, where I hoped I'd find Dr. Zacarias. I also hoped I was crafty enough to come up with a way to get her to talk to me about Erin.

Even though I was anxious about whether or not I'd accomplish that, I figured there was no reason not to enjoy the animals. As I made my way across the property, I made a few detours to check out the elephants, the giraffes, and the big cats.

My favorite stop was the Monkey House. I joined the crowds of enthralled visitors who couldn't tear themselves away from the gold lion tamarins with their bright red-orange fur and contrasting dark faces, the wise-looking owl-faced guenons, and the tiny pygmy marmosets.

But my favorites were the comical squirrel monkeys, who acted like a bunch of kids who'd just burst onto the playground after a morning of math and spelling lessons. Only these guys had a jungle for a playground. Instead of swinging on swings and sliding down slides, they redefined the word *frenzied* as they darted across tree branches, swung from vines, and leaped onto light fixtures, acting as if they were chasing each other even though it was usually impossible to tell who was running after whom.

I finally reached a low concrete building that had to be the Animal Health and Research Center. It was fairly large, stretching all the way back to the edge of the property, and was tucked away in the most remote corner of the zoo. It was also hidden behind a barricade of trees, no doubt to keep visitors from noticing it.

Here goes, I thought as I strode inside, reminding myself that this was hardly the first time I'd talked myself into a place I didn't belong.

Directly inside I found myself in a small reception area. It had an air of quiet dignity, thanks to the upholstered chairs, the copies of *National Geographic* neatly stacked on the wooden coffee table, and the framed oil paintings of lions, elephants, and giraffes on the walls. A young woman wearing a pale turquoise sweater set sat behind a high counter. An ID tag instead of a string of pearls hung around her neck. In addition to a telephone with a complex set of buttons, her desk was cluttered with a collection of small stuffed animals that I had a feeling were available at the gift shop.

I spotted a pair of double swinging doors just beyond the lobby. From the growls and chirps emanating from the other side, I suspected that was where the Animal Health part of the building was located.

"Can I help you?" the receptionist asked with a pleasant smile.

"I'm here to see Dr. Zacarias," I replied as confidently as I could. "She's expecting me. In fact, I'm running a little late."

I held my breath for the three seconds it took her to reply. "In that case, I'll walk you over to her office. Dr. Zacarias hates to be kept waiting. Besides, I have to go back to the administration area to drop something off."

I couldn't resist adding, "If you have time, I'd love to get a quick tour of your medical facilities."

"Sure," the young woman said. "We have to walk in that direction anyway."

I followed her as she pushed through the swinging doors. They opened onto a long corridor with rooms shooting off both sides.

"This is where we provide medical care for all the animals," the receptionist told me. "We have an entire team of veterinarians right here. Since this place runs twenty-four/seven, the vets have staggered schedules so someone's always available. We also have all the equipment and medications we need to treat the animals on-site. A lot of the equipment is the same as what you'd find in a hospital for humans. For example, we use the same type of incubators for our baby animals and the same kind of X-ray machines.

"Some of the other machinery we have here performs the same functions as what you'd find in any ordinary veterinary clinic, only it's on an entirely different scale," she continued. "Over here, we have a five-ton crane. That's used to lift the largest animals we have, usually after they've been sedated."

"Do you use a CO_2 pistol to anesthetize them?" I asked.

"That's right. One of the vets shoots them with a dart while they're still in their cages. Then we bring them here in a truck or whatever's needed to transport them."

Gesturing toward another room off the same hallway, she said, "Over here is our operating room. It has the usual equipment like heart monitors and oxygen hoses. But our operating table is outfitted with hydraulic lifts to help us manage the elephants and the other large animals. And of course we have really big cages where we keep the animals that have come in for treatment. We also quarantine any new animals that are brought in from outside the zoo."

"It sounds as if the vets are kept pretty busy," I commented.

"It's true; one of the animals always seems to need care," she agreed. "Just this morning, the vet on duty removed a tumor from an aardvark and stitched up a male bison that had been gored by another male in the herd. Then we discovered that one of our tigers is pregnant.

"But the vets' routine also includes doing daily rounds every single morning, checking every animal on-site. And all the vets meet twice a week to discuss the animals that are under their care as well as any other concerns they have about their health and well-being. Dietary issues are really important. If an animal is overweight or underweight, adjustments are made in the food they're given. The vets' job also includes immunizing the animals, screening them for infectious diseases, checking for parasites, and taking care of their teeth. And in the event that one of our animals passes, they do extensive postmortem studies to figure out the cause of death."

"But there are also scientists here who do research, aren't there?" I asked. "Dr. Zacarias, for example."

"That's right, we do have researchers on staff," the receptionist replied, nodding. "Their main concern is finding better ways of taking care of the animals in captivity. Diet is a biggie, and so is reproduction. Environmental factors are also something they're constantly learning about.

"Working with zoo animals makes it really easy for scientists like Dr. Zacarias to do research. The animals are so much more accessible than they would be in the wild. For instance, we've been able to measure the levels of certain hormones in the urine of rhinoceroses. We found that rhinos' peak fertility only lasts for about two days, once a year. Knowing this makes it much easier for us to understand the way they reproduce. And most of the animals that are in zoos these days were born in captivity. That means we have tons of information about their parents and in some cases their grandparents and even their great-grandparents. That's especially useful for studying anything that's related to genetics.

"The one thing we don't do is change the way the animals live," she noted. "Our goal is to replicate their natural environment as closely as we possibly can, so for example, we'd never interfere with their social structure or bring in a species of animal that wasn't part of their natural habitat."

We walked a few more steps, then passed through a second set of swinging doors. On the other side were offices that looked as if they'd been designed to house humans, not ailing animals.

"That's the end of the tour," the receptionist told me with a shrug. "And Dr. Zacarias's office is right here."

"Thanks," I told her sincerely. I only hoped Erin's boss would be half as forthcoming.

The door of Annalise Zacarias's office was partially open. I waited until the receptionist had disappeared behind the swinging doors before knocking on it softly.

"Yes, what is it?" a woman's thin, high-pitched voice replied.

I pushed the door open and found a frail-looking woman sitting behind a tremendous wooden desk. She wore her white hair tightly braided and coiled at the back of her head, giving her the look of the headmistress at a boarding school—perhaps one located in Munich or Vienna. Her outfit was equally stern: a black blazer, a white blouse, and a gray paisley scarf worn almost like a necktie.

Perched on her slender nose was a pair of thick glasses with gold wire frames, the chain that held them around her neck dangling from either side. The metal matched the large pin she wore on her jacket lapel, which was in the shape of a chimpanzee.

I assumed that her taste in jewelry was a sign that somewhere in there lurked a sense of humor. That is, until I realized that the primate theme dominated her office's decor. There were at least twenty framed photographs scattered on the walls, almost all of Dr. Zacarias posing with some type of monkey. The background, a dense canopy of trees strewn with vines, told me they had most likely been taken in Africa.

Some of the photos, especially the black-and-white ones, featured a considerably younger version of the office's occupant. In those pictures, her baggy pants and dated hairstyle reminded me of Katharine Hepburn in her heyday.

A few of the photographs were of Dr. Zacarias with other people. I recognized Dian Fossey, who lived among mountain gorillas in Rwanda for almost two decades, and Jane Goodall, who studied chimpanzees in Tanzania. Both women also founded research centers dedicated to understanding and conserving the animals that had been the center of their lives.

Dr. Zacarias certainly traveled in impressive circles. Either that or she was good at talking world-renowned primatologists into posing for the camera.

Aside from the photo gallery, half a dozen posters that featured various primates hung on the wall. The floor-to-ceiling bookshelves were crammed with books, which according to their titles were mainly about primates. Even Dr. Zacarias's coffee mug was adorned with the face of a grimacing monkey, along with the words *Don't Monkey With Me 'Til I've Had My Coffee!*

"Dr. Zacarias?" I asked as I stepped inside the office.

She positioned her glasses on her nose and peered at me with dark eyes filled with distrust. "That's right. Is there something I can help you with?" She spoke with a British accent.

"My name is Jessica Popper," I began. "I'm a veterinarian, and—"

"Do you have an appointment?" she interrupted sharply.

I swallowed hard. "Yes," I lied. "I called yesterday and was told I could meet with you this morning."

"Really." Frowning, she added, "This is the first I'm hearing about this. With whom did you speak?"

"I . . . I didn't get the name of the person who answered the phone," I replied vaguely.

Dr. Zacarias sighed. "Well, since you're here, I suppose I can spare a few minutes. What is it you want?"

Now that I'd gotten her attention, I was going to have to do some quick thinking. Taking a deep breath, I said, "As I mentioned, I'm a veterinarian, and while my practice has always focused on the usual cats, dogs, and horses, lately I've been getting more and more interested in exotics." Glancing around the office, I added, "Actually, I'm mainly interested in primates."

"I see." Her eyes remained fixed on mine with such unrelenting steadiness that I felt like a butterfly pinned to a mounting board. Still, I've become pretty good at staring right back. It's a technique that often comes in handy.

"I understand you're doing some important work," I went on. Deciding that it was safe to make some assumptions, given the photos on the wall, I added, "Especially in Africa."

Sitting up a little straighter, she said, "I'm sure you've heard about the research center I founded in

Kenya. Of course, that was long before I came to the zoo. It was something I did completely on my own."

I hope she doesn't pull a muscle from patting herself on the back, I thought dryly.

Aloud, I said, "I was wondering if you'd be interested in taking me on. As a volunteer, of course. I'd be happy to tell you more about my background, but I think you'd find that I could make a valuable contribution to your research."

Dr. Zacarias was silent for a few seconds. "I don't know if you're aware of this, Dr. . . . I'm sorry, what was the name?"

"Dr. Popper. Jessica Popper."

"Dr. Popper," she repeated. Somehow, she made my name sound like something distasteful. "I'm sure you're highly qualified. However, I'm afraid the timing of this meeting isn't the most opportune. In fact, after the experience I had with the last veterinarian who worked for me, I've been putting a lot of thought into whether or not it's a good idea. You see, there was recently a rather nasty incident that involved my last employee. I don't suppose you heard about Erin Walsh in the news?"

"Erin Walsh?" I exclaimed, feigning surprise. "I know her! Not well," I added quickly. "But she was in my class in vet school at Cornell. I didn't know she works here."

"She did." Dr. Zacarias hesitated before explaining, "She seems to have met up with something . . . unpleasant."

Unpleasant? I thought, struggling to keep from reacting. Getting caught in a rainstorm is unpleasant.

Having your back fender smashed in a parking lot is unpleasant.

Being murdered goes way beyond unpleasant.

"What happened to Erin?" I asked, doing my best to sound innocent.

"Apparently she was murdered." Dr. Zacarias's thin mouth twisted downward, as if she was informing me that her former employee had done something untoward—like shopping online on company time.

"That's horrible!" I cried. "Poor Erin. Her family must be beside themselves. Her parents, of course... and was she married?"

"Yes. To another veterinarian, I understand. Fortunately, she had no children."

"It must be a terrible loss for you too," I commented. "As well as everyone else who works here at the zoo."

Dr. Zacarias pushed her glasses farther up the bridge of her nose and peered at me. The phrase *The better to see you, my dear* popped into my head.

"Erin Walsh was not well liked," she said simply.

"Really?" This time, my surprise was genuine. "That's strange. I seem to remember Erin as quite personable. She also struck me as someone who was very excited about working with animals."

"Let's just say that your former schoolmate was a rather...*ambitious* young woman." Her tone was sour. "Perhaps even too ambitious for her own good. That caused quite a bit of negative feeling around here, since we all try to work together as a team."

Ambitious? I thought, confused by the way she spat out the word. I'm sure Erin had high aspirations.

After all, she had always been the type of person who expected a lot of herself.

But somehow Dr. Zacarias made her sound like some ruthless villain in a political novel, one of those despicable power-hungry individuals who'll do anything to get ahead. And that characterization just didn't fit with the Erin Walsh I'd known.

Before I had a chance to construct a question that would help me clarify her meaning, however, we were interrupted by a knock at the door.

"Dr. Zacarias?" a soft-spoken woman asked timidly as she stepped into the office. She was dressed in jeans and a T-shirt, a work outfit so casual that I concluded she must be one of the researchers on the esteemed primatologist's staff. "I just wondered if you had—oh, I'm sorry. I didn't realize you had someone in here."

"Amanda, please wait for me in your office," Dr. Zacarias said icily. "I'll get back to you when I can."

Even though the young woman hadn't done anything but knock on the door and attempt to ask what sounded like a simple question, Dr. Zacarias's tone implied that she'd just committed some unpardonable sin.

"Uh, sure. Sorry." The younger woman's face reddened, and I could practically see her self-confidence eroding away before my eyes.

Their brief interaction made me glad I wasn't really interested in working with Dr. Zacarias. It also gave me a better understanding of what Erin's life must have been like while she was working under her.

"Is there going to be a funeral?" I asked as Amanda

turned and slunk away. I was anxious to bring the conversation back to the point at which we'd left off. "If there is, I'd like to go—"

"Frankly, I don't know about any of that," Dr. Zacarias interrupted. "As I told that impudent police detective who stopped by, I didn't see much of Erin over the past few weeks. Over the past months the zoo has undertaken a massive fund-raising effort. Since I'm one of the more high-profile figures on staff, I've been given the job of entertaining potential donors. I even helped plan the gala fund-raising dinner held a few weeks ago, which was quite a success, if I do say so myself."

"I'm sure there are a lot of people who are impressed by all you've accomplished," I commented. "And getting people excited about your research must be a great way to motivate them to contribute." Given the way I was buttering her up, I was afraid I was going to have to start taking cholesterol medication.

"Ye-e-es," she said in a way that made it clear she was questioning my sincerity. "Now, if you'll excuse me, Dr. Popper, we'll have to discuss your newfound interest in primates at some later date."

"Of course," I said. Maybe I'm not that good at flattery, I thought, but at least I can take a hint.

I actually felt relieved as I walked out of Dr. Zacarias's office. In fact, I was so busy appreciating having escaped from the oppressive atmosphere in her office that I jumped when someone touched my arm.

"Sorry," the same young woman who'd interrupted us apologized. "I didn't mean to startle you."

Up close, she looked younger than I'd originally

thought she was. But that could have been because she wasn't wearing any makeup. The freshly scrubbed look of her skin emphasized her large blue eyes and the freckles sprinkled over her nose and cheeks.

"You caught me daydreaming," I said with a smile, giving the first excuse I could think of.

"I've been known to indulge in some of that myself," she said, returning the smile. "I don't mean to be nosy, but I couldn't help overhearing you asking about the funeral plans for Erin Walsh. I don't imagine Dr. Z knew anything about it, and I'm afraid I don't either. But I can give you the name and number of a friend of hers who might."

"I'd appreciate that," I said politely, even though Kimberly had already told me there wasn't going to be a formal funeral.

"I have that information in my office," she said. "It's right down the hall."

I followed her to a small room that was very much like Dr. Zacarias's office in that books about primates were crammed onto the bookshelves and the bulletin boards fastened to the walls were covered with pictures of apes. The one major difference was that instead of there being one desk inside, there were three, leaving little space for moving around.

"It looks like you're kind of crowded in here," I commented, surveying the room from the doorway.

Amanda smiled sadly. "Not as crowded as it used to be." Gesturing toward one of the desks, she added, "That's where Erin sat."

"I see." I noticed that no one had had the heart to pack away her things yet, which made it look as if she was likely to walk in at any second. Knowing that wasn't going to happen cast an air of melancholy over the room.

"I know, it's an incredible tragedy," Amanda said, as if she'd read my mind. "We're all feeling it. Fortunately, we'll be leaving soon. Those of us who are working with Dr. Z will be spending most of the summer doing field work."

"In Africa?" I asked.

"That's right. In Kenya, at her research center." Lowering her voice, she added, "Her bark is a lot worse than her bite. She's really quite brilliant. And she's done so much to advance our understanding of primates' mating habits."

"I understand she's quite accomplished," I said.

"She sure is. But you didn't come here to talk about Dr. Z," Amanda said brusquely. "Let me get you Walter's card."

She leaned over one of the desks, reaching into a drawer and pulling out a business card. "You can contact him at this number," she said, handing it to me.

I glanced at the card, which was embossed with the name Walter Weiner. Below it were a telephone number and address. "Does he work here too?"

"Heavens, no. He started working here at the zoo a few months ago, but he was only around for a short time. He's a computer consultant. Dr. Zacarias brought him in to help us streamline some of our operations. Believe it or not, these days even studying the mating behavior of chimps requires spreadsheets and PDF files. But while he was working here, he and Erin became pretty . . . close."

The way she said the word *close* made my ears prick up like Lou's whenever I ask, "Where's the ball?"

"I'm sure he's made a point of finding out all about the funeral arrangements," Amanda continued. "In fact, I should probably get in touch with him myself."

"Thanks," I said, trying to sound casual even though my heart was doing flip-flops over the discovery of this special friend of Erin's. "I'll give him a call."

As I walked down the hall, away from both Amanda's and Dr. Zacarias's offices, I pondered the possibility that Erin had taken up with this computer consultant. Frankly, I found it pretty hard to believe. Even if my intuition was correct and Ben really had been exaggerating about the perfect state of their marriage, Erin had never struck me as someone who would be unfaithful. She was simply too honorable a person.

Then again, if Amanda's insinuation was correct, it meant that there was one more thing about the Erin Walsh I had known in vet school that had changed dramatically.

It also meant that in terms of the murder investigation, I'd found someone else worth questioning.

Chapter 7

"The quizzical expression of the monkey at the zoo comes from his wondering whether he is his brother's keeper, or his keeper's brother."

—Evan Esar

My visit to the zoo ended up being considerably shorter than I'd expected, thanks to Dr. Zacarias's lack of interest in speaking with me. Yet rather than using the extra time to take care of wedding-related errands, I couldn't resist swinging by Walter Weiner's address instead.

According to my trusty Hagstrom map, his street was only half a mile or so off the Long Island Expressway. True, the town he lived in was about as far away from Riverton as a person could get without actually leaving Long Island. It was so far west, in fact, that it was practically at the Queens border. But I wasn't about to let a little detail like one more ridiculously long drive get in my way. Not when I thought of myself as Jessie Popper, Queen of the Road.

Besides, I made good time. And I had no trouble locating the address that matched the one printed on Walter's business card. It turned out to be a narrow brick row house that was wedged closely between its neighbors. The homes immediately to the left and the right looked as if they were occupied by families, thanks to the colorful plastic toys littering their tiny front yards. By comparison, Walter's looked stark. The only personal touch I spotted was the lace curtains hanging in every window—not exactly what I'd expect from a single guy.

I rang the doorbell and waited. As I did, I tried to picture the person I hoped I'd find at home, the man that Amanda had intimated had been "more than friends" with Erin. But as I tried to decide whether he'd embody the classic tall, dark, and handsome look of a Calvin Klein model or the blond preppy look favored by the Abercrombie & Fitch catalog, the door opened. I blinked, totally caught off guard by finding myself face-to-face with a man who was short, pudgy, and balding. Not at all the kind of guy I could imagine a beautiful, vibrant young woman like Erin Walsh falling for—especially if doing so put her ten-year marriage at risk.

"Are you Walter Weiner?" I squeaked, wondering if the answer to this puzzle was something as simple as mistaken identity.

"That's me," he replied, looking confused. "Who are you?"

I took a deep breath, trying to get over my surprise. "My name is Jessica Popper. I was friends with Erin Walsh. I thought you might be willing to give me a few minutes of your time. I'd really appreciate the chance to talk to you, since I understand you were a friend of hers too."

He paused for just a moment before saying, "Sure. Come on in."

"Thanks." As I stepped inside, I noticed that the jeans and cotton-poly button-down shirt Walter was wearing both fit him badly. In fact, it was difficult to picture any self-respecting person looking into the mirror of a dressing room and thinking, I'll take it!

Once I was in his compact living room, however, I was too surprised by the decor to notice any other details about the man's personal appearance. The faded flowered wallpaper looked as if it hadn't been updated since the house was built, which had probably been at least a half-century earlier. The same went for the faded Oriental area rugs and the furniture, which included a sagging brown couch with yellowing crocheted doilies on its rounded arms and a couple of pole lamps with beaded fringe edging the shades. Hanging on the walls were paintings of kittens and little girls. Overall, the place looked as if it had been designed with the Little Old Lady decorating theme in mind.

Superimposed over the worn, dusty furnishings, however, were clues about the man who spent his life here. Stacks of books filled at least half the available floor space. But rather than dignified, old-fashioned-looking volumes that would have fit in with their surroundings, most were paperbacks as thick as phone books, with brightly colored lettering on their spines. Their titles consisted of what looked like words from another tongue. *Mac OS X 10.5. NetBSD 4.0 RC3. DragonFly BSD 1.10.0.*

I quickly realized they weren't dictionaries for languages spoken on other planets. They were software manuals.

I also noticed that sitting on tables and shelves of a few low bookcases were glass tanks. I counted at least a dozen. But it was too dark to see what was inside them, since the blinds were drawn and there wasn't a single light on. I was tempted to suggest that he switch on one of those beaded lamps, but decided it wasn't really the polite thing to do.

"Nice house," I commented, glancing around.

"Thanks. I inherited it from my grandmother."

Ah. So that explained why this dark little hovel looked like the set for a stage production of *Arsenic and Old Lace.*

Walter didn't appear to have inherited any little old lady–style manners, however. In fact, he stood awkwardly in the middle of the room, staring at me with steel-gray eyes half-hidden by the thick lenses of his black plastic-framed glasses, until I asked, "Do you mind if I sit down?"

"Oh. Of course not."

As I lowered myself onto the brown couch—half-expecting a cloud of dust to emerge as my butt hit the cushions—Walter sat down in the rocking chair next to the fireplace.

"So how do you know Erin?" A pained expression crossed his face as he said, "Sorry. I mean, how *did* you know Erin?"

"We went to veterinary school together, at Cornell," I replied.

Even though I'd been in Walter Weiner's company for less than three minutes, I already had serious doubts about Amanda's insinuation that this man and Erin had been linked romantically. And his physical appearance was only a small part of it.

"So you're a vet, just like Erin," Walter said, nodding. "Do you work with exotics too?"

"I'm afraid not. My practice mainly consists of the usual dogs, cats, and horses. Occasionally a reptile or bird comes my way. But never lions or tigers or elephants."

"Too bad."

"I understand that you're a computer consultant," I commented.

"That's right. But I really love animals, including the ones you just mentioned. Which is one of the reasons I really admired what Erin did. I loved the fact that she was so smart and so accomplished. Her determination to get into primate research totally blew me away. And not only was she brilliant; she was also extremely dedicated. She had a real passion for what she did."

I was slowly beginning to understand what Erin might have seen in Walter. For one thing, he had clearly worshipped her. And I got the impression she wasn't someone he'd developed a crush on simply because of her physical beauty. He seemed to see her for what she really was. He truly appreciated her—perhaps more than her own husband did.

But I could also see how attractive he became when

he was animated. As he talked about Erin, his gray eyes glowed. In fact, he took on an entirely different appearance, something that went far beyond what any stone-faced Calvin Klein model could pull off.

"I get the feeling you and Erin were pretty good friends," I observed.

"I thought the world of her," Walter replied ardently. "She and I became very close while I was doing a consulting project at the zoo."

"I'm sure that's bound to happen when two people work together regularly," I commented. I studied his expression, trying to figure out whether his version of "closeness" meant what Amanda had implied.

"It was much more than that," he insisted. "Erin was a very special person. She was one of those rare women who's as beautiful on the inside as she is on the outside."

Frankly, Walter didn't impress me as the type of man who'd had all that much experience with women, either beautiful ones or any other kind. Then again, I'd certainly misjudged people before.

"How long did you and Erin work together?" I asked. I was doing my best to sound as if I was making pleasant conversation instead of giving him the third degree.

"Just a few weeks," he replied. "I was hired by the head of the primatology department to update the software used to track their research data. To be honest, I could have done a lot of it from home. But once Erin and I became friends, going into the place where she worked every chance I could became fun."

"She felt that way too." I hoped I didn't sound as if

I was making this up as I went along, which of course was exactly what I was doing. "In fact, that's why I wanted to meet you. I'd heard so much about you—"

"Erin talked about me?" he interrupted. I couldn't tell if he was pleased or panicked.

"Of course she did," I replied evenly. "She talked about all the people she worked with. You and Dr. Zacarias..."

At the mention of Dr. Zacarias's name, the muscles of his face tightened.

"I can't imagine that Erin had anything good to say about that battle-ax."

"She didn't, as a matter of fact." I chose my words carefully, since by this point I was *really* winging it. "The two of them didn't seem to get along very well."

"Oh, Erin got along fine with everybody," Walter insisted. "She was too nice, if that's possible. She certainly was where Zacarias was concerned." His bitter tone told me that it was his strong dislike for the woman that prevented him from honoring her with the title "Dr." "That old witch is so egocentric that it was inevitable that she would feel threatened by someone as smart and capable as Erin."

"You know, I got the same impression when I spoke with her earlier today." Doing some quick thinking, I added, "I dropped by the zoo to pick up some of Erin's things. Personal items. Ben was too distraught to do it, so I volunteered."

I searched his face again, this time to see if he reacted to me mentioning Erin's husband. But he still seemed to be wallowing in his hatred of Dr. Zacarias.

"Walter," I continued, anxious to find out more

about Erin's boss, "when I was talking to Dr. Zacarias, she made a strange comment about Erin being ambitious. But I got the feeling she meant it in a bad way. Did you ever see that side of Erin?"

Walter snorted. "As if *she's* one to talk."

"What do you mean?"

"Annalise Zacarias is one of the most ambitious people I've ever met. And I'm not talking about her having a true passion for animals or an undying devotion to advancing the field, the way most scientists do. I'm talking about someone who'd do anything to get ahead. Someone who'd run over her own mother if it would help get her name in some scientific journal— or even something as insignificant as a hometown newspaper. Anything at all that would make her look good. Believe me, that woman gives new meaning to the term *cutthroat*."

I swallowed hard, no doubt because of his use of the word. Was Dr. Zacarias cutthroat enough that Erin's ambitions might have driven her to murder?

"Walter, do you have any actual evidence that Dr. Zacarias has done things that other scientists might consider . . . unethical?" I asked.

Another snort. "Erin told me that when she started working for her and saw what she was like, she looked into her background to see if anyone else had had the same experience she was having. Once she started asking around, she got quite an earful. Before Zacarias came to the zoo, she was a university professor. Apparently she was famous for making her graduate students put in ridiculously long hours. I understand she wouldn't even let them go home over Christmas break, not even for a couple of days.

"Erin also found out that a few years ago, one of Zacarias's students wrote up the research he'd spent two years doing, then gave her the manuscript to review before submitting it to a scientific journal for consideration. The next thing he knew, she had published it under her own name—without even mentioning his. And at scientific meetings, she was in the habit of publicly humiliating people in her field. She had a way of phrasing the questions she asked about their research in a way that made it sound as if they'd done something wrong—or even downright sleazy."

His tone more bitter than ever, he concluded, "That woman has been nothing but unscrupulous throughout her entire career, all in the name of self-aggrandizement. The idea of her even implying that Erin was anything but ethical makes me want to put my fist through a wall."

The vehemence of his reaction took me aback. He was certainly doing an effective job of discrediting Dr. Zacarias, as well as the primatologist's assessment of Erin's character. Then again, if Walter and Erin really had been lovers, it made perfect sense that he would become so defensive of her in the face of even an implied criticism.

On top of that, Walter must realize that at some point the police would find out about their relationship—and that he could well become a suspect in her murder. That was another reason that he might be trying to move the spotlight onto Dr. Zacarias, accusing Erin's boss of all manner of unscrupulous tactics.

But before I had a chance to pursue the topic of Dr. Zacarias and her relationship with Erin any further, Walter said, "I'm sorry about going on like this. I'm afraid that just hearing that woman's name sets me off."

"I understand completely," I assured him. I took advantage of the awkward silence that followed to glance around the living room. "If you don't mind me asking, what's in all these tanks?"

He brightened. "That's right; you're a veterinarian. So you'd probably be interested in seeing my own personal zoo."

Gesturing toward the glass tank sitting on a low table just a few feet away, he said, "I don't think of them as pets. More like . . . collectibles. Or curiosities. Wonderful beings that I like to keep around because I find them so fascinating. Let me show you."

I had just assumed that the tanks contained hamsters or guinea pigs or some other cute furry creatures. But when I followed Walter halfway across the room to one of the tanks and glanced into it, I instinctively jerked backward.

"What on earth . . . ?" I cried.

"That's a black widow spider," Walter said, sounding awestruck as he leaned over and peered at the eight-legged creature inside.

"I know what it is," I replied, thinking, *What I don't* know is why anyone would consider the most venomous spider in North America a collectible— even though contrary to popular belief, its bite rarely kills humans. After all, a rare coin or a ceramic figurine isn't likely to send you to the hospital if you handle it incorrectly—or if it manages to escape from the china closet.

"She's a beauty, isn't she?" he said, sounding awestruck.

When I glanced over at him, he was beaming like a proud father. "It's a female?"

"That's right."

"If I'm not mistaken," I commented, taking another step farther away, "it's only the female that's poisonous to humans."

"I'm impressed by your knowledge of arachnids." His eyes still fixed on the inch-long, shiny black spider crawling across the bottom of the tank, he added, "They're nonaggressive, of course. Unless something disturbs their web or if one gets trapped inside someone's clothes. In that case, they inject a neurotoxin. Their bite is rarely fatal, of course, but it does cause some nasty symptoms like muscle spasms, vomiting and diarrhea, and numbness. There are two species in the United States, the northern and the southern. This one's the northern black widow. See? She has a row of red spots running along her abdomen and two bars underneath. The southern black widow has a red marking shaped like an hourglass on its underside."

"Interesting," I said, edging away a little farther. The only thing I hate more than spiders is snakes. Scorpions, maybe, but I don't encounter many of those. Fortunately. "I seem to recall that the only other spider in the United States that's poisonous to humans is the brown recluse."

"That's exactly right!" Once again, Walter sounded pleased that someone had at least some interest in an area that was clearly his passion. "And I happen to have a beautiful specimen right over here."

I could practically feel spiders crawling all over my skin as I politely followed him to another glass tank. This one was sitting on a spindly round table that looked better suited to displaying hand-painted ceramic poodles. But inside there was a brown recluse, all right. The light brown arachnid had six eyes of equal size, arranged in pairs. Maybe they were an optometrist's dream, but I could barely stand to make eye contact with the creepy little fellow.

Walter, meanwhile, looked as if he was in spider heaven. He had the same look on his face that most men get when they're looking at pictures of Angelina Jolie.

"Like the black widow, this guy only bites when somebody's disturbed him." Once again, Walter's feelings of admiration were reflected in his voice. In fact, he was talking about a creature that gave most of us the willies as if it was some charming maverick, the rakish bad boy of the spider world. "It usually takes a few hours for signs of the bite to show. Then it becomes a red lesion with black in the center. It's also itchy and really painful. The symptoms that go with it are pretty nasty too: fever, vomiting, headache, muscle pain. The bite is rarely fatal in humans, but children have been known to die from it. The cause of death is generally kidney failure, seizures, shock, or hemolysis. That's—"

"I know what that is," I interrupted with a shudder. "The breaking open of red blood cells."

"Exactly." Walter beamed. "Not a pretty sight.

Which is a good reason to stay away from these guys."

My strategy exactly. "But you don't," I pointed out. "Stay away from them, I mean."

He shrugged. "I realize they don't exactly make warm and furry pets. It's not as if they come running over to you when you walk in the door, and you certainly can't play Frisbee with them. But I still find them endlessly intriguing."

I had a feeling there was an unspoken *don't you?* tacked onto the end of that sentence, but I wasn't about to extol the wonders of a pet that could kill you. Or at least cause vomiting, seizures, and diarrhea. Puppies, kittens, and gerbils were looking better and better every minute.

"There are still a few specimens I'd love to add to my collection," Walter went on. "Mainly a *Heloderma horridum*—a Mexican beaded lizard. They're venomous, of course, one of only two types of lizards that are. The other is the Gila monster. But of course I'd never keep either of them, since CITES lists them both as endangered. CITES is the Convention on International Trade in Endangered Species of Wild Fauna and Flora."

I was only half-listening, since another thought had just occurred to me. "You don't have any snakes, do you?"

"Unfortunately not," Walter replied. "I used to have a terrific boa named Feather, but he kept escaping. I had no choice but to find him another place to live."

I glanced around nervously, hoping that Feather

hadn't found his way home the way dogs that have been given away sometimes do.

"But I have a few other interesting roommates," he continued. "A tarantula and a few scorpions...Hey, have you ever seen a death stalker?"

"No, I haven't," I told him, thinking, Nor do I have the slightest bit of interest in adding it to my life list. "I'm sure they're fascinating creatures, but I'm afraid I have to get going." To drive home my point, I glanced at my wristwatch. "Goodness! I'm really running late."

"Too bad. Maybe next time."

By that point, I was more than ready to get out of there. Before I left, however, I had one more question.

"By the way," I asked casually as I eased toward the door, "there's something I wanted to ask you about. I remember Erin mentioning a fund-raiser the zoo held a few weeks ago."

Walter looked startled. "She told you about that?"

"Only that she went to it. For some reason, the way she spoke about it gave me the impression that it was..." I fumbled for the right word. "Significant."

"I don't know anything about it," he replied, his face blank. "I mean, I didn't actually work at the zoo, so there was no reason for me to get involved in something like that."

"I see." With a shrug, I said, "I just thought I'd mention it since Erin acted as if it was pretty important to her."

"Like I said," he repeated, "I wasn't there. And she never said a word to me about it."

His response was a little too vehement, and I would

have loved to press him harder. There were other questions I would have liked to ask as well, mainly if he was able to decipher any of the strange combinations of letters Erin had written on her cocktail napkin.

But I wasn't quite ready to be that forthcoming. Not when I had yet to figure out if Walter shared a common trait with the animals in his possession: that when provoked, he was capable of delivering a fatal bite.

Chapter 8

"These can never be true friends: hope, dice, a prostitute, a robber, a cheat, a goldsmith, a monkey, a doctor, a distiller."

—Indian proverb

While I'd thought about little besides Erin's murder in the days that followed the tragic event, on Friday morning I had no choice but to focus on what was probably my most demanding obligation of the week: doing a weekly television spot.

As I raced into the parking lot of Sunshine Multimedia's headquarters, I checked my watch and saw that I was running late. I climbed out of my car and charged across the asphalt, knowing I'd need a minute or two to collect myself before I went on the air to do my weekly television spot. I'd need at least another ten to make my hair look like something besides a lion's mane.

I'd started doing the show back in the fall. Turning me into a media star had been Forrester's idea. Actually, it was more like he was the one who roped me into it. He told the show's producer about me, and before you could say, "We'll be right back after this commercial break," she hounded me until I finally agreed to come into Channel 14's studio.

I thought I was just meeting her to prove that I possessed absolutely no charisma. But the next thing I knew, I was the star of the station's new fifteen-minute TV show about pet care, *Pet People*.

Once I got the hang of it, however, I kind of enjoyed it. It was fun to share what I knew about taking care of animals. Besides, I took the show seriously. I felt responsible for providing viewers with worthwhile information that would benefit both them and their pets.

The only hard part was coming up with a different topic each week, especially since Patti Ardsley, the producer, loved demonstrations. Apparently the shows' ratings were highest when they featured real, live animals. My theory was that it was because putting Fido or Fluffy in front of a camera—on live television, no less—practically guaranteed disaster. But she insisted it was the cuteness factor that made the difference.

In the past, my experiences as a stage mother pushing my offspring into the spotlight hadn't exactly gone smoothly. In fact, I'd sworn that the days of bringing members of my own menagerie to the studio were over.

But because desperation is so often the mother of invention, I'd recruited representatives of both the canine and feline categories for today's show. The feline came in the form of Tinkerbell, who I was lugging toward the entrance of the building in a cat carrier. She had yet to make her television debut, and I was hoping for the best.

Finding an appropriate dog had been more of a challenge. Max was an obvious choice, but he possessed a little too much star quality. The last time I'd had my feisty little terrier on *Pet People*, he'd stolen the show, largely because he'd picked a fight with the camera. As for Lou, he tended to get stage fright.

The only other obvious possibility was Frederick. Unfortunately, Betty and Winston were going to miss their beloved dachshund's first television appearance, since at the moment they were en route to the airport. But I promised to get them a tape of what I was certain would be a stellar debut. Why wouldn't it, when so far he'd behaved like the ideal companion? He was trotting alongside me at the other end of a leash, curious about his new surroundings but not overwhelmed by them.

"Who have we got here?" Patti asked when she poked her head into the green room a few minutes before showtime. As always, *Pet People*'s producer was dressed in a crisp, businesslike suit, and her layered light brown hair was styled as meticulously as if she and Katie Couric shared the same hairdresser. Yet to me, she always looked like a high school senior on Bring Your Daughter to Work Day.

"This is Frederick," I replied, proudly pointing to my furry fawn-colored companion. At the moment, he was watching the TV in the corner, mesmerized by a commercial for a wart remover. "He's a wire-haired—"

"Excellent," Patti interrupted. "Love the visuals. I see you have a cat too. That's great, since we'll be hitting both demographics."

"Demographics?" I asked. Even though I'd been doing this show for a good nine months, I still wasn't fluent in televisionese.

"Demographic categories," she explained impatiently. "We'll be hitting both the dog people and the cat people."

I'd barely had a chance to think about my natural abilities as a marketing mogul before Marlene Fitzgerald, who doubled as the production assistant on the show and Patti's personal assistant, appeared.

"All set?" she asked, as cheerfully if we were going to Disneyland instead of putting on a TV show.

Before I had a chance to answer, she shepherded me and my two sidekicks to Studio A, the station's one and only studio. Marlene was as perky as Patti, with long blond hair and an effervescent smile that made her look as if she was eternally running for class president.

While at first I'd found the idea of being on television frightening, I'd quickly learned that doing a television show was far from intimidating, even when it was live. In fact, it was so low-key that I sometimes felt as if I was making a home movie. The process pretty much consisted of just four of us—Patti, Marlene, the cameraman, and me—putting on the entire show in a small room with black walls and lots of cables. At times, it was difficult to comprehend that what seemed like such an intimate experience was actually being broadcast into thousands of people's homes.

Still, I knew there was a danger in getting too comfortable. I had to keep in mind that just because I couldn't see the people who tuned in didn't mean they couldn't see me. Which is why I did my best to act poised and professional as the red light on the camera began to glow and Patti gave the five-second countdown, saying, "Five, four, three..." and then using two fingers to finish.

"Welcome to *Pet People,*" I began confidently, "the program for people who are passionate about their pets." Believe me, I'd already gotten past the humiliation of pronouncing a sentence as awkward as the one about Peter Piper and his pickled peppers.

I'd also gotten used to the set, which basically consisted of a stool behind a high counter. Behind me was a riotously colorful display of stuffed animals. What a zebra with rainbow stripes and a fuzzy fish covered in fake fur had to do with a veterinary practice was beyond me. Still, I had to admit that the bright colors and different textures did create an interesting background.

"Today I'd like to talk about your pets' teeth," I said, looking directly at the camera. "Most of us don't particularly enjoy going to the dentist, but we do it anyway because we know how important it is to take good care of our teeth. The same is true for your pets. Yet a recent study indicated that roughly two-thirds of pet owners don't make sure their dogs and cats get the level of dental care that the American Animal Hospital Association recommends.

"As a result, signs of oral disease appear in eighty percent of dogs and seventy percent of cats by the time they're three years old. And dental problems don't just affect your animal's teeth. They can lead to heart disease, lung disease, and other serious health problems.

"For all those reasons, it's a good idea to brush your pets' teeth every day. It's also wise to get them used to it while they're still young." I held up Frederick, who up until that point had been snuggling in my lap. "I'll demonstrate on Frederick, a wire-haired dachshund who's agreed to help me out today. Right, Frederick?"

I noticed almost instantly that my assistant had gone from laid-back to fidgety. I didn't know if it was the bright lights or the microphones, but he'd finally figured out that something unusual was happening.

I stroked the silky fur on his head, hoping he would remain calm. "With a dog," I chirped into the camera, "start by dipping your finger into beef bouillon. I have a small bowl right here that I prepared ahead of time. Then rub it on his teeth and gums like this." Cradling Frederick with my left arm, I dipped my right index finger into the bowl and inserted it into his mouth. "Once he's gotten used to the process, you'll be able to wrap gauze over your finger and—ouch!"

I cast my co-star a look of disbelief. "Frederick, what do you think you're—" Suddenly remembering that we were both on camera, I laughed as if having a dog sink his teeth into my flesh was the most amusing thing that had happened to me all day. "My little friend isn't used to being on TV, so no doubt he's a little nervous."

I dipped my finger into the broth again. "Okay, Frederick," I said, continuing my happy-go-lucky approach. "This isn't going to hurt. In fact, you'll like the taste of the—"

"Gr-r-r-r..."

Sweet little Frederick clearly wanted no part of teaching viewers about oral hygiene. I checked the monitor and saw that the cameraman had chosen this particular moment to zoom in for a close-up. All I could see on the screen was Frederick's mouth, magnified about a hundred times. His teeth were bared and his lips twitched threateningly.

What is it about television that brings out the worst in everybody? I thought with dismay. No wonder TV stars' antics are all over the tabloids!

"Okay, it looks as if Frederick is a little camera shy," I said, trying to sound as if I was in control. "But what you can do with *your* pet"—the implication being that unlike Frederick, the dogs belonging to the concerned pet owners watching at home knew how to behave—"is rub the teeth and gums with a circular movement, paying special attention to the gum line. You can eventually move on to a toothbrush that's specially designed for pets, along with cat or dog toothpaste. But don't use toothpaste that's made for humans, since it can cause stomach problems."

During my short monologue, Frederick had gone from fidgety to squirmy. When he found he couldn't break free of my grasp, he started to howl.

Actually, it was more like he was baying at the moon. In fact, from the way he was carrying on, I wondered if Frederick was part werewolf. There had to be something supernatural going on here, since never before had I heard this even-tempered little dog emit more than a friendly "woof, woof."

I noticed that Patti was making a slit-my-throat motion with one hand. Even I knew that was televisionese for Let's move on, shall we?

"Perhaps Tinkerbell will let me demonstrate," I said to the camera.

I deposited Frederick back in my lap and pulled over the cat carrier positioned nearby on the counter. When I let my tiger cat out, she just stood there, blinking. I actually felt relieved that she was temporarily disoriented, since I hoped it would make her a bit calmer than usual.

Instead, the minute she laid eyes on Frederick, she arched her back and began to hiss.

"Tinkerbell!" I cried. "You *know* Frederick! He's a friend! For heaven's sake, he's your next door neighbor!"

My pussycat didn't seem to have heard me. Neither did Frederick. Before I knew what was happening, he leaped off my lap, she jumped off the counter, and the two of them began streaking around the tiny studio.

I glanced at the television monitor and saw that the expression on my face was identical to the one generally worn by the victim in a horror movie. In the background, I could hear the sound of hissing and snarling. As I opened my mouth to speak, I was interrupted by a loud crash as one of my guest stars collided with some unknown object that undoubtedly cost an insane amount of money.

"Goodness, it looks as if Frederick and Tinkerbell are fighting like cats and dogs!" I said feebly.

I glanced at Patti, hoping she would be chuckling. Instead, her expression made it clear that she was anything but amused.

She was also rolling her hands in the air, another bit of televisionese I'd mastered.

"Let's go to the phones!" I cried, desperately grabbing the telephone in front of me on the counter. "Surely one of our viewers has a question. Please feel free to call in. *Please!*"

Never before had I been so relieved to talk to someone about mange. I was equally glad that a large burly man appeared from out of nowhere, captured Frederick, and carried him off, leaving Tinkerbell with no one to fight with.

Still, the fifteen-minute segment seemed to stretch on for hours.

When I finally burst out of the studio with Tinkerbell in my arms, I encountered Patti standing in the hallway.

"I thought that went rather well, don't you?" I joked.

She just glared.

That's the trouble with TV people, I thought as I slunk away. They have absolutely no sense of humor.

• • •

By late Friday afternoon, I'm always pretty wiped out—and today was no exception. It had been a long week. Even Sunny was looking a little ragged around the edges. Her crisp Brooks Brothers blouse was starting to look wilted, and if I wasn't mistaken, there was a scuff on her shoe.

But even though the workday was over, we still had work to do.

This was the day of the move. Nick and I were relocating to the Big House and Sunny was moving into the cottage.

Kind of like a game of musical chairs, I decided as I pulled into my driveway. Even though Betty's chair happens to be on a 747 which at the moment is three thousand feet in the air, en route to Italy.

"Is it okay if I start unpacking some of the stuff from my car?" Sunny asked eagerly as soon as we'd greeted every member of my menagerie and I'd done my usual water bowl check. "I didn't bring much. Just some clothes and a few books and CDs."

"In that case, why don't you bring in your things while I start lugging mine over to Betty's?"

I grabbed my laptop and a shopping bag stuffed with jeans, shorts, and T-shirts and started out the door. Sunny had already opened the trunk of her sporty green Elantra and was lifting out a huge cardboard carton of books packed so full the seams threatened to rip open.

I wondered if somehow she'd confused the definitions of the words *house-sitter* and *roommate*.

"Sunny," I said nervously, "I hope you understand that you're only going to be here for a week and a half."

"I know." Glancing down at the box, she apologetically added, "I'm a fast reader."

I was about to point out as diplomatically as I

could that the only free shelf space in the entire cottage was the gaps between the spice jars she'd arranged so methodically when I heard the distinctive sound of tires crunching against gravel. I turned and saw Suzanne Fox's car careening up the driveway, shaving a few leaves off the trees she narrowly escaped colliding with.

Her shiny red BMW, a vehicle so sporty she looked as if she'd taken a wrong turn on the Indianapolis Motor Speedway and ended up on the LIE, jerked to a halt, its front fender mere inches away from Sunny and me. Interestingly, she wasn't any better at parking than Marcus Scruggs was.

Perhaps that explained why the two of them had been an item for a while. I certainly couldn't see any other reasons that made even a lick of sense. In fact, I'd been more relieved than anyone when she finally saw him for what he was, although that wasn't until the going got tough and he got going—by running in the opposite direction.

"Hey, Jessie!" Suzanne cried happily as she sprang from the car that had always reminded me of a giant M&M. "Skipping town?"

She flicked back her stylishly layered hair, as bright as her BMW, albeit a different shade of red. In honor of the warm June day, she was wearing white shorts that gave new meaning to the term *short* and a hot pink tank top that gave new meaning to the word *hot*. The fact that my pal has more curves than a mountain road made her outfit all the more startling.

Suzanne had certainly come a long way in revamping her image since our days as bio majors at Bryn

Mawr College. Back then, she'd worn her thick red hair in a long braid that hung down her back, a style that screamed "farm girl." Her fashion statement had been similarly low-key. Like me, she'd favored jeans and T-shirts, the more faded the better. And while she could already have been described as pleasingly plump back then, she'd rounded out even more during her twenties and early thirties.

She and I had pretty much lost touch when she went off to veterinary college at Purdue University in her home state of Indiana at the same time I went to Cornell. But we reconnected after she moved to Long Island to start a practice in Poxabogue, a tiny community on eastern Long Island. Her clinic happened to be smack in the middle of the chichi Bromptons, the summer playground of the rich, the famous, and the frequently rude. That meant her client list included a few celebrities and their dogs. In some cases, both had appeared on the cover of *People* magazine.

I wasn't sure if it was her new location that was responsible for her magical transformation into a femme fatale or her recent return to the dating scene following her divorce. But whatever it was, she'd pulled it off with amazing speed and skill.

"I'm not going far," I replied. "I'm just doing some house-sitting and dog-sitting while Betty and Winston are on their honeymoon. And Sunny, my new assistant, is going to be staying in the cottage, taking care of Prometheus and Leilani."

After I'd introduced her to Sunny, Suzanne turned to me and placed her hands on her hips. "Okay, Jessie, I'm not going to beat around the bush, even though

I've been told in no uncertain terms to keep this a secret from you." She paused to take a deep breath. "I'm planning a wedding shower for you."

"A wedding shower?" I was as pleased as I was surprised. "For *moi*?"

"I know, I know. I just broke one of the major rules of wedding shower planning by spilling the beans."

"That's really sweet, Suzanne," I told her sincerely.

"Actually, I can't take full credit," she continued. "Okay, I can't take *any* credit. Dorothy put me up to it."

"Dorothy?" For a moment, I was delighted that my soon-to-be mother-in-law had done something so thoughtful. But then I realized that her motivation was more likely something along the lines like Doing the Proper Thing, rather than Doing Something Nice for Jessica.

"Apparently she originally railroaded Betty into doing it," Suzanne explained. "But when she and Winston decided to go on their honeymoon and were going to be away next Saturday night—that's the date Betty picked—Dorothy put me in charge. Which means I need you to give me a list of people you want me to invite and their phone numbers. I also need a list of the foods you'd like served. Oh, and the name of the stores where I can get them. Also, any decorations you think might be appropriate and the presents you'd like to receive."

Suzanne is quite the party planner, I thought wryly. Rachael Ray must be quaking in her boots.

"You might as well tell me what time you'd like it to start," she continued. "And where you'd like to have it. Hey, maybe we could do it right here in the cottage. Since you won't be staying here, I can really surprise you."

I was about to thank her for all the thought and hard work she was putting into this when I heard more gravel-crunching. Surprised, I glanced up and saw that a pickup truck was pulling into the driveway.

What did I do to deserve such popularity? I wondered.

The fact that I didn't recognize either the truck or the German shepherd sitting shotgun in the cabin confused me even further. As for the driver, I couldn't see his face. That was because of the strange angle at which he was forced to wedge his car into the driveway, thanks to Suzanne's creative, origami-like approach to parking.

"Who's that?" Suzanne demanded, putting her hand above her cornflower-blue eyes as if she was an Apache scout. I had a feeling that what had caught her attention was the fact that the driver was of the male variety.

"Ya got me," I replied with a shrug.

And then, for the next few seconds, we were both silent. No doubt it was because we were both rendered speechless by the awe-inspiring sight before our eyes.

Climbing out of the pickup truck was what looked like a god from mythological times. The man, who stood at least six feet tall and had a lean build with shoulders as broad as a football player's, could only be described as a hunk. His tight, dark blue T-shirt showed off his sculpted muscles. His tight, dark-blue jeans showed off some of his other assets. His short hair was blond, streaked even blonder in spots from the sun. His features were so perfect that you had to wonder if somewhere Brad Pitt was sobbing over the fact that he was no longer the handsomest man in the world.

"Why, *hello* there!" Suzanne cooed, immediately arranging her Mae West frame into a Mae West stance.

"Hello," he returned with a curt nod. "I'm looking for Dr. Popper."

Once he got closer, I could see that his eyes were as green as a shamrock on St. Patrick's Day. So I wasn't surprised when he added, "I'm Kieran O'Malley."

"I'm Jessie Popper," I told him once I'd finally caught my breath.

Suzanne cast me such a scathing look that I wondered if *she* had planned on claiming to be Dr. Popper. Anything to prolong her interaction with this living, breathing page out of *GQ*.

I cast her a dirty look of my own, thinking, Every woman for herself.

"Is there something I can help you with?" I asked sweetly.

It was only then that I remembered I was currently in the process of planning my wedding—a wedding that involved place cards, ice sculpture, and even surprise showers that weren't actually a surprise. Oh, yes, and a lifelong commitment to one Nicholas Burby.

I cleared my throat, a gesture that seemed to clear my head as well. "Of course," I said in my normal voice. "You're Trooper O'Malley from the New York

State Canine Unit. I was told to expect a call from you."

I'd gotten a call a few weeks earlier, asking if I'd be willing to add some of the dogs in the New York State Canine Unit to my list of patients. Of course I said yes. In order to foster a good working relationship, the dogs lived with their handlers in addition to working with them. And with state troopers residing all over the state, the dogs received their medical care from local veterinarians, rather than one central facility.

Once I'd found out I was going to be working with state troopers and their dogs, I did a bit of Internet research. I learned that the New York State Canine Unit had more than sixty canine teams that specialized in explosive detection or narcotics detection, with three additional bloodhound teams used for tracking. The unit had started in 1975 with three troopers and three dogs purchased from the U.S. Army. While Crow, Miss Jicky, and Baretta were trained by the Baltimore Police Department, in 1978 New York began its own training.

These days, most of the dogs were donated by Humane Societies, breeders, and private citizens. Dogs and handlers trained together at the department's training center in Cooperstown for twenty weeks. In addition to basic obedience and agility, they learned specialized skills like tracking, building searches, and narcotics or explosive detection.

"I happened to be close by, so I figured I'd stop over," Trooper O'Malley explained. "It seemed easier than playing phone tag."

"How did you find my address?" I asked, surprised.

He shrugged. "I'm a cop," he replied matter-of-factly.

"Personally, I've always thought that law enforcement was *such* a fascinating career!" Suzanne interjected, her voice as breathless as if she'd just run a marathon. "Looking danger in the eye must be an everyday occurrence for someone like you."

Kieran O'Malley grinned. "I'll admit I've got a few stories to tell."

"Did I hear Jessie say you're with the canine unit?" Suzanne asked.

"That's right. In fact, that's why I'm here. Skittles, come heel!"

He'd barely gotten the words out before the muscular German shepherd that had been sitting patiently in the truck leaped out and positioned herself beside him as if she was his shadow. Yet from the steely look in the beautiful dog's dark brown eyes, it was clear that this powerful animal was nobody's shadow.

"Here's my girl," Officer O'Malley said proudly. "Skittles, sit!"

The dog dutifully lowered her butt to the ground.

"Skittles is *such* a cute name," Suzanne purred, fluffing out her hair as if she'd begun channeling Farrah Fawcett. "How did you *ever* come up with it, Officer O'Malley?"

"Please, call me Kieran," he drawled. "It's a custom in the department to name every new dog after the last trooper killed on duty. In this case, it was a man named Stanislaus Kraminski. But his nickname was

Skittles because he loved candy so much." Smiling fondly at his partner-in-crime-fighting, he said, "The name Skittles suited this little girl much better than Stanislaus or Kraminski."

"I'm going to be treating some of the dogs who work with the state troopers," I explained to Suzanne. "The dogs in the canine unit live at home with their handlers. I've just been hired to work with the troopers who live on Long Island."

"I'd love to get involved in something like that!" Suzanne cooed. "I'm a veterinarian too."

Between all the cooing and purring, Suzanne sounded as if she was one of the patients instead of a doctor. In fact, I had to look closely to make sure the woman standing next to me was the same one I'd stayed up all night with during our pre-vet years at Bryn Mawr, memorizing the body parts of a fruit fly and doing dissections. This version of Suzanne reminded me a little too much of Betty Boop. At the moment, she was draped across Kieran's pickup truck like a model in a spark-plug ad, batting her eyelashes as if she'd gotten soap from a car wash in them.

"It sounds as if you live nearby," she murmured. "What town?"

"Bright Shores," he replied.

"Really!" Suzanne exclaimed. "I live in West Brompton Beach. Goodness, that practically makes us next door neighbors."

Right, I thought dryly. If your backyard happens to be thirty miles wide.

Kieran didn't seem to be any better at Long Island geography than my gal pal.

"West Brompton Beach, huh?" he said lightly. "You're right. You and I live so close to each other that maybe we should get together sometime. Compare notes on our favorite restaurants, stuff like that."

Like Suzanne, his voice had changed. His posture too. At first I thought I was the only one who'd noticed. Then I realized that Skittles had as well.

And Kieran's loyal sidekick didn't seem to approve of all the sparks that were suddenly flying. She drew herself up a little higher and stuck out her chest. And then, her ears pricked and her eyes bright, she emitted a no-nonsense growl.

"Quiet!" Kieran barked.

Being a well-trained animal, Skittles followed his command. But that didn't keep the German shepherd from glaring at her master.

I'm with you, Skittles, I thought grimly. I'm running a veterinary practice, not a dating service for the hormonally challenged.

"Let me give you my phone number," Suzanne offered. With a giggle, she added, "You know, I don't think I told you my name. It's Suzanne Fox."

Kieran's grin widened. "Fox, huh?"

Somehow, the double meaning of my girlfriend's last name never seems to be wasted on her male admirers.

"I'll just give you one of my cards," Suzanne went on. "It has both my office number and my cell phone number...."

As she stepped forward to hand Kieran her card, Skittles tensed. The massive dog's upper lip flared upward, just a millimeter or two, in what I recognized as a snarl.

Kieran and Suzanne were too busy playing the roles of Romeo and Juliet to notice.

"Great," Kieran said, tucking the card into his pants pocket. "I'll give you a call, Ms. Fox."

"Anytime, Trooper O'Malley," Suzanne cooed.

I cleared my throat. "Maybe I should take a look at Skittles," I suggested, gesturing toward the clinic-on-wheels parked a few feet away. "Since you're here and all."

A look of confusion crossed Kieran's face. For the moment, at least, he'd clearly forgotten all about why he'd come to my house.

"Oh. Sure." He snapped to attention. "Skittles, heel!"

Skittles seemed relieved that once again she was the center of her master's attention. As for Suzanne, she was already sashaying toward the cottage, her hips swaying so far from side to side you'd have thought she was giving rumba lessons.

"I'll just wait inside," she called over her shoulder. Fixing her eyes on Kieran, she added, "It was *so* lovely meeting you. I look forward to seeing you again. *Soon.*"

Skittles let out a yelp. I had to suppress the urge to do the same.

• • •

Since this was the first night Nick and I would be spending in the Big House, I wanted to mark the occasion by doing something sensational.

Besides, Friday evenings had had a special meaning for Nick and me for a long time. Both of us were so busy during the week that we'd begun setting aside this one night of the week as a chance to relax and reconnect. This past year had been particularly tough. His first year at the Brookside University School of Law had been as demanding as boot camp, but it had lasted nine months instead of six weeks. Embarking upon his first internship at a law firm wasn't much easier. As if the long hours and nonstop pressure weren't bad enough, the poor man had to iron a shirt every morning.

I decided to take advantage of the magnificent kitchen that was now at my disposal by cooking an elegant dinner. My version of an elegant dinner anyway. That meant ravioli smothered in Bolognese sauce. Homemade, of course—not by me but by the wizards at Papa Luigi's Italian Market.

I picked up a bottle of Chianti too. For the dessert course, however, I stuck with an American classic: Ben & Jerry's Cherry Garcia. Besides, I told myself it was possible that either Ben, Jerry, or the ice cream's namesake had some Italian blood in them. To maintain the theme of fine dining, I served it in the crystal bowls I found in the butler's pantry instead of straight out of the carton.

"This isn't too shabby," Nick commented as the two of us sat at opposite ends of Betty and Winston's dining room table. Since it was long enough to seat fourteen, I practically had to squint to see him.

Not that it wasn't worth it. The table was covered in a lacy cream-colored tablecloth that matched the napkins we'd both felt obligated to place in our laps. A fresh bouquet of cream-colored roses that Betty had left for us to enjoy sat in the center, flanked by two ornate silver candelabras holding six pale pink candles. A chamber music CD added to the elegant and extremely romantic ambience.

Even though I'd been busy shoving pasta into my mouth, I paused long enough to say, "Not at all. In fact, I could definitely get used to this."

Nick set down his fork. "You know, Jess, once I'm out of law school and I've started working, we should be able to buy a house. With our combined salaries, I mean."

Is it getting warm in here, I wondered, or did Papa Luigi put too much garlic in the tomato sauce?

Here I was still trying to get used to the idea of being someone's lawful wedded wife, with my wedding day looming ahead in the not-distant-enough future. And now my betrothed was suddenly throwing real estate into the deal. Mortgages, taxes, circuit breakers, cesspools, lawns that required mowing, leaves that required raking, shingles that required painting...it was enough to take away anyone's appetite.

I took a big gulp of wine, then mumbled, "I'm happy living in the cottage."

"Sure," Nick replied. "The cottage is great. For now. But before long, we'll want more space. A two-car garage. A laundry room. And we'll probably want to do some renovations. You know, to make our place exactly the way we want it.

"Besides," he continued as matter-of-factly as if he

was talking about the Yankees, "at some point we'll want to start a family."

"I have a family," I squawked. I gestured toward two of my children, who at the moment were sitting on the floor next to me with their pal Frederick, as alert as Beefeaters guarding the crown jewels. Of course, I knew perfectly well that all three of them were merely hoping that some random morsel of people food would drop onto the floor.

"Right." Nick chuckled. "But I'm talking about family members who don't have to be walked twice a day."

"Oh."

By now, I'd *really* lost my appetite. If talking about real estate made my stomach so tight that it would no longer accept food, talking about the pitter-patter of little feet was enough to launch a full-scale anxiety attack.

It wasn't that I didn't *want* children. It was just that whenever I thought about having them, it seemed like something in the distant future. One of those things it was difficult to imagine actually happening, like losing one's teeth. Or hair. Or any other body parts that had the potential to drop off much further along in one's life.

I'm not saying that having children should be viewed in such a negative way. It's just that it sounded so darned scary. In fact, discussing it was as likely to ruin a romantic dinner as talking about global warming or nuclear warfare.

Nick must have read my mind. Either that or he

correctly interpreted the stricken look that was no doubt on my face.

"But we don't have to make any decisions about that now," he said with a gentle smile. "Instead of the future, we should be concentrating on the present."

Yes, I thought, the present is much easier to cope with. Especially since it involves nothing more demanding than finishing up this bottle of Chianti and moving on to the Ben & Jerry's course.

• • •

After dinner, Nick volunteered to do the dishes. He insisted it was only fair, since I was the one who'd played the role of executive chef, or at least executive food shopper.

I decided to use my free time by grabbing my computer and my purse and parking myself on one of the silk brocade-covered Victorian couches in Betty and Winston's living room. Tinkerbell jumped up beside me and meowed crossly at the machine in my lap, telling it in no uncertain terms that that was her spot. When it failed to respond to her threats, she finally gave up and settled down on a lavender beaded throw pillow that Betty had brought back from Morocco or Majorca or one of the other exotic places she'd traveled to.

I reached into my purse and pulled out the Xerox copy of the cocktail napkin that I'd been carrying around. Spreading it out on the couch next to me, I studied it, hoping that somehow what I was looking at would start to make sense.

100 Brown BB +
NGIPPL IFAWCI
A2RX X ☺

It looked just as mysterious as it had the first time
I'd seen it. Still, I didn't lose heart.

In the old days, I thought as I clicked on the
Internet Explorer icon, people needed a decoder ring
to figure out this kind of thing. In modern times, we
had something a heck of a lot better.

As soon as the Google page loaded, I typed in "100
Brown," then hit Enter.

As I expected, a long list of links came up. Unfortunately, they all appeared to be links to websites that were selling something with the words *100*
and *brown* in them, including 100 Christmas lights
on brown wire, a 100% brown leather recliner, 100
brown baby-proof electrical outlet covers, and 100
brown corrugated shipping boxes. There was also a
link to the website of a radio station that considered
Van Morrison's recording of "Brown-Eyed Girl" one
of the top 100 hits of all time.

Maybe I would have done better with one of those
decoder rings.

But I was hardly ready to give up. Next I Googled
"NGIPPL." After a few seconds, Google politely informed me that my search did not match any docu-
ments. It also suggested that I make sure all words
were spelled correctly or try different keywords.

"You're not trying very hard," I muttered churl-
ishly.

Next I tried Googling "IFAWCI." Not surprisingly,

I got the same response—and the same unhelpful suggestions.

I expected the same for A2RX, but learned that A2RX was part of an equation that had something to do with a perturbed harmonic oscillator and odd coherent states. At least, according to some physicist in Russia.

I was so absorbed in what I was doing that I didn't even look up when Nick came into the room and snuggled up next to me.

"Hey," he murmured, gently brushing away a strand of hair that had fallen into my eyes.

"Hey, yourself," I returned, wondering if I should Google "odd coherent states."

"This is our first night as lord and lady of the manor," he reminded me. "Shouldn't we be taking advantage of all the finery around us?"

"You mean like the big-screen TV in Winston's study?" I teased.

"Actually, I was thinking of the king-size bed in the master bedroom." Kissing my neck, he said, "Didn't you tell me once that Betty gets her sheets at some fancy store in the city? What do you say we check them out and see what we've been missing?"

I had to admit, that sounded like a lot more fun than trying to decipher Erin Walsh's mysterious scribblings.

"I think that's an absolutely stupendous idea," I replied.

Having Nick and me sleep in the master bedroom had been Betty's idea. It was the nicest bedroom in the house, and she'd wanted to make sure our stint as house sitters was as luxurious as possible. The room was huge, with a gigantic four-poster bed, antique dressers, and elegant drapes that reminded me of the curtains in a theater. The dear woman had even thought to leave chocolates wrapped in gold foil on the pillows as a special welcoming gesture.

But we'd barely slipped between Betty's silky Italian sheets before my cell phone trilled.

Nick groaned. "It's Friday night. Don't your clients ever leave you alone?"

"It's your mother," I informed him, glancing at caller ID as I grabbed my phone off the spindly table next to the bed.

"Don't answer it!"

But it was too late. "Hello, Dorothy," I greeted my future mother-in-law cheerfully, trying to sound as if I wasn't lying in bed naked with her son.

"Jessica," she said brusquely, "I'm calling because I have a question."

"Shoot," I replied, immediately wondering if I'd just made a Freudian slip.

Dorothy hesitated. "It's a question about wedding showers."

Ah, I thought. Such a popular topic these days.

"If someone was throwing a person's future daughter-in-law a wedding shower—a surprise shower, mind you—and that person happened to live far away— say, a distance of well over a thousand miles—do you think that person would be obligated to travel such a long distance, at great personal expense, no less, and I'm not even going to mention the inconvenience, to attend that daughter-in-law's surprise wedding shower?"

This was beginning to sound like the legalese Nick was learning in law school, all that business about the party of the first part and the party of the second part.

"No, Dorothy, I don't," I replied. "In a case like that, I think a friendly phone call the day after would be just fine. And maybe a card or a short note."

"Oh, thank you!" Dorothy cried. "For your input, I mean. This happens to be something, uh, a friend of mine is dealing with."

"Your friend certainly sounds like a very caring, sensitive person," I said, astounded by how good I was getting at this. Still, I had to admit that I wasn't exactly disappointed that my future shrew-in-law wouldn't be attending my not-very-surprising surprise shower.

"Boy, are you a master of laying it on thick!" Nick commented with a grin after I'd put my cell phone back on the table. "Before you know it, you're going to have that impossible mother of mine wrapped around your finger."

I'd settle for having her stay in Florida, I thought. But I didn't want to waste the rest of the evening thinking about such an unsavory subject. Not when there were much more savory ones to concentrate on.

"Now, where were we?" I asked, turning to Nick and purring as if I'd earned a Master's degree at the Suzanne Fox School of Charm.

He'd barely had a chance to refresh my memory before my cell phone trilled again.

"If it's my mother calling back . . ." Nick muttered.

But when I glanced at caller ID, I saw that it wasn't Dorothy Burby. It was Forrester Sloan. And the fact that he was calling this late on a Friday night told me this was more than just a social call.

"I'm sorry, Nick, but I have to take this." I tried to ignore his loud sigh as I answered with, "What's up, Forrester?"

"Hey, Jess," he said. "Sorry to call you so late."

"No problem," I assured him. My heartbeat was already speeding up. While Forrester had never been shy about his interest in me, I couldn't remember any other time that he'd called me at this hour on a Friday night.

Which meant he had to have a good reason. "Is this about Erin's murder?"

"I'm afraid so," he replied somberly. "I just got off the phone with Falcone. The results of the autopsy are in."

The seriousness of his tone was making me more and more anxious.

"And?" I prompted.

"I have to warn you, Jessie. This is kind of . . . disturbing."

"Tell me," I demanded.

Forrester took a deep breath. "It seems that right before Erin was murdered, she was attacked by a deadly scorpion."

Chapter 9

"I learned the way a monkey learns—by watching its parents."

—Prince Charles

A scorpion!" I exclaimed. I glanced over at Nick and saw that he looked just as shocked as I was. "I know. It sounds crazy," Forrester said, sounding dazed. "But it seems that while the medical examiner was performing what he expected to be a routine autopsy, he noticed some strange markings on Erin's arm. He decided they looked like insect bites, so he did a little extra toxicology testing and found what he thought was some kind of venom in her blood.

"Apparently Dr. Stokes had never encountered anything like it before," he continued, "so he contacted somebody at the natural history museum in New York. It turned out that what he'd found was the venom of a scorpion called—wait, let me make sure I've got the name right—the yellow fat tail scorpion. Apparently it's found in North Africa and parts of

Asia. It also happens to be one of the deadliest scorpions in the world."

Forrester paused. "But interestingly enough, Dr. Stokes was convinced that it wasn't the venom that killed Erin. Even though it was in her system, everything he found points to strangulation as the cause of death."

So many questions swam around in my head that I didn't know which one to ask first. But even though everything in the room suddenly looked blurry, one thing was perfectly clear.

And that was that the surprising findings from Erin Walsh's autopsy pointed straight at Walter Weiner, the man who was as infatuated with creepy crawling creatures as he had been with the murder victim.

• • •

"What was all that about?" Nick demanded as soon as I'd hung up.

I was about to pour out the details of this bizarre new twist in Erin's murder when I remembered that my interest in this subject wasn't exactly something that Nick was likely to be particularly enthusiastic about.

I knew perfectly well that he had good reason to be concerned. After all, on more than one occasion I'd come horrifyingly close to suffering the same fate as the poor individual whose murder I was investigating.

But this time was different. The victim's sister had specifically requested my assistance. Besides, as Kimberly had pointed out, the fact that Erin had called me to ask for help right before she was killed meant that I was involved, whether I liked it or not.

I decided to take a matter-of-fact approach. "That was Forrester Sloan," I said. "I don't know if you remember him. He's a reporter at *Newsday*—"

"Believe me, I remember him," Nick assured me. His icy tone told me he also remembered that Forrester had been pursuing me practically since the day we'd met.

"Anyway," I continued, "he just talked to Falcone. The medical examiner discovered that right before Erin was strangled to death, she was stung by a deadly scorpion. One that's only found in Africa and Asia."

"Whoa," Nick said breathlessly. "That's horrible. And very weird."

Not to mention potentially revealing, I thought.

"But why did he call *you*—especially so late at night?"

A look of comprehension crossed Nick's face almost as soon as he'd gotten the words out, telling me that he'd already answered his own question. "Jessie, please don't tell me you've been investigating another murder."

"This isn't just any murder investigation," I insisted, trying to remain calm. "This is one I've been involved in all along. Nick, I'm the person Erin called to ask for help right before she was killed."

"But you hardly knew her!" he countered. "You told me yourself that you hadn't talked to her in years!"

"I know. But that just makes the fact that she called

me at five-thirty on the morning she was murdered all the more meaningful.

"Besides," I continued, "Erin's sister, Kimberly, asked me to help. She wants me to try to figure out the meaning of some mysterious notes Erin made on a paper napkin a few weeks ago, the same night she attended a fund-raiser for the zoo. Kimberly said Erin acted strange when she asked her about them, so she thinks that whatever she jotted down might have something to do with her murder."

Nick flopped onto his back. "I don't believe this! Jess, have you forgotten that you and I are getting married three weeks from tomorrow?"

"Of course I haven't!"

"Isn't that what you should be concentrating on?" he demanded. "Instead of running around sticking your nose into places where it doesn't belong—and where it might even get cut off?"

"Your mother is planning practically the entire wedding by herself," I pointed out. "She's turning out to be a real angel."

He groaned. "I never thought I'd hear anyone, especially you, refer to Dorothy as an angel!"

"But she's been an enormous help." I was about to tell him about her being so organized that she'd put Suzanne in charge of planning my surprise wedding shower. But I decided that at least somebody should be surprised.

"So you thought that I'd simply accept the fact that, once again, the woman I love, the woman I'm about to *marry,* is going to put her own safety and possibly her life in danger by investigating another murder," Nick grumbled. "You just assumed that I'd go along with it."

"Actually," I said casually, "I thought you might help."

"*What?*"

"You were a private investigator for years, Nick. There are so many things you're an expert at that I don't know a thing about." I reached across the bed and began running my fingers lightly along his chest. "You're so good at being sneaky."

I could tell he was weakening. In fact, the tension in the room was dissipating with amazing speed. "Sneaky, huh? You mean that in a good way, right?"

"Definitely! Besides," I said, now moving my fingers around and around in a gentle swirling motion, "as a wedding present you could think of helping me figure out who killed Erin."

"Oh, yeah?" he replied. "I didn't know the groom was expected to give the bride a wedding present."

Doing my best to keep a straight face, I said, "It's an old Lithuanian custom."

"And here I had no idea the woman I was about to marry was Lithuanian."

"Only a small part."

"No kidding." Nick's voice had gotten low and husky. "Do you mind if I try to figure out which part?"

"I think that's an excellent idea," I told him. Wriggling closer, I added, "In fact, that's the best idea I've heard all day."

• • •

Now that I knew Erin had been stung by an exotic scorpion, possibly one that lived in a tank in Walter Weiner's house, I was anxious to find out more about the true nature of her relationship with him. But my plan was to start with someone other than the man himself.

Saturday morning, right after Nick and I gorged ourselves on the buttermilk pancakes he whipped up, I punched Kimberly Walsh's home number into my cell phone.

"Kimberly? It's Jessie Popper."

"I was hoping you'd call," she replied sincerely. "Have you heard the latest? About what the autopsy revealed, I mean?"

"Yes. As a matter of fact, it raised a few questions that I'd like to talk to you about. Can I stop by this morning?"

"Of course. Let me tell you how to get here. . . ."

Kimberly lived in a condominium complex that had recently sprung up alongside the Northern State Parkway. For decades, the large plot of land had been a nursery that bore the name of one of the early Dutch families that settled Long Island in the 1600s. And then, practically overnight, the neat rows of flowers and ornamental shrubs magically morphed into a hundred townhouses, all painted a sunshine yellow that was at least as colorful as the blossoms they replaced.

While the grounds had once been covered with greenery, the developer had apparently pulled everything out by the roots and started again. As a result, the few trees that had been planted in the rich, dark brown soil were still scraggly.

Yet some of the residents, including Kimberly, had planted a few flowers of their own. Hers burst out of large terra-cotta pots lined up in back of the throw rug–size plot of land accompanying each two-story townhouse. The bright pink-and-white impatiens spilling over the sides went a long way in giving the place a friendly, welcoming appearance.

Kimberly answered the door even before the loud, melodious doorbell had stopped echoing through the interior. She was dressed in jeans and a black T-shirt. It was a somber outfit that I imagined matched the somber mood reflected in her slumped shoulders and the drawn look on her face.

"Thanks for coming over," she greeted me. "Let's go into the kitchen. I just made a fresh pot of coffee."

As I followed her through the spacious apartment to the kitchen in back, I saw that it was as bright and sunny as the exterior. Instead of yellow, however, the walls were painted a glaring shade of white. Kimberly had used their starkness as a backdrop for her own taste in decorating, which incorporated restful pastels like pale blue and green with tiny floral patterns. The decor was decidedly feminine, with too many ruffled throw pillows and baskets of dried flowers for my taste. Still, it definitely looked as if she'd put a lot of effort into making the place her own.

I could see the anxiety in her eyes as she filled two white ceramic mugs, then pushed one toward me across the gray-and-white granite counter. I decided not to waste time on chitchat.

"Kimberly," I said as I lowered myself onto one of the counter-height stools, "I have kind of a difficult question I'd like to ask you."

She laughed coldly. "Believe me, everything I've had to deal with this week has been difficult. Why should today be any different?"

I realized that no matter how hard I struggled to find the right words, there was only one way to phrase the question I'd come here to ask. Even so, I took a deep breath before asking, "Do you think it's possible Erin was having an affair?"

I braced myself for a string of protests, a loving sister's insistence that there was no way her sister—a married woman—would ever have strayed.

Instead, Kimberly was silent for a long time, as if she was giving my question serious consideration.

"If you'd asked me that question even a year ago," she finally said, her eyes fixed on the still-untouched coffee in her mug, "I would have said it was impossible. But given the tension in her marriage over these past few months, I could imagine Erin looking elsewhere for whatever she wasn't getting from Ben."

Narrowing her eyes inquisitively, she asked, "Do you have any idea who she might have been seeing?"

I nodded. "A man named Walter Weiner."

I searched her face for a reaction. Instead, she just looked at me blankly. "I never heard her mention him. Who is he?"

"Someone she worked with at the zoo."

"I see." She finally paused to sip her coffee. "Is this what you mentioned was related to the scorpion business?"

"Possibly," I replied. "I made a point of dropping by his house a couple of days ago, right after I went to the zoo. Someone who worked with Erin intimated that she and Walter were close."

"What is he like?"

"He certainly isn't as good-looking as Ben," I replied thoughtfully. "Not nearly as charming either. But it was impossible not to see how crazy about Erin he was. He really seemed to care about her."

"Then, unlike Ben, I guess we can leave him off our list of murder suspects," Kimberly said dryly.

"Not necessarily."

"But if he was as crazy about my sister as you seem to think, why would he have wanted anything bad to happen to her?"

"Because something in their relationship—if there really was one, that is—could have gone wrong," I replied. "For example, what if he really did adore Erin and in fact had big plans for their future together, and then she told him she wanted to end the affair?"

Kimberly took another sip of coffee while she thought about that scenario.

"I see what you're saying. I suppose he also could have pressured her to leave Ben and she refused." As if she suddenly remembered what had precipitated this discussion in the first place, she abruptly asked, "But what does this new piece of information about the scorpion have to do with him and Erin?"

I took a deep breath. "Kimberly, Walter keeps some pretty unusual creatures as pets—including a scorpion that's called a death stalker."

"Oh, my God," she breathed. In a choked voice,

she asked, "Does he have one of those yellow tail thingies? The kind the police think attacked Erin?"

"I don't know," I said. "But whether he has one or not, I bet he'd know how to get hold of one. And even though they're apparently pretty dangerous, he'd probably feel comfortable enough around them to handle one without getting stung himself. He's also likely to know enough about their habits to have created a situation in which one would have attacked poor Erin."

"Walter Weiner," Kimberly said softly. It was almost as if she was trying out the name to see how it sounded. "I wonder if he was at that fund-raiser."

It was the very question that had been gnawing at me ever since I'd talked to him. While he'd claimed that he knew nothing about it, he had looked shocked when I brought it up.

His reaction had left me determined to find out more about his involvement in the event the next time I saw him.

And I intended to make that soon.

• • •

Even though the news about the scorpion had made Erin's devoted co-worker look like an extremely strong suspect, that didn't mean her husband wasn't still under suspicion. And while I'd already had a chance to talk to the man himself, I was just as anxious to meet his business partner. After all, he was the one who had helped elevate Ben's economic status to a level that included such highly coveted luxuries as impractical white carpeting and outdoor planters filled with fake flowers.

So I decided to spend Saturday afternoon paying Donald Drayton an unannounced visit. As was so often the case, the precise piece of information I was looking for—Donald Drayton's home address—was readily available in the Norfolk County phone book.

While I was delighted that I tracked him down so easily, I couldn't say the same about the place he called home. In fact, I couldn't help grimacing as I pulled up in front of the Drayton residence. And it wasn't because the house had been constructed on such a tremendous scale that it made Ben and Erin's McMansion look like a starter home. It was because every detail of the place made it look like a set from *The Sopranos*.

Whoever had designed the house seemed to have been hell-bent on squeezing in every architectural element possible, whether it made visual sense or not. No fewer than six two-story columns were lined up in front, as straight and tall as the guards at Buckingham Palace. But the building also featured semicircular Palladian windows, an overly large porch crammed with archways, and on top, a cupola that reminded me of a single candle poking out of a huge birthday cake.

Even the grounds did little to disappoint in the race to achieve the ultimate in bad taste. A tremendous rose-colored marble fountain dominated the front lawn, no easy task given the fact that it stretched as far and wide as a potato field. The monstrosity was a tall, complicated affair adorned with cherubs frolicking with what from the street looked like half a dozen pink goats. As if that wasn't tacky enough, water spouted from the most unlikely places.

Parked on one side of the house was a sleek silver sports car. While I'm no car expert, even I knew enough about the ones favored by the rich and famous to recognize it as a Maserati. Sitting on the other side like a second bookend was a boat big enough to be called a yacht, its white fiberglass exterior gleaming in the bright June sun.

Like Ben Chandler, Donald Drayton was clearly enjoying great success in the business world.

Is there really so much money in pet supplies? I thought, wondering, at least for a moment, if I was a fool for not rushing to join Ben Chandler and Marcus Scruggs in their pursuit of animal-related commerce.

I rang the doorbell, expecting a maid to answer the door. I pictured some poor woman who was forced to wear a black dress and a white apron, just like a character out of a British period film. Instead, when the door finally opened, I found myself face-to-face with a teenage girl—although thanks to her rail-thin frame, hollow cheeks, and shabby clothes, she could have *passed* for the maid. Or the Little Match Girl, moonlighting as a housekeeper to make ends meet.

But the girl's condescending gaze, which made me feel about as welcome as a Jehovah's Witness, told me she was no housekeeper. So did the badly faded jeans that were practically sliding off her narrow hips. They had the Juicy Couture logo on the pocket, a distinctive curlicue that broadcast the fact that they retailed for about two hundred bucks. And this diva wore Prada, even though this particular shirt, which was plain black but probably cost more than a month's rent at the cottage, didn't fit any better than the overpriced jeans. Thanks to its deeply cut neckline, it kept slipping off, revealing a pair of bony shoulders.

Her dark brown hair, long and sleek, was cut blunt. Her eyes were ringed in black, making her look as if she hadn't slept for days. Either that or she was a little-known member of the Addams Family, perhaps Morticia's long-lost niece. A small nose ring festooned one nostril. Gold, of course.

She wasn't alone. Unfortunately, her companion couldn't seem to keep from howling as if it was a full moon and not the sun that at the moment was lighting up the sky. In fact, the beagle she was dragging around by the collar seemed to be half-beagle, half-hyena. It made Frederick and his on-camera antics look amateurish.

"I hope you're not selling anything," Morticia's niece greeted me nastily. "We boil salespeople in oil."

Nice girl, I thought.

"Actually, I'm paying a social call," I told her, doing my best to remain polite. "I was wondering if Donald Drayton is home."

At least that's what I tried to say. Given the fact that the dog hadn't stopped letting out one ear-piercing shriek after another, I wasn't sure she'd heard a word.

"Maggie, shut *up*!" the girl screamed. Grimacing, she added, "This dog is so nutty. She's always been like this, ever since she was a puppy. She does this every time somebody approaches the house. Even if it's only one of us!"

I was tempted to suggest that the family invest in a few sessions with a good dog behaviorist. But this hardly seemed like the time or place.

"Look, come inside," she said impatiently. "Once she gets used to you, she'll quiet down."

As soon as I stepped into the foyer of the palatial house, the beagle's howling simmered down to a whine that was nominally less irritating. But then another high-pitched voice rang out from the back of the house.

"Nicole, I don't want you having any friends over right now!" a woman screeched in a voice capable of shattering glass. "I told you this isn't a good time! And will you shut that damn dog up?"

"It's not for me!" Nicole yelled back. I suppose I should have been heartened by the fact that she didn't address her mother any more politely than she talked to me.

"Then come back in here and finish eating!"

"I'm not hungry!"

"You're never hungry! You're practically a skeleton and you still won't eat. I'm calling a doctor on Monday, Nicole. A *psychiatrist*! The one who was on *Oprah* last week!"

"She thinks I have food issues," Nicole told me with a sneer. "If you ask me, she's been watching too much *Dr. Phil*." She rolled her eyes. Miraculously, all that caked eyeliner didn't crack.

"Is your father home?" I asked.

"No-o-o," Nicole replied in the same petulant

tone. "He's probably out making money. Oh, right, it's Saturday. So he's probably out playing golf with a bunch of stuffy old businessmen who can help him make money." Gesturing toward the back of the house, she added, "But my wicked stepmother's here if you want to talk to her."

Ah, I thought. A stepmother. That helped explain why I felt as if I'd walked into an updated version of *Who's Afraid of Virginia Woolf?* with an all-female cast.

"Actually," I said, "it's your dad I wanted to—"

"Who is it, Nicole?" the shrill voice demanded.

"It's some lady who wants to talk to you!" Nicole yelled back.

No wonder Maggie howls every time somebody comes to the door, I thought grimly.

Before I had a chance to attempt to explain once again that it wasn't her stepmother I came to see, I heard loud heels rapping sharply against the floor of what had to be a very long hallway. Finally, a woman emerged into the front hallway from what I assumed was the kitchen.

However, what she'd been doing in a kitchen was beyond me. She was dressed as if she was going to the opera, not whipping up a batch of brownies. Not when chocolate was guaranteed to leave unsightly stains on a clingy white minidress.

The woman didn't appear to be much older than Nicole. Twenty-five, maybe, only a decade or so older than her stepdaughter. And like her stepdaughter, she was bone thin. I wondered if that eating disorder specialist she was planning to call offered a family rate.

But there was one thing about her that didn't fit the rest of her frame: her large, balloonlike breasts, which took center stage thanks to her dangerously low neckline. I suspected that, like the dress and high heels, they were something she'd paid a lot for.

Her hair, meanwhile, looked as if it had been styled in a cotton candy machine. Fortunately, it wasn't pink. It was pale yellow, as if the spun sugar was pineapple flavor. Or maybe lemon. Her heavily made-up eyes were also an unusual color, an unnatural shade of turquoise that could only be achieved with tinted contact lenses.

Still, her startling hair and colorful eyes paled beside her eyebrows. The originals appeared to have been shaved off, or perhaps she'd gotten too close to the gas while preheating the oven for those brownies. Either she or someone who didn't like her very much had drawn substitute eyebrows with what appeared to be a Sharpie. The two dramatic arches made her look perpetually surprised. She, too, had clearly spent a long time smearing various powders and creams all over her eyelids. I got the feeling extreme eye makeup, like whining and howling, ran in the family.

As she crossed the room toward us, her dangerously high heels struck the wooden floor even more loudly. But my ears weren't the only sensory organs that were suffering. So was my nose, which suddenly had to cope with way too much perfume.

Her approach also motivated Maggie to launch into another round of howls.

"Nicole, take that beast outside right now!" she

screeched. Turning to me, she said in a voice that wasn't much friendlier, "What is it you want?"

"My name is Jessica Popper," I said as calmly as I could, given the fact that I felt as if I was standing in the center of a three-ring circus. "I went to school with Ben Chandler and Erin Walsh. I wanted to personally extend my sympathy to your husband, since he and Ben are business partners."

"Oh. Is that all." Donald Drayton's wife looked taken aback, probably because I was actually doing something thoughtful.

"Donny's not here," she told me in a voice as sharp as her high heels. "I'm his wife. Darla Drayton." She spoke hesitantly, as if she was carefully considering each piece of information she offered before revealing it.

"In that case, I hope you'll tell him that I dropped by." Deciding that it probably wasn't a bad idea to keep my options open, I added, "I'll try again in a day or two."

Darla simply stared at me for at least five seconds. "You could have just called, you know," she finally said. "Or sent a note."

"Yes, but I wanted to extend my sympathies in person," I replied. "Erin's death is such a tragedy. One that affects all of us who knew her and cared about her."

"Thank you." Darla said simply. Just saying those two words seemed like an effort. "Now if you'll excuse me, I'm sure you understand that I have other business to attend to. This is an extremely busy time. Difficult too."

"Of course. I'll let myself out."

I'd already seen enough. Donald Drayton had not only found a way to make a lot of money during his lifetime; he'd used it to acquire the classic trophy wife. Like the overpowering fountain on the front lawn, the Maserati, and the yacht, Darla was one more accessory that showed the rest of the world that he was a true champion in the game of Whoever Has the Most Toys Wins.

As I stepped out the front door, relieved to be inhaling fresh air again instead of choking on perfume, I found Nicole sitting on the grass, her face buried in the soft fur of Maggie's neck. She glanced up when she heard me, looking surprised at having been found out. A little embarrassed too.

"Sorry," Nicole said, looking up at me and blinking.

"About what?" I asked.

"That my stepmother is such a loser."

For the first time, I saw that beneath the eye makeup and nose piercing, there was a little girl who was as unhappy and unsure of herself as any other fifteen-year-old stuck in a bad living situation.

"You know," I told her, gesturing toward the beagle wrapped in her arms, "you might find it worthwhile to consult with a professional dog trainer. It's not my area of expertise, but I'm pretty sure there are some simple behavioral modification techniques that would help break Maggie of her bad habits."

"Really?" The girl brightened. "That would help make life at least a little more peaceful around here."

I reached into my purse. "Here's my card. Give me

a call. In the meantime, I'll ask around and see if I can get you the name of somebody who's good."

"Thanks." Nicole still looked surprised as she stuck my card into the back pocket of her jeans, the one with the swirling yellow logo. I suspected that what had caught her off guard was the fact that somebody—a grown-up no less—was being nice to her.

I really did intend to find Nicole a professional who could help make living with Maggie a little easier. It occurred to me that Marcus might know somebody. For all I knew, there was even a behaviorist in that snazzy new practice of his.

But there was another reason I wanted to talk to Nicole again—alone. A reason that was much more important than a beagle with bad habits.

And that was the wealth that Donald Drayton and his business partner, Ben Chandler, seemed to be enjoying. Not only its magnitude, but also the fact that it seemed to have come to both of them fairly recently, perhaps even since they had struck up a partnership.

Questions about all the money that was suddenly floating around nagged at me. And I had a hunch that Donald Drayton's disgruntled daughter might be just the person to help me answer them.

Chapter 10

"An American monkey after getting drunk on brandy would never touch it again, and thus is much wiser than most men."

—Charles Darwin

I waited until Sunday morning to ask Nick about the favor that had been pressing on my mind for days. Even though we'd talked about him helping me investigate Erin's murder, the subject was still hot enough that I knew I had to handle it with oven mitts.

In fact, I took that quite literally. I made a batch of blueberry muffins and served them still warm from the oven for breakfast, hoping that loading him with tasty carbs would buy me a little extra goodwill.

"Nick, do you remember the other night?" I asked as he popped a good third of a muffin into his mouth. "The first night we spent here at Betty and Winston's house?"

"I certainly do," he said with a leer. "In fact, if you'd like to try an instant replay—"

"I was thinking about what you said, not what you

did," I corrected him. "You agreed to help me investigate Erin's murder, remember?"

I hoped he would have forgotten that he never actually made a commitment to helping me. It was more like he'd stopped protesting when I made that suggestion, thanks to a little distraction.

No such luck.

Warily, he said, "Jess, I thought I made it pretty clear that I'm not crazy about you getting involved in another murder investigation. It's simply too dangerous."

Now there was a point that was hard to deny. "Would you feel better if I promised not to get myself into any compromising positions?"

"You mean that you'd stick to behind-the-scenes stuff? Doing research, brainstorming with Erin's sister...that kind of thing? Maybe talking to a few people who might know something?" He paused to take a deep breath. "I guess what I mean is, would you avoid putting yourself into any situation in which you might get hurt...or worse?"

"I suppose I could do that," I assured him, thinking, At least as much as possible.

Besides, I reminded myself, words like *dangerous* and *unsafe* are open to interpretation, aren't they?

"In that case, I suppose I could help out a little," he finally agreed.

"Fabulous!" I exclaimed. "And it just so happens that I already have an assignment for you. Not only does it fit the description of being totally danger-free, it's also a perfect match for your unique qualifications."

"I can't wait to hear what it is," he said dryly.

I decided to ignore his lack of enthusiasm. After all, I knew better than to look a gift horse in the mouth.

"Okay, here's the situation," I told him. "Ben Chandler, Erin's husband, has a business partner named Donald Drayton. He's apparently been very successful at whatever it is he does."

"Wait a minute," Nick interjected. "If this Donald guy is Ben's business partner, doesn't that mean you already know what he does?"

I grimaced. "Let's just say that while Ben is quite successful, no doubt because of the venture the two of them undertook together, his pal Donald is big-time successful. We're talking a Maserati, a yacht, and a huge ugly house outfitted with every gaudy design element you can imagine."

I decided not to mention that the symbols of Donald Drayton's success included a classic trophy wife. While my take on Darla Drayton was that she fit nicely into that category, I still felt I should give Donny and Darla the benefit of the doubt. After all, when you came right down to it, who knew what really drew two people together?

Nick had pulled out a pen and was jotting down the names and details I mentioned in the date book he always carried around in his shirt pocket.

"And what's the nature of this business venture of theirs?" he asked.

"A chain of pet shops. Embarrassingly enough, they're named the Pet Empawrium. That's E-M-P-A—"

"I got it," Nick interrupted.

"There are eleven stores," I continued, "five of them on Long Island."

"Pet stores, huh?" Nick thought for a few seconds. "That doesn't exactly strike me as the road to riches. At least not at the level you're describing."

"Me either. Which is why I'm curious about what else Donald Drayton might be into. And given your background as a private investigator, that seems like exactly the type of information you'd be great at tracking down for me."

"That does sound like something right up my alley." Frowning, he asked, "But what if it does turn out that this guy is into something sleazy? What do you think that might have to do with Erin's murder?"

"Frankly, I have no idea," I admitted.

"So Donald Drayton isn't a suspect?"

"Not at this point. But by finding out more about him, I'll be finding out more about Ben."

"I see. So Erin's husband *is* a suspect."

I shrugged. "The spouse always is. You know that as well as I do."

Nick shut his date book and stuck it back in his pocket. "I'll work on it as soon as I can. But for now, I think we should get back to our earlier discussion. I believe we were talking about an instant replay of Friday night—"

When the annoying trill of a cell phone kept him from finishing his sentence, he groaned.

"Whose is it this time, yours or mine?" he asked.

"Mine. Sorry." I grabbed my pocketbook and pulled out my cell phone.

Caller ID told me it was Suzanne. I answered anyway.

"Good morning, Suzanne," I began, subtly trying to make the point that Sunday morning is unofficially private time in households throughout the land. "Nick and I are kind of in the middle of something. Would you mind if I called you ba—"

"Jessie, I think I'm in love!" Suzanne cried.

"That's great," I replied, wondering which part of *Nick and I are kind of in the middle of something* she didn't understand. "But right now, I'm afraid I—"

"I'm talking about Kieran, of course. The man is absolutely amazing."

Just for a moment, her dreamy voice took me back to our college days. That is, the days when she and I were still both teenagers and fully believed that there really was such a thing as Mr. Right.

"Oh, I know what you're thinking," she went on dreamily. "That the incredible attraction between us is just physical. That it's simply the fact that he's a total hunk—and that the sex is beyond fabulous—that's got me in such a state."

More information than I need! a voice in my head shrieked.

"But honestly, Jessie, that's only the beginning," Suzanne continued. "Kieran is smart, funny, affectionate . . . and he does the sweetest things. Like right after our first date last night, he took out a felt-tip pen and wrote my phone number on the back of his hand, just to make sure he'd always have it with him. Isn't that cute?"

The man didn't exactly get a tattoo, I thought. Still, I supposed it was a nice gesture.

At that point, Nick stood up and began collecting dishes to bring to the sink. I cast him an apologetic look, then geared up for another attempt at cutting her off. But to add insult to injury, at that moment I got a beep through call waiting. Sunday morning was no time to be so popular.

When I glanced at caller ID, however, I recognized the area code on the screen. It belonged to Jack Krieger, the close friend of Ben Chandler's from our vet school days who I'd been anxious to speak with.

My heart began to pound for reasons that had nothing to do with Kieran O'Malley's many outstanding attributes.

"Suzanne," I interrupted, "I'm really happy for you. But right now, I have to—"

"This afternoon, he's taking me to a friend's house for a barbecue," she gurgled. "Another trooper who's in the canine unit. Jessie, do you believe that he's already introducing me to his friends?"

"Suzanne, I have to hang up now," I insisted as the second call-waiting beep sounded. "I don't mean to be rude, but I have another call and I really have to take it."

I might as well have been trying to use logic on Leilani. "Next week," she gushed, "we're going to—"

"Good-bye, Suzanne," I said firmly. "I'll call you later."

With that, I clicked a magic button and all of a sudden found myself talking to Jack instead of Suzanne.

"Jack?" I began. "Thanks for calling me back. I wasn't sure you'd remember me."

"Of course I remember you, Jessie."

As soon as I heard his calm, almost monotonic voice, I experienced total recall. In fact, it was hard to believe that a solid decade had passed since I'd last spoken to him.

"It was nice to hear from you," he continued in the same unhurried way. "Too bad it's because of such a tragedy."

"So you heard about Erin," I said. "I wasn't sure if you knew."

"Yeah. Kenny Storch called me. Remember him? I think he heard about it from Sarah Cleary, who was also in our class. Word travels fast." He was silent for a long time before adding, "Pretty awful, isn't it? Did you go to the funeral?"

"Erin's family didn't want anything public. They just had a small family thing." Choosing my words carefully, I added, "If there had been a funeral, I would have let you know, since you might have wanted to come down for it. I remember that you and Ben were really close."

"Yeah, we were," he replied. "For a while anyway."

Something in his voice told me that he still hadn't gotten over whatever it was that had ruined their friendship. Which made me more curious than ever about what that had been.

"Looking back," I continued, "it seems kind of surprising that you and Ben were such good friends back in vet school. Ben was so outgoing. Brash even. And you were so much more introverted. I guess what I mean is that the two of you were so different."

"More than you know," he said under his breath.

This struck me as the perfect time to pounce.

"Jack," I said hesitantly, "I always wondered what happened between the two of you. You and Ben were inseparable for years, and then suddenly it all just fell apart."

He was silent for what seemed like a very long time. Finally, he said, "Yeah, that sounds like a pretty accurate description."

"I suppose your differences finally started getting in the way," I went on, still fishing. "As time goes on, people grow apart—"

He let out a contemptuous snort. "If only it was that simple. The real problem was that Ben Chandler turned out to be a cheat."

"*What?*" I cried, prompting Nick to glance over at me questioningly.

"You heard me," Jack said. He hesitated before saying, "His true nature finally came out, thanks to the Pharmacology final."

"I—I don't understand."

"Look, enough time has gone by that I might as well be honest about what happened at the end of our final year. Basically, Ben claimed he was so busy studying for all his other exams that he just didn't have time to study for that one." Jack's voice was dripping with so much acrimony that it was hard to believe he was describing something that had taken place ten years earlier. "I remember him saying that that was no reason for him to flunk out and be forced to give up his dream of becoming a veterinarian.

"The night before the Pharm final, Ben came to my room," he continued. "I don't know if you remember, but he and I were sharing a house with a couple of other guys. It was late, probably one or two in the morning. I was still up, trying to stuff as much information into my head as I could. Ben knocked on my door, and when I opened it, he looked really upset. When I asked him what was wrong, he told me that if he didn't find a way to pass the Pharm final, he wasn't going to graduate."

"What did you say?"

"I offered to help him cram for the test," Jack replied matter-of-factly. "I said I'd make coffee and the two of us could stay up all night, study until noon the next day if we had to, since that was when the test was scheduled.

"That was when Ben came inside and closed the door. I knew from the way he was acting that something funny was going on." He paused. "Once he was sure nobody else in the house could hear, he offered to pay me a thousand dollars if I'd let him cheat off me during the test."

I gasped. Nick abandoned the dishes and sat down at the kitchen table again, the muscles in his face tense.

"I said no, of course," Jack said bitterly. "In fact, I told him in no uncertain terms where he could stick his thousand bucks."

"But Ben graduated with the rest of us," I pointed out.

"Yup." In a steely voice, he said, "I always figured

184 • Cynthia Baxter

he found somebody else who needed that thousand bucks a lot more than I did.

"After the exam," he continued with the same rancor, "Ben couldn't look me in the eye. In fact, we never spoke again. Not that it mattered to me." Almost as if he was thinking aloud, he added, "At least he had the sense to be embarrassed that I finally knew him for who he really was."

"What about Erin?" I asked gently. "Did she ever find out about this?"

"She didn't hear anything about it from me," Jack replied. "And the next thing I knew, the two of them announced that they were getting married right after graduation."

He was silent for a long time. "Maybe I should have said something to her. At the time, I guess I figured it wasn't my place. But to be perfectly honest, I thought the world of Erin. At first, I was happy that Ben got himself such a prize. But by the time they decided to get married, I was convinced he didn't deserve her. Erin was pretty amazing. Much too good for that jerk."

I realized then that Jack had also cared deeply for Erin, perhaps even more deeply than he felt Ben's best friend should have. But that was a subject I couldn't bring myself to pursue.

"Jessie," he asked in a strained voice, "do you think things might have gone differently if I'd spoken up? For Erin, I mean."

"I honestly don't know," I told him.

But I was thinking, Maybe they would have, Jack. And they might also have gone differently for you.

• • •

The news about Ben Chandler's true character gnawed at me all day. Even Nick's contention that there was a big difference between cheating on an exam and murdering someone didn't do much to comfort me.

I was still trying to come to grips with what Jack had told me about Erin's husband that evening, when I found myself with some downtime. Nick was in the shower, Max was gnawing on his poor pink plastic poodle, and Tinkerbell was stalking a dust bunny.

Lou, meanwhile, was playing Hide the Tennis Ball Under the Couch. Even though I knew he'd soon be summoning me, barking the command, "Jessie, retrieve!" I curled up on the couch with Cat beside me and turned on my laptop. I e-mailed a few veterinarians I knew in the area, including Marcus Scruggs, asking for the name of a good animal behaviorist who might be capable of helping a really bad opera singer who'd been reincarnated as a beagle.

Then I checked my inbox, relieved to see that as usual the weekend had been quiet. When I spotted an e-mail from Betty, I let out a joyful yelp. She'd had a couple of days to settle in at her Tuscan villa, and I was looking forward to her report on how her honeymoon was going. Especially since it was such a crowded one.

Greetings, Jessica—or as we say in Tuscany, *Saluti!*

Tutto sta andando bene—which means everything here in Italy is going just fabulously! Even though we just got here, we've already grown accustomed to living in the lap of luxury, Italian style. We're staying in a gorgeous white stucco villa with a red tile roof, overlooking the rolling hills of *la Toscana*. It has a huge swimming pool, exquisite gardens, and a charming patio that's perfect for dining by moonlight. *Molto romantico!*

It's so lovely having Winston's children with us. It's the first chance they've really had to get to know me, and me them. We all sit down to breakfast together every morning. Then we usually take a day trip together. There's so much to see in *la Toscana bella!* Best of all, Fiona seems to be having a wonderful time. What a dear child! I treasure the time she and I get to spend together.

Better run, since there's so much to do. My best to both you and Nick—and of course Cat, Tinkerbell, Max, Lou, Prometheus, and Leilani. As for my darling Frederick, please give him a big hug and tell him I miss him terribly!

Hugs and kisses,
Betty

I let out a deep sigh of relief. Thank goodness Betty and Winston's honeymoon is working out after all, I thought. In fact, it even sounded as if Betty was enjoying all that company.

By this point, I'd gotten a response to one of the e-mails I'd sent to other vets I knew. I printed out the name and phone number of a behaviorist, who fortunately happened to live nearby.

I planned to put it to very good use.

• • •

Even though Monday was jam-packed with appointments, I made the time to squeeze in a quick visit to the Drayton household. And I purposely scheduled my detour into their neighborhood in Walt Whitman Hills in the late afternoon, hoping that by then Nicole would be home from school. On my way, I dropped Sunny off at the cottage to perform some more of her organizational magic. This was one house call I wanted to make alone.

As I pulled up in front of the Draytons' eyesore of a house, I noticed that the silver Maserati was gone. In its place was a white Mercedes. I wasn't familiar with the various models the Mercedes-Benz company produced, but I had a feeling this was one of their higher-priced buggies.

As I neared the front door, Maggie's ear-piercing howls shattered the silence of the otherwise quiet residential street, as the heavy wooden front door did very little to muffle the sound.

At least the Draytons' beagle hasn't been cured of her bad habits in the last forty-eight hours, I observed. A good thing, too, since it's those very habits that are providing me with the excuse I need for paying a second visit.

The cacophonous canine chorus continued as the door opened. But at least it was Nicole who answered the door. This time, instead of wearing expensive pre-ripped jeans that cost even more than the unripped ones, she was dressed in a school uniform that consisted of a gray blazer and a gray-and-navy-blue plaid skirt. She stood in the doorway, stooping over with her fingers looped around the errant beagle's collar.

"Quiet, you stupid dog!" she cried, her shrill voice almost as irritating as Maggie's barks.

Once she focused her attention on me, a look of confusion crossed her face. "Can I help you with—oh, that's right. You were here on Saturday."

"That's right," I said cheerfully. "I'm Jessie Popper. The veterinarian, remember?"

"Right." But she still looked confused about why I was standing on her doorstep.

"I offered to get you the name and number of a good animal behaviorist," I reminded her. "Somebody who could help you break Maggie of her howling problem. I found somebody, but then I realized I didn't have your phone number. I was on my way to a house call just now that happened to take me right through your neighborhood, so I figured I'd stop by and see if you were home."

"Great," she said. "We could sure use some help with this monster."

As if to emphasize just how true that statement was, the unruly beagle's howls got even higher and louder.

"Can I come in?" I yelled over the noise.

"I guess."

Nicole retreated inside the house, dragging Maggie by her collar and commanding her to be quiet. Not surprisingly, her words had absolutely no effect.

Fortunately, once the novelty of a newcomer's arrival wore off, the beagle's howls quieted down enough that Nicole and I could finally hear each other.

"Here you go," I said, handing her an index card on which I'd written the animal behaviorist's name and phone number. "This is someone a friend of mine recommended, so she's probably pretty good."

"Thanks," Nicole said, glancing at the card. "Now all I have to do is get my dad to spring for it." Sullenly, she added, "I'll start working on Darla as soon as she gets back from her stupid Pilates class. You see, the trick is to get *her* to ask him, instead of me. He never says no to *her*."

My ears pricked up. The more I learned about the dynamics of the Drayton household, the more intriguing they seemed.

"So...is there anything else I need to know?" Nicole asked. "About this animal whatever-you-call-it, I mean."

She had apparently realized that there was no reason for me to continue standing in her living room. So I did some fast thinking.

"Before I go, could I trouble you for a glass of water?" Fanning my face with my hand, I noted, "It's pretty hot out there."

"No problem."

Nicole disappeared into the back of house, with Maggie trotting after her. I took advantage of being alone to do some exploring.

Interesting, I thought as I wandered through the room, my eyes darting around as if I was a member of a S.W.A.T. team. There's not a book or a magazine or even a newspaper in the place. Even the shelves are covered with expensive-looking collectibles, rather than anything containing the printed word.

I also noticed that there was scarcely anything personal in the room. Like Ben and Erin's house, the Draytons' residence looked as if it was some designer's dream. I got the feeling this grand living room was simply waiting for someone from *Architectural Digest* to come by and photograph it.

I was actually startled when I happened upon something that indicated a real, live family dwelled within these rooms. The floor-to-ceiling shelves tucked away in a back corner of the living room were lined with photographs, most of them in silver frames. One was a photo of a little girl—Nicole, no doubt—all dressed up in a pink ruffled party dress. Another was a picture of Maggie when she was still a puppy. A third was a shot of Darla, lounging on the family yacht in a skimpy black bikini.

I picked up the fourth photograph, the one featuring Nicole standing next to a balding middle-aged businessman in a red polo shirt. His arm was draped around her shoulders and they were both grinning at the camera. Behind them stood a low, ramshackle building that looked like a stable, with a large grassy field stretching out beyond.

"I didn't know what kind of water you wanted," Nicole said as she returned, this time holding a glass. "We have Perrier, San Pellegrino, Evian...this is Evian."

Tap water would have been just fine, but I accepted the glass without comment.

"Thanks, Nicole." Glancing at the photograph in my hand, I commented, "I was just looking at this photo of you and your father. That is your dad, right?"

She glanced over my shoulder. "Yeah. That's him."

"It looks as if this was taken at a stable. Do you ride?"

"I used to," Nicole replied dully. "My dad too. It was something we did together every Sunday. There's a stable nearby where we would rent the same horses every week. They were our favorites."

As I put the photograph back, I commented, "It must be nice, being so close to your father."

She shrugged. "We're not that close anymore. In fact, these days, we hardly spend any time together."

"I guess once a girl gets to be a teenager, she doesn't have much time for her parents anymore," I observed.

"It's not *me* who has no time," she shot back. "It's *him*. And it's all because of that wicked witch he married."

I wasn't surprised by her comment, since Darla Drayton hadn't exactly struck me as the type of person who would spend her afternoons baking cookies with her stepdaughter in order to create goodwill. In fact, she exuded about as much warmth as this house.

"I guess it's not easy getting used to a stepmother," I observed.

Nicole snorted. "Not if she's somebody who wants a stepdaughter about as much as she wants cellulite," she replied angrily. "Especially since my father is so crazy about her that he doesn't seem to want his own daughter around either. As soon as *she* came into the picture a couple of years ago, it was like I ceased to exist. Sometimes I think I should just forget about my friends and my school and move to California, the way my mother did." Scowling, she added, "Except that she's just as busy with *her* new spouse."

"I see," I said quietly. And I did.

"You wouldn't believe the way Dad and Darla are living it up," Nicole continued in the same bitter tone. "You'd think they were Marie Antoinette and King Whatever-his-name-was."

It sounds as if Donald and Darla are reveling in their dramatic increase in prosperity, I reflected. Just like Ben and Erin.

"First came this monstrosity of a house," Nicole went on. "I mean, honestly. Have you ever seen anything so grotesque in your life? Then my father started buying himself toys like that stupid boat and that stupid car. But that was nothing compared to all the stuff he bought for Darla. Ridiculously gaudy jewelry, designer clothes . . . do you believe she has a pocketbook that cost twelve hundred dollars?"

I kept my observations about Nicole's own preference for expensive designer clothing to myself. Besides, what she was saying about her father and stepmother's buying habits seemed to skyrocket them to an entirely different level.

"Then there are all the trips," Nicole added. "I mean, the two of them travel so much you'd think they wouldn't even be able to remember what country they were waking up in."

"Where do they like to go?" I asked, expecting her to name the world's most desirable and expensive destinations. The French Riviera, Tahiti, St. Bart's . . .

"Africa," Nicole replied disdainfully. "South America.

Weird places like Indonesia and Thailand and a few I've never even heard of. Sometimes I wonder if they're just going to the far corners of the world so they can get away from *me*."

Interesting, I thought. Ben Chandler is working his butt off while his business partner is on a nonstop honeymoon.

Then again, it didn't exactly sound as if Donny and Darla were flying all over the globe so they could soak up the sun and sip umbrella drinks on some beautiful beach. In fact, their vacations sounded a lot more adventurous than I ever would have expected.

Aloud, I said, "I'm sure that's not the case, Nicole. It sounds as if they're simply trying to enjoy their money."

"Oh, it's definitely all about the money." She practically spit out her next words. "As long as it's in the showiest, most obnoxious way possible. And as long as it doesn't include *me*."

Nicole seemed convinced that the arrival of her silicon stepmother was responsible for the dramatic changes in her father's lifestyle. But I wasn't so sure.

As for all that money, I had yet to learn where it was coming from. But what interested me more than the sports car, the yacht, and the sparkling new wife were the trips. Somehow, I couldn't picture Darla rafting down the Amazon or trekking through mud in a pair of Manolos en route to the great temples of Thailand.

It just didn't fit. And the fact that something odd appeared to be going on in the Drayton household made me realize it was time to add Ben's business partner to my list of murder suspects.

• • •

I was still pondering the juxtaposition of three such different personalities within the Drayton household as I pulled into the slow lane of the Expressway. I jumped when my cell phone began to trill. I automatically checked caller ID, and while I'm usually vigilant about not using my cell phone while driving, the fact that Kimberly Walsh's number had come up made taking the call irresistible.

"Hi, Kimberly," I answered.

"Are you busy today?" she asked, her breathlessness telling me immediately that something was up.

"I'm on my way to a house call," I said, "but I've got some free time later. Where are you?"

"I'm at Erin's house. I've been cleaning out her stuff. Ben kept insisting that he'd do it, but I barged my way in."

She was silent for a few seconds before she said, "Jessie, you'd better come over here as soon as you can. I found something I think you should see."

Chapter 11

"I feel more comfortable with gorillas than people. I can anticipate what a gorilla's going to do, and they're purely motivated."

—Dian Fossey

As soon as I finished my calls, I rushed over to Ben and Erin's house. In fact, I made the trip in record time. The urgency of Kimberly's tone—not to mention her mysteriousness—made it hard to resist stepping on the gas pedal a little harder than usual.

My heart was thumping as I knocked on the door. Kimberly opened it within seconds.

She greeted me with a nervous smile. "I'm glad you made it."

"It sounded important," I replied, stepping into the foyer.

Her smile faded. "I think it is."

I followed her up to the second floor and down a very long hallway. At the end was the master bedroom. Like so much of the rest of the house, it was decorated entirely in white. Everything sparkled, from the wall-to-wall carpeting to the bedspread to the silk throw pillows. I felt as if I was watching a bleach commercial.

The room was absolutely huge. Between the square footage and the cathedral ceiling, the king-size bed looked like a piece of dollhouse furniture. The space included a sitting area with a couch and an upholstered chair, two tremendous walk-in closets that were practically rooms in themselves, and a big-screen TV that probably made the room's occupants feel as if they were spending the night at the multiplex.

But what impressed me most was that there were two bathrooms—not one—jutting off opposite sides of the room. His and hers, one with peach-colored walls and the other painted a masculine beige.

If there was ever an invention to promote marital harmony, I thought enviously, this is it.

I reminded myself that I'd come to see whatever Kimberly had stumbled upon, not to develop a bad case of House Envy.

"What did you want to show me?" I asked.

Frankly, I didn't know what to expect. A packet of flowery love letters from Walter, perhaps, indicating that in addition to being a lizard aficionado, he had a talent for writing mushy poetry? Some sign that Erin had been leading a secret life, like an ID card from the CIA, the FBI, or the DEA?

Or maybe something as basic as a gun, hidden between two thongs in her underwear drawer?

A wave of disappointment swept over me when Kimberly ducked into one of the walk-in closets and emerged carrying nothing more intriguing than a plastic bag with the red Target logo.

"I found this hidden in the back of the closet," she announced, handing it to me.

What could this possibly tell us about Erin? I wondered as I took the bag. That Erin liked cute housewares and inexpensive designer clothes?

Without looking inside, I reached in and pulled out the first thing I touched. As soon as I saw what it was, I understood why Kimberly had called.

It was a home pregnancy test, still wrapped in cellophane.

I cast her a look of surprise before reaching into the bag again. This time, I took out two items. One was a scrapbook covered in a cheery fabric decorated with teddy bears. The other was a book entitled *30,000 Names for Your Newborn.*

"Erin was *pregnant*?" I asked breathlessly.

"The funny thing is, I don't think that she actually was," Kimberly replied, her voice wavering. "If she had been, it would have been discovered at the autopsy."

Gesturing toward the stack of brand-new items, she added, "But she clearly thought she was."

She took the bag from me and pulled out a small slip of paper. "The receipt was still in the bag. It's dated two days before she was murdered."

"Whoa." I took a few seconds to think about the implications of this unexpected new development. "So the question is, who did Erin think was the father, Ben or Walter?"

Kimberly nodded. "And the second question is, if

she told one or both of them she thought she was pregnant, what kind of reaction did she get?"

I lowered myself onto the edge of the bed. "If it was Ben," I said thoughtfully, "I suppose he could have seen the arrival of a child as an intrusion into their marriage. He might be one of those men who wants his wife all to himself."

"Could be," Kimberly agreed. "I always thought he was kind of a baby himself, so maybe he resented the idea of having to share Erin's attention with someone else—even his own child."

Bitterly, she added, "Or maybe he was worried about how expensive a baby would be. Or how much damage a toddler could do to his new white couches and carpets."

"It's also possible he knew their marriage was on the rocks," I mused, smoothing out the yellow satin bow on the scrapbook's front cover. "Maybe he'd suspected that Erin was having an affair. Or maybe he was having one of his own. If either was the case, another possible scenario might be that he was planning to leave Erin and saw the baby as a tie to her that he just didn't want."

Nodding, Kimberly commented, "Every one of those theories sounds plausible."

"And what if Erin thought Walter was the father?" I continued, still thinking out loud. "Maybe he became enraged because he thought a baby would ruin their affair. That it would take all the romance out of their secret trysts. Or maybe her announcement prompted Walter to insist that she leave Ben once and for all."

"And if she refused," Kimberly added, "he might have flown into a rage."

"Or maybe Erin told Walter she was ending their affair because she thought she was pregnant with Ben's baby," I suggested.

Of course, another possibility was that Erin had kept her suspicions that there was a baby on the way to herself.

After all, she hadn't actually used the home pregnancy test yet. The wisest thing to do would have been to wait until she was completely certain about her condition before breathing a word to anyone. Erin wasn't only a mature, responsible woman. She was also a doctor. I would have thought she'd have known that waiting until she'd taken the pregnancy test was the smartest, most reasonable thing to do.

Then again, I wouldn't have thought she was capable of having an affair either. But of course the circumstances of people's lives could make them do all kinds of unexpected things.

And the reactions they got from other people could be dramatically different from what they expected.

Those other people could certainly include Walter. Quiet, nerdy, peculiar Walter. While he appeared to have worshipped Erin, no one could deny that he was a little strange.

Besides, he remained on my suspect list for reasons other than the fact that he was the only person in her life who actually kept scorpions as pets. I was also troubled by his insistence that he hadn't been at the zoo fund-raiser, even though the way he reacted to my question indicated otherwise.

Suddenly I had a brainstorm.

"Kimberly," I asked hesitantly, "would you mind if I borrowed the jacket Erin wore the night she stuck that cocktail napkin in her pocket?"

A startled look crossed her face. "Of course you can borrow it." Still looking confused, she added, "Do you mind if I ask why?"

I simply replied, "I just want to try something. I'll let you know afterward if it worked."

I didn't want to promise more than I could deliver. But as far as the jacket was concerned, I definitely had something up my sleeve.

●　●　●

It wasn't until Wednesday that I managed to set aside a block of time to pay another visit to Walter Weiner. Now that I'd discovered that Erin had believed she was pregnant, I was more anxious than ever to learn whatever I could about him. After all, the man might not only have been her lover, he was also a lover of scorpions. In addition, I wanted to find out once and for all whether or not he'd been at the zoo fund-raiser.

Which was why I made sure my fashion statement for the day included the black velvet jacket Kimberly had lent Erin that night.

Just as I'd hoped, I found Walter at home. As he opened the door, his eyes were glazed, as if I'd caught him in the middle of concocting a particularly complex computer program. Either that or the lenses of his glasses were so thick they couldn't help making him look distracted.

"Oh, hello," he greeted me, blinking as if he was

confused about why he'd found me standing on his doorstep once again. "Jessica Popper, right?"

"That's right. I hope this isn't a bad time...."

"I'm actually kind of busy—"

"In that case," I interrupted, "I'll make it quick."

Reluctantly, he opened the door a little farther. As I stepped inside, I noticed he was staring at my jacket. Of course, it was possible that he was simply horrified that someone had the poor judgment to wear velvet on a warm June day. But my radar told me otherwise.

"Is something wrong?" I asked, pointedly glancing down at my outfit.

Looking a little flustered, he replied, "No, not at all. It's just... your coat. I feel like I've seen it before."

So Walter *was* at the fund-raiser, I thought, the event at which Erin made those mysterious markings. The question is, why did he lie about having been there?

Even more importantly, what had happened that night?

Aloud, I said, "It's a pretty jacket, isn't it? But I didn't come here to talk about clothes."

Gingerly I lowered myself onto the couch. I couldn't help wondering if I was about to sit on a venomous member of the animal kingdom, one clever enough to find a way to break for freedom.

Folding my hands neatly in my lap, I began, "I guess you heard about the information that came out of the medical examiner's report. I mean Dr. Stokes's findings that Erin was stung by a scorpion shortly before she was murdered."

"Yes," Walter replied somberly. He sat down in the

rocking chair, the same place as during my last visit. "Amanda Cooper, who works at the zoo, called to tell me. Apparently somebody from homicide questioned Zacarias, since she was Erin's boss and all, and word got out."

I studied his face, searching for some reaction. A flicker of guilt or remorse in his eyes, perhaps, or even a telltale twitch in his cheek. But I didn't pick up on anything the least bit incriminating.

In fact, the muscles of his face drooped a little further, as if he was having as difficult a time dealing with this new development as I was.

I decided to ask the questions I'd come to ask anyway. "I remembered that you were interested in scorpions, so I thought you might be able to give me some information about them."

"I'm certainly no expert," he replied with a little shrug. "I do find them fascinating, however. I believe I told you I have a death stalker."

Precisely why your name popped into my head as soon as I heard the news, I thought.

Aloud, I said, "You did mention something about that. In fact, that's why you were the first person I thought of when I decided to do some research on my own. I was hoping you could educate me a bit."

"I don't know what you might find helpful," Walter said thoughtfully. "I can tell you that scorpions are arthropods with eight legs. They're in the class Arachnida, which also includes spiders, ticks, and mites."

Not exactly what I was looking for. "I guess what

I'm most interested in is what makes them so dangerous," I said.

He brightened, as if I'd finally come up with a topic
of conversation he could get excited about. "Actually,
even though there are more than fourteen hundred
species of scorpion worldwide, only a few are considered medically important—meaning dangerous to humans," he said. "Scorpions tend to live in areas where
fresh water is available, the same way people do.
That's why they're estimated to account for somewhere in the range of eight hundred deaths a year.

"And contrary to what some people think, scorpions don't bite, they sting," he went on, with the same
level of intensity. "The venom they inject doesn't
come from anywhere near their mouths. It comes
from a very sharp, pointed organ called the aculeus
that's commonly referred to as a sting. It's located at
the posterior tip of their abdomen. They inject the
sting into a soft place and then activate muscles in
their venom gland, located at the rear of the abdomen,
to inject the venom. The process is kind of like giving
someone an injection with a hypodermic needle."

The image made me shudder. But rather than wanting him to stop, I wanted him to go on.

"What part of the world does the one that stung
Erin, the yellow fat tail, come from?" I asked.

"*Androctonus australis* is mainly found in northern
Africa—Algeria, Egypt, Morocco, and a few other
countries," Walter explained. "But it's also in India,
Israel, and Saudi Arabia. It probably causes more ill-
ness and death than any other scorpion in Africa and
Asia, simply because it's so common. It's not that big,

204 • Cynthia Baxter

only about four inches long. But it has a thick yellow cauda—that's the tail—that's really powerful."

I bit my lip. "Do you think Erin would have been in terrible pain? And if she was, would she have experienced it for very long?"

"I'm afraid that getting stung by a yellow fat tail would be extremely painful." Walter grimaced. "In fact, the pain at the injection site would be pretty horrific. A few minutes later, numbness would set in. See, the venom consists of a protein mixture that interacts with sodium ion channels in nerve cells, which means it interferes with electrical conduction and disrupts autonomic function. Since it's a neural toxin, it spreads through the circulatory system really quickly and symptoms begin appearing within minutes.

"Over the next hour or so, the symptoms become worse and worse," he continued. "In fact, anyone who's left untreated is likely to die from cardiac arrest or respiratory difficulties or some other autonomic problem."

"I see." I swallowed hard, a reaction to the dryness in my mouth. "And how rare are these yellow fat tail scorpions? In this part of the world, I mean."

"It's legal to keep them as pets, if that's what you're asking," Walter replied. "That doesn't necessarily mean you can walk into your average pet store and buy one. You'd have to get one from a specialty store or a supplier. But those are both easy enough to find, especially on the Internet."

"So it wouldn't be that difficult for someone to get their hands on one," I commented, thinking out loud.

Walter laughed, but it was a cold laugh that wasn't

meant to be associated with anything funny. " 'Getting their hands on one' is the last thing anybody would want to do. Believe me, as much as I enjoy keeping a death stalker here at the house as part of my collection, I always make a point of handling him with long forceps. I make sure my fingers never come close enough for him to sting me."

"Would Erin have known that?" I asked. "I guess what I mean is, is it possible this was an accident?"

"Unlikely," Walter replied. "Erin never had any reason to work with scorpions directly, but the few times she came over to my house, she knew enough to keep away from the one I have. She saw me use forceps every time I handled the death stalker. She was too smart and too familiar with the dangers of a scorpion—*any* scorpion—to take any chances."

Aha, I thought. So Walter and Erin's relationship *did* extend beyond the office. I wondered if the police had uncovered that interesting little fact—and whether they, too, considered the lizard-loving Lothario a suspect.

I glanced around, trying to imagine how Walter's living room would look if it was lit by candlelight. Somehow, I just couldn't picture it as a love nest. Maybe it had something to do with the spiders. The grandmotherly knickknacks didn't help either.

"Besides," Walter went on, "despite their reputation as vicious aggressors, scorpions don't just run up and attack people. They don't sting unless they've been provoked. Which means Erin had to have surprised the one that stung her."

"I see." And I did see, with sickening clarity. Somehow the murderer had arranged for a yellow fat tail scorpion to come into close enough contact with Erin's arm so that it stung her over and over again. As a result, she'd been in excruciating pain. She had undoubtedly been hideously frightened, too, since she would have quickly figured out what was happening—and what was likely to happen from that point on. Between those two reactions, Erin had probably started to scream—which might have prompted her attacker to finish the job by strangling her.

Yet if this really was the way the scenario had played out, it could also mean that whoever had arranged for the scorpion to sting Erin hadn't been particularly familiar with them. Otherwise, the person would have known that death wouldn't have come instantly.

Or maybe that was part of the plan, I thought grimly. Maybe the murderer had *wanted* Erin to suffer.

Walter shrugged. "I don't know what else I could possibly tell you that would make a difference at this point."

"This information was very helpful," I assured him.

"I guess all that really matters is that Erin is dead," he said, the expression on his face reflecting his sorrow.

The vulnerable look on his face told me it was time to ask the $64,000 question.

"Walter," I began, choosing my words carefully, "from the way you talk about Erin, I can't help feeling that you really cared about her."

"Of course I did," he answered quickly. "We were...friends. Close friends."

Here goes.

"I get the sense that you two were much more than friends," I said gently. "That the two of you were bonded by something much stronger."

He blinked as if he was startled by my frankness. Then a look of alarm crossed his face.

I braced myself for a string of protests. Instead, he replied defensively, "It wasn't just some squalid affair, if that's what you're thinking. I was in love with her."

I was still trying to come up with an appropriate response to his unexpected confession when he let out a deep sigh. "I guess there's no reason to try to keep it a secret anymore. It's bound to come out through the cops' investigation."

"How long had you been seeing each other?" I asked in the same soft voice.

"A few months," he replied. "Not long after I started consulting for Dr. Zacarias at the zoo, Erin and I started hanging out together as much as we could. We just clicked, you know? We had so much in common. We both loved animals and we shared a fascination for exotics...

"But there was something else too. Almost from the beginning, I sensed a sadness in her. A loneliness, in a way, but something that went even deeper. She seemed...disappointed."

"Disappointed in what?" I probed.

He shrugged. "I don't know. Not her work, that's for sure. She loved what she was doing, especially her research at the zoo. It was more like she was disappointed in her personal life."

Ben, I thought automatically.

Walter took a deep breath, as if he was trying to get past a flood of emotion so he could go on. "Anyway, it tapped into the way I've been feeling too. It was as if the two of us were kindred spirits. And the more time we spent together—at work, I mean—the stronger the feeling became.

"I began to sense that she felt it too. We started spending time together that had nothing to do with our jobs. Like at the end of the day, instead of packing up and going home, she'd come to my office. We'd sit and talk for a long time. At first, she made excuses about wanting to avoid rush-hour traffic. But after a while she stopped pretending there was any reason for her to put off going home aside from the fact that we really liked each other. Being together just felt so good. It felt so . . . so *right*."

His eyes took on a faraway look, almost as if he was gazing into the past. In a soft, almost reverent voice, he added, "And then we became lovers. It happened at work, on one of those nights when she clearly didn't want to go home. We were talking, and it kept getting later and later . . . and by that point just about everybody had left for the day. We had the office to ourselves."

With a little smile, he added, "Maybe an office doesn't seem like the most romantic place in the world, but there was something in the air that night. Something special. An electricity, kind of, as if we both knew what was going to happen. It was dark by that point, and it felt as if we were the only two people in the world. That probably sounds crazy...."

It didn't sound crazy at all. Not to me. I knew the exact feeling he was talking about. And the dreamy way he was speaking made me experience it as if it was actually happening.

"It was a magical night," he said wistfully. "And like I said, it wasn't about the sex. It was about the two of us acknowledging the connection between us and finally deciding not to hold back anymore."

"And her husband?" I asked softly, trying not to sound judgmental. "Did Erin ever talk about leaving him?"

Walter shook his head. "She was much too loyal. At least that was what I assumed. The fact is, she was reluctant to talk to me about him at all." His voice hardening, he added, "Even though I suspected from the start that he was the root of whatever unhappiness she was experiencing."

Suddenly his expression changed. "I'm sorry. I shouldn't be dumping all this on you. You didn't come here to listen to the pathetic details of my personal life."

On the contrary, I thought.

"I appreciate you being so open with me, Walter," I told him sincerely. I wasn't entirely sure he hadn't had anything to do with Erin's murder, but his openness motivated me to take a chance by being open with him too. As I reached into my purse, I said, "This is something I haven't shown to anyone, but I'd like to know if it means anything to you."

I handed him the Xerox copy of the cocktail napkin I'd been carrying around.

"What is this?" he asked, frowning.

I hesitated. I still wasn't positive that Walter was someone I could trust. But I had to come up with some sort of answer.

I decided to go with the truth. Or at least an abbreviated version of it.

"They're notes Erin made," I said. "Can you make sense of any of it?"

I held my breath as he studied the sheet of paper. He remained silent for such a long time that I assumed the odd assortment of letters meant as little to him as it did to me.

Until he said, "Sure I can. At least if you split them up."

"What do you mean 'split them up'?" I asked, aware that my heart had begun hammering in my chest.

He leaned forward to show me the page. "See, these letters here that look like 'NGIPPL'? I'd bet anything it's supposed to be 'NG' and 'IPPL.'"

"But what does that mean?"

"Well, it could mean a lot of things," he continued. "But NG could stand for National Geographic and IPPL most likely stands for the International Primate Protection League. As for these other letters—IFAW and CI—they probably refer to the International Fund for Animal Welfare and Conservation International." Nodding, he added, "Yeah, that would make sense. After all, they're all organizations that share a common goal. Erin told me all about them."

"What goal do they share?" I asked, even though the answer was fairly obvious. By this point, my heart was pounding so loud I was afraid he could hear it.

"Animal conservation," he replied soberly. "They're all dedicated to fighting the illegal animal trade."

A chill went through me.

Was it conceivable that whatever happened that night, as well as what happened to Erin a few weeks later, was related to something as huge and as horrific as the worldwide smuggling of animals? The very idea was too devastating to contemplate.

At least, at first. But the more I thought about it, the more sense it began to make. True, this was an area I didn't know much about. But it was entirely possible that on the night of the fund-raiser, Erin discovered that someone she knew was involved in it.

After all, when she started working at the zoo, she began moving in a sphere in which people dealt with exotic animals as a matter of course. Then again, these were individuals who spent their entire lives caring for them and studying them and preserving them. It was hard to believe that anyone that dedicated would be capable of using their knowledge and connections for such evil purposes.

I also had to consider Erin's husband and his business partner. They, too, were in the animal business.

Still, peddling dog collars and cat food was light years away from engaging in illegal smuggling. The malignant practice grossly endangered both the animals and the buyers, not to mention the fragile balance of the entire planet. And it was done out of nothing but sheer greed.

I swallowed hard as the image of Ben's ostentatious house flashed through my mind. It was followed by a mental picture of Donald Drayton's mansion, complete with all his expensive boy toys. I also thought about what Nicole had told me about those trips her dad and Darla had been taking, to the most unlikely places. Asia, Africa, South America . . . the very places most exotic animals came from.

Yes, it was possible. Extremely possible. Especially since the very source of my suspicion was handwritten notes made by Erin herself.

I realized that having deciphered at least part of Erin's scribblings from that night hadn't put me any closer to figuring out who had murdered her. But my sense was that I'd just traveled light years in terms of figuring out why.

Chapter 12

"An example from the monkey: The higher it climbs, the more you see of its behind."

—German proverb

As I drove home at the end of the day, I was still brooding about the possibility that Erin's murder had been in some way related to the illegal animal trade. This new twist was so unexpected that I found myself wavering between being convinced that I'd finally stumbled upon some solid evidence and thinking that her paramour's interpretation of what she'd written had to have been dead wrong.

But one thing was certain: My top priority was finding out whatever I could about this despicable practice.

Reaching home was a great relief. As I let myself into Betty and Winston's house, I braced myself for the enthusiastic welcome I always got from my animals. I wasn't disappointed. In turn, I made sure they knew that I'd missed each and every one of them too.

I would have given Nick an enthusiastic greeting, too, but the absence of his car told me he hadn't made it home yet. Even though he was just an intern at the law firm, he was already working insane hours. Still, I didn't mind having the mansion all to myself. There was definitely something to be said for living in the lap of luxury.

Even my animals were getting used to the good life. Max had already staked out Betty's couch as his favorite place to hang. Despite his tough terrier demeanor, he loved resting his head on her lavender satin pillow. Lou liked to park himself in front of the fireplace. Since it was June, he hadn't seen us light a fire in it, but he still seemed to find it cozy. In fact, both dogs looked kind of annoyed that I'd showed up, forcing them to leave such comfortable spots to come over and greet me. Lou kept yawning in my face, as if he wanted me to know that I'd disturbed his afternoon repose.

My cats had also made themselves at home. Since Cat wasn't able to leap up onto the furniture without assistance anymore, she followed the same strategy as at the cottage: She napped on a chenille rug in front of Betty's refrigerator. This soft rug happened to be a lot bigger than mine, since Betty's restaurant-size Sub-Zero refrigerator was a lot wider than the one squeezed inside my tiny kitchen at the cottage. Tinkerbell preferred circulating around the entire house, trying out beds, chairs, window seats, assorted cushions, and any garment that may have accidentally fallen to the ground.

It'll be tough going back to real life, I thought with

a sigh, yanking off my chukka boots and socks so I could feel the soft fibers of Betty's carpets against my toes. I poured myself a glass of Harvey's Bristol Cream from a crystal decanter, sank onto the soft couch next to my luxury-loving Westie, and opened my laptop.

As soon as I logged on to check my e-mail, I saw that I'd gotten another message from Betty. I clicked on to that one first, eager to know if her Tuscan honeymoon was still as glorious as her first e-mail had made it sound.

HELP!!!!

I can finally write the truth, now that that meddlesome daughter of Winston's has FINALLY left the room. Honestly, she treats me as if I'm her second daughter. Worse yet, she treats me the way she treats her poor husband!

Not that Rupert deserves better. I found out there's a good reason he's so successful in the cutthroat world of investment banking. Jessica, the man is crazed. He's up at five every morning, jogging. Jogging—in Italy, a country where the most popular sport is eating pasta! Over breakfast, he insists on holding the newspaper in front of his face. Then he reads the day's stock prices—aloud! He's always planning, planning, planning. As he's drinking his third cup of espresso, he'll say, "Let's visit some of the local wineries this morning. We'll leave at ten. I'll drive. On our way, we can practice conjugating Italian verbs. We'll stop for lunch in that charming town we drove through a few days ago on our way back from touring the olive groves. We'll be home by three, take a swim, shower, then gather for cocktails at five. Are you all with me?"

Of course, Chloe is someone who does NOT want to be told what to do. So her response is invariably to argue with him. She'll start listing reasons why his ideas are bad—too hot, too far, too crowded, too unwholesome (that's the wineries). Poor little Fiona just sits there, looking as if she wishes she could jump into the huge bowl of oatmeal her mother insists that she eat for breakfast every single morning. (If I hear "Plenty of yummy-yummy and oh-so-healthy oat bran, Fiona, dear" one more time, I may throw the entire bowl out the window!). Every chance I get, I sneak that poor girl into town and buy her the biggest dish of gelato I can find.

James and his French model aren't getting along very well either. It seems his idea of a vacation in the Italian countryside is going on all-day bike trips. Fabienne's idea is lying by the pool, perfecting her tan. They spend so much time arguing that neither of them gets to do much of either.

Winston and I have hardly had a moment alone. Each one of them—Chloe and Rupert, James and Fabienne—keeps coming to us to complain about the other. I feel like a marriage counselor, not a newlywed!

I miss you all terribly. I wish we'd simply stayed home!

Poor Betty! I thought.

I was suddenly aware of an uncomfortable tightening in my stomach. But I knew the reaction in my guts was only partly because of Betty's difficulties as a brand-new bride. It was more because I saw it as a sign of what might lay ahead of me.

True, Nick didn't have any intrusive children. But he had a mother who was more aggravating than the entire cast of *Cheaper by the Dozen*.

Yet that was only one reason that even now, with my wedding just weeks away, I still had trouble picturing myself actually walking down the aisle.

And the prospect of appearing in public dressed like an oversized cupcake smothered in white butter-cream frosting wasn't the problem either. As scary as playing the starring role in a wedding ceremony seemed, I knew that in the grand scheme of things, that would turn out to be the easy part.

It was the business of intertwining my life with someone else's that gave me the heebie-jeebies.

Not that I didn't love Nick. I did. I loved him to pieces. But there was another side of me that I couldn't ignore. That was the side that couldn't wear turtlenecks for fear that the soft, innocent-looking fabric would somehow grow tighter and tighter around my neck until I suddenly found myself unable to breathe. The side that had chosen to work out of a clinic-on-wheels instead of staying inside a cluster of rooms all day as if I was under house arrest—or at least office arrest.

The side that had done everything possible to avoid saying yes to Nick's marriage proposals until I realized that I wanted him in my life so badly that the idea of him giving up on me was simply too painful to bear.

And that was the side that, at the moment, was

making me feel as if I'd just sipped cleaning fluid instead of sherry.

When my cell phone rang and the familiar number on the screen warned me that Suzanne was calling, I groaned. If there was anyone on the planet who was a poster child for the devastating effects of following one's heart, it was Suzanne Fox.

"Hi, Suzanne," I said, hoping my wariness wasn't reflected in my voice. "What's going on?"

"What's going on?" she repeated crossly. "I'll tell you what's going on. I'm thinking of breaking up with Kieran."

Even though she was clearly trying to sound as if she was a woman in control, I could hear the telltale waver in her voice. I had a feeling this was going to be a long conversation. I put my laptop on the coffee table, replaced it with the first pussycat I spotted, and settled back against the cushions.

"Trouble in paradise?" I asked. "So soon? How can that be?"

"Skittles doesn't like me," Suzanne stated simply.

It took me a few seconds to remember who Skittles was—and what a presence she was in Kieran's life.

Still, while many a dog has ruled the roost the way Skittles apparently did—a situation that I had to admit sounded a lot like my own—I couldn't believe that she, and not Kieran, had final say when it came to the man's love life.

"I'm sure Kieran is extremely attached to his dog," I said. "But surely who he dates isn't up to—"

"And as far as Kieran's concerned, she's the head of

the household," Suzanne insisted. "The queen of the condo. The light of his life. Should I go on?"

Please don't, I thought.

Especially since I was convinced that she was exaggerating. She had to be. There was no way I was going to believe that a German shepherd was coming between Suzanne and the man that only three days earlier she had interrupted a blueberry muffin-fest to gush about. True, Skittles and Kieran worked together. Lived together too. But that didn't mean that one could overlook the simple fact that she and Kieran didn't even belong to the same genus, much less the same species.

"Suzanne, I think you're blowing this way out of proportion," I told her, distractedly scratching the head of the gently snoring Westie beside me as I watched Tinkerbell attack a thread that had come loose on my jeans. "Of course Kieran and Skittles are close. They're partners. They spend the entire day together. They're . . . they're the Cagney and Lacey of the New York State Canine Unit! But you're his girlfriend, for heaven's sake! How could their relationship, if you can even call it that, interfere with yours?"

"I'll tell you what," Suzanne replied petulantly, "I'll give you a chance to see what goes on for yourself. Why don't you come to dinner at Kieran's place Friday night?"

"I'd love to. What time?"

After she'd told me Kieran's address and given me a rough idea of how to get there, I asked, "Is there anything I can bring?"

She snorted. "If I were you, I'd bring a hostess gift.

A Nylabone would be perfect. King-size. Or maybe I should say *queen* size."

I hoped I would prove her wrong.

I also hoped the main course wouldn't be Purina Dog Chow.

I'd barely hung up before my cell phone trilled again. I assumed Suzanne was calling me back, most likely to ask me about what to serve, what time to serve it, whether to use cloth napkins or paper, and every other decision that goes into making dinner for more than one person. But when I glanced at the caller ID screen, I saw that Patti Ardsley, the producer of *Pet People,* was calling.

"Hi, Jessie!" she said, greeting me with her usual buoyancy. In fact, she sounded as if she'd been getting perkiness pointers from a Jack Russell terrier. "All set for this Friday's show? I can't wait to hear what you'll be talking about!"

"Uh..." Not the most intelligent response, I realized, but I'd been busted. While I usually call the station early in the week to let someone know what topic I'll be discussing on the next show, this week I'd been so busy that I'd forgotten all about my upcoming TV spot. Still, I wasn't about to admit that any more than I was about to admit that I didn't have an idea in my head.

I wracked my brain—a brain that happened to be overloaded, thanks to my distress over Betty's e-mail, Suzanne's telephone call, and the prospect of my own future as half of a married couple.

"I'm sure you have something wonderful in mind," Patti prompted pertly.

"As a matter of fact, I thought we'd do something a little different," I replied, stalling for time.

"Great! I can't wait to hear what it is!"

Me, either, I thought, fighting off pangs of panic.

And then, before my brain had a chance to take control of what my mouth was doing, words I never thought I'd hear myself utter flew from my lips: "I'm inviting a friend of mine on the show. A veterinarian named Marcus Scruggs."

"Fabulous!" Patti was practically percolating. "Getting some new blood on the show is a fabulous idea! Jessie, I don't know where you come up with these brainstorms of yours."

Low blood sugar? I thought woefully.

"I know," I agreed, nearly choking on my own words. "Sometimes I'm just too creative for my own good."

"Marcus Scruggs," Patti repeated slowly, as if she was writing it down. "Wonderful! I'll mention his name in the teaser. Something like, 'This week, in addition to learning from Channel 14's resident expert, Dr. Jessica Popper, viewers will get a totally different perspective from her accomplished guest, Dr. Marcus Scruggs!'"

Accomplished, up for debate. Different, definitely.

But one thing was for sure. The next time someone asked me if I worked well under pressure, I'd be sure to respond with a resounding *no*.

• • •

It wasn't until late morning on Thursday that I found the time to check out my local branch of Pet

Empawrium. While I was curious about Ben Chandler's new venture, what I was really hoping for was the chance to check out his business partner, Donald Drayton.

"Wow," I muttered as I turned into the parking lot and took a good look at the one-story brick building that housed Donald and Ben's enterprise. It was almost as big as a department store. I knew the days of the tiny hole-in-the-wall pet store crammed with leashes, catnip, canned food, and a few budgies and goldfish were pretty much over. But based on size alone, this place elevated shopping for pet supplies to the same level that warehouse stores like Costco had raised food shopping.

I entered through glass doors that automatically slid open at my approach. Instantly some poor unfortunate individual whose work clothes consisted of a dog costume stepped in front of me. The fuzzy orange-red canine bore just enough of a difference from Clifford the Big Red Dog not to get sued, with a Hefty bag–size head, long floppy ears, and at eye level, tiny slits that were barely big enough to keep him from walking into any fire hydrants.

"Arf, arf, welcome to Pet Empawrium," he greeted me, sounding considerably less enthusiastic than my real dogs did whenever we were reunited.

"Down, boy," I automatically replied.

It turned out that a talking dog the size of a grizzly bear was just the beginning. Pet Empawrium was not only tremendous in terms of square footage, the fact that it was lit brightly enough to perform surgery gave it an open, airy feeling even though it was packed with endless rows of shelves, tremendous cardboard bins overflowing with merchandise, and enough live animals displayed in cages and tanks to render school trips to the zoo obsolete. Some displays were decorated with bigger-than-life cutouts of the animal the goods were designed for, while others had balloons printed with eyes, ears, and whiskers floating above them. A few featured blinking lights.

An overly cute version of "How Much Is That Doggie in the Window?" blared from hidden speakers. There was even a coffee bar tucked away in one corner, no doubt to rejuvenate tired shoppers enough that they'd have the energy to pile more stuff into their shopping carts. I could imagine Marcus Scruggs drooling at the very sight of all that commerce packed into a single establishment.

Yet despite the overwhelming amount of merchandise, I didn't spot a single salesperson. In fact, the only people in the store appeared to be a few shoppers who were wandering through the aisles, looking as confused as I was.

Doesn't anyone work here, I wondered, aside from the Clifford wannabe?

After doing some wandering of my own, I finally spotted three employees, identifiable by bright red shirts with the words *Pet Empawrium* embroidered on the pocket in bright yellow. They had congregated in the back of the store around an eye-catching display of pooper-scoopers.

I walked over and planted myself two feet away from the little group, then stood there for at least thirty seconds hoping that sooner or later one of them would notice me. When I realized that the presence of a mere customer wasn't enough to stop the chubby thirty-something guy from pontificating about the weaknesses of the latest Xbox video game, I interrupted, "Excuse me, can anyone help me?"

The pudgy gameboy stopped mid-sentence. All three glanced over at me, looking surprised that someone had actually dared to ask them to stop yakking long enough to do their job.

"I'm on break," announced the only female member of the group, an emaciated teenage girl pierced with so much metal that I hoped she stayed inside during thunderstorms. She immediately stalked off, as if even addressing a customer during her official downtime compromised some moral code.

"I have eight cartons of birdseed to unpack," insisted a middle-aged man with coffee-colored skin and dead-straight black hair. The name JOSE was embroidered on his shirt, underneath the company logo.

That left the video game guy, whose name tag identified him as Justin. He didn't look like a Justin. He looked more like a Peabody or a Quincy.

I flashed him my friendliest smile. "Then maybe you can help me."

He sighed. "If it's not on the shelves, we're out of it."

Except for birdseed, I thought dryly.

"Actually, I've never been to this store before," I said, sounding as chirpy as one of the canaries on display nearby beneath a "Bird Buy of the Week" sign. "I'm having some trouble finding my way around. I mean, this place is so darned big."

Justin just stared at me with blue eyes so pale that they looked like they'd been colored in with a wet watercolor brush. I noticed then that only one of them was focused on me. The other stared dully into space.

"In fact," I went on, feeling like a Chatty Cathy doll whose wiring had run amok, "I'm surprised that a store this size has so few employees."

"Welcome to corporate America," Justin shot back. "If you want to meet the oppressed underclass, you've come to the right place."

Actually, most people probably came here to buy leashes and chew toys, but I didn't bother to point that out. At least I'd finally figured out that the way to get Justin's attention was by appealing to his disgruntlement over being a member of the downtrodden proletariat—even though I'd have bet my autoclave that he owned every single video game ever manufactured for that Xbox of his.

"It sounds as if working at Pet Empawrium doesn't rank very high on the job satisfaction list," I said, trying to sound sympathetic.

"Oh, it can be extremely satisfying," he replied snidely. "That is, if you like working long, grueling hours for minimum wage. With lousy health benefits. And no dental whatsoever."

"I see." What I saw, however, was Donald Drayton's mansion hovering in front of me like a mirage, along with his yacht and his expensive sports car.

"But you probably added the Pet Empawrium to your to-do list for some reason other than discussing its exploitative working conditions," Justin continued.

"What is it you're interested in adding to your hoard of material possessions today?"

Here goes. I cleared my throat nervously, then said, "I was wondering if you had any exotics. Any *unusual* exotics."

Justin's eyes narrowed. "What do you mean by 'unusual'? Are you talking about, say, giant African land snails?"

Now, there's a pet that's always up for a rollicking game of Frisbee, I thought. "Maybe."

"They're illegal, you know," he replied.

"Okay, then maybe something that isn't illegal but is still interesting. You know, the kind of animal most people don't have."

He cast me a skeptical look. "Don't tell me you're one of those party girls who likes to bring weird animals to clubs so that everyone will think you're cool."

Since when have giant African land snails replaced Fendi bags as the ultimate in trendy accessories? I wondered.

"I just happen to like animals that are kind of different." Unfortunately, I thought, that penchant doesn't necessarily extend to *people* who are kind of different. "What about scorpions?"

"What about scorpions?" Justin asked cautiously.

"Do you carry any?"

"Scorpions make very cool pets," he said with an approving nod. "But we don't carry them. Too dangerous."

No kidding, I thought.

"What if I wanted one anyway?" I persisted.

He stared at me for what seemed like a very long time. "You'd have to talk to Mr. Drayton."

"Who's Mr. Drayton?" I asked, putting on my Miss Innocent face.

"The owner of this fine establishment. The entire chain of Pet Empawriums, in fact. Or, if I remember my Latin correctly, Empawria."

"Ah. The Man."

"Precisely." Justin and I were finally communicating.

"And you're in luck," he continued. "He happens to be here today. See, he moves around from store to store with the stealth of a tiger. That way, we never know when he'll be checking up on us. But I caught him sneaking in this morning when I came in."

"Really?" Both my palms and my armpits were already growing damp.

"In fact, he's probably watching you right now."

"Watching me?"

"Our security system." Justin smiled coldly. "Mr. Drayton's way of keeping his eye on us. Of course, it means he's also keeping an eye on the customers. Like you."

I glanced around nervously.

"Oh, you can't see him," he said. "But he can see you. See, that's the whole idea."

Justin made shopping for pet supplies sound like breaking into CIA headquarters.

"I'd really like to speak with him," I said. "Could you find out if that's possible?"

"We're here to serve," Justin replied with a little bow. "Right this way."

When I followed him up a flight of stairs at the back of the store, I was confronted with a dozen television screens. They lined an entire wall of the first of many rooms that overlooked the selling floor. Each one provided a clear view of a different spot somewhere inside or outside the store. A few metal desks were placed directly underneath them, along with a phone, a mug filled with pens, and other assorted office supplies that made it look as if a secretary or perhaps a security guard sometimes sat here.

"See? This is where Dr. Evil runs his empire," Justin said in a low voice. "At least at this branch."

Donald Evil—er, Drayton—certainly believes in keeping track of what's going on, I thought, gulping. I only hoped I wasn't getting in over my head.

I trailed after Justin, following him down a long hallway. Interestingly, when he knocked on the door at the very end, I noticed that he slumped his shoulders and ducked his head down. I knew enough about body language to understand that Long Island's own version of Che Guevara had just gone from courageous to cowed.

I began to understand why as soon as I heard a gruff voice from inside snarl, "Come in!"

"Mr. Drayton?" Justin said softly, opening the door a few inches.

"What?" The single syllable sounded as friendly as a Doberman's bark. A really peeved Doberman.

"Somebody wants to see you," Justin replied in a high-pitched voice that made him sound about eight years old. "A customer with some special interests."

"Fine," Drayton replied, still sounding annoyed. "Send 'em in."

As I stepped into Donald Drayton's hideaway, I saw that his control center looked more like something out of *The Office* than something from an Austin Powers movie. As for the man himself, I already knew what he looked like, since I'd seen that photograph of him and Nicole taken during the days when the father-and-daughter team still spent their Sundays together.

But I didn't expect the king-size belly, something that had clearly developed since he'd given up horseback riding. Nor did I expect an expensive suit that looked as if it had missed a few of its regularly scheduled appointments with the dry cleaner. Drayton's left hand, so pudgy and red that it reminded me of a baked ham, was decorated with a diamond pinky ring. The rock was so huge I wondered if he inadvertently left scratches on glass wherever he went.

"Something I can help you with?" he demanded in the same grouchy voice.

He sounded hurried, so I got right to the point. Taking a deep breath, I said, "I may be interested in purchasing a rare exotic animal."

He didn't look the least bit surprised. "Have a seat," he said, gesturing toward the chair that faced his desk. He studied me for a few seconds before asking, "What kind?"

How about a yellow fat tail scorpion? I thought.

Aloud, I said, "I'm not sure. Something different. You know, the kind of thing that not just anybody owns."

Once again, Drayton hesitated. "I can probably get

you what you want," he finally said, still staring at me as if he was trying to use his X-ray vision to read my mind. "But you'll have to be more specific."

"Maybe you could just tell me what's available," I said, doing my best not to squirm.

He shrugged. "Like I said, you need to be specific about what you're looking for."

"How about—oh, I don't know, a gorilla?" I joked.

I expected him to chuckle. Instead, he frowned thoughtfully and said, "Not cheap. But not impossible either."

I was stunned. Was it possible he was serious? He certainly seemed to think I was.

Remembering Justin's comment about the latest in outlandish accessories, I casually asked, "How about giant African land snails?"

"A lot easier—and a lot cheaper," he replied matter-of-factly.

But also illegal, I thought.

"Let me think about it," I told him. "Now that I know that I can pretty much get what I want, I'll need some time to consider my options, and how much I want to spend."

"Whatever," he replied, waving the ham hock at the end of his arm in the air. "Let me know when you're ready to talk price."

"I certainly will."

As I stood up to leave, a little voice nagged at me. True, I'd already found out that from the looks of things, Drayton's business did indeed extend far beyond what it appeared to be. But even though I'd just witnessed his willingness to supply me with any kind of pet I wanted, I still wanted to know more.

Mainly, whether he was just showing off or if he meant business.

"By the way, is there a rest room I could use?" I asked.

"Downstairs, behind the doghouses," he replied.

"Uh, this is kind of an emergency."

He looked startled, but didn't hesitate before saying, "Down the hall. Second door on the right."

"Thanks." Funny, that ploy never seemed to fail. Especially when I put on a look of desperation—and the person I was asking was male.

"Close the door on your way out," Drayton instructed, picking up the phone.

Rats, I thought. And here I'd hoped to do a little eavesdropping while I was inside the belly of the beast.

But I quickly realized that a closed door meant that I would be able to poke around without him seeing me. And that for someone as creative as I was, a closed door wasn't enough to keep me from doing some of that eavesdropping.

First I dashed into the rest room, wanting to make it look as if I really was facing some bodily crisis. I washed my hands, then leaned against each of the small room's four walls, anxious to see if I could hear anything interesting. *Nada.*

When I stepped out into the hallway again, I tried to look relieved, just in case anyone was watching. But no one else appeared to be around. I also noticed that none of the television screens in front of me featured the hallway I was standing in. Which gave me the perfect opportunity to do a little of that spying I wanted to do.

I moved toward Donald Drayton's closed door, walking on cat feet. The fact that I could hear his voice but no one else's told me he was still on the phone.

"... a delivery. A very special delivery," I heard him say. "How does tomorrow sound?"

I crept closer, my heart pounding so loudly that I was having trouble hearing Drayton over the noise.

"I knew you'd be pleased, Mr. Santoro," I heard Drayton say. Even though his voice was muffled, I could tell that he was pretty pleased himself. "I told you we'd be able to come through for you."

So a customer named Mr. Santoro was about to get a delivery, I thought. A very special delivery.

Which made me curious about who Mr. Santoro was—and whether the delivery he was so pleased about was a particularly large amount of dog food or something much more interesting.

I crept away from the door, heading back to the security area I'd passed through before. I'd noticed on the way in that while Drayton had installed state-of-the-art security equipment, his love of technology didn't extend to office supplies. I thought I'd spotted an old-fashioned Rolodex sitting on top of the desk, and sure enough, there it was.

After stealing a quick glance behind me, I rifled through the cards, past the M's and the P's, and on to the S's. Bingo! There was a Santoro listed. Louis Santoro. An address too. Two twenty-five Hillsboro

Drive in the village of Lloyd Cove. I committed it to memory.

I'd barely put back the Rolodex when I heard the floor creak, which I took as a sign that Drayton was about to emerge. The last thing I wanted was for him to find me here, playing Nancy Drew. So I scuttled down the stairs, doing my best not to make any noise.

When I spotted Justin a few aisles ahead, my heart sank. I had assumed I'd have to stop to give him an update. But surprisingly, he actually appeared to be helping another customer. Either that or enlisting her aid in the revolution.

I eased my way toward the front entrance, relieved that I'd managed to slip right past him without being noticed. At the moment, my head was too full for me to make small talk.

Things were clicking into place with amazing speed. It appeared that Donald Drayton, Erin's husband's business partner, dealt in exotic animals, including illegal ones. That reinforced Walter's interpretation of the initials Erin had written down: that they were all the names of organizations that were dedicated to fighting that very practice. It seemed increasingly clear that once Erin had found out what Ben and his partner were up to, she began making plans to do something about it.

That still didn't tell me who had killed her. But I was certainly developing a better understanding of the unsavory world she'd stumbled into—and how high the stakes were for those who were part of it.

• • •

As I was coming out of the store, breathing freely for the first time since I'd gone in, I noticed a gleaming white Mercedes speeding into the parking lot. It was hard not to, since it zoomed by me so quickly I instinctively jumped back. After it shot behind the building and out of sight, I braced myself for the sound of metal crunching against metal.

By the time I rounded the corner, however, I saw that the car had safely made it into a parking spot. Two spots, actually, since the driver seemed to have made a point of straddling the yellow line that divided two separate spaces.

As I was about to cross the asphalt so I could get to my VW, I noticed that the person climbing out of the passenger side was Nicole Drayton. Then another familiar face popped out the other side. Just like the last time I'd seen the two Drayton women together, I couldn't tell whether Nicole or her stepmother was wearing more eye makeup.

I surmised that Darla had picked up her stepdaughter from school, since Nicole was dressed in the same gray blazer and plaid skirt I'd seen her wearing on Monday. I couldn't imagine her allowing herself to be seen in public in the same outfit twice in one week unless she had no choice.

As for the missus, she was wearing denim shorts and a lime green tank top, its fabric stretched so tight and its neckline plunging so deeply that she made my flashy pal Suzanne look like a member of a religious order. She was also wearing heels. Granted, they had probably come from the sandals department, since they were made of some coarse brownish material that looked like rope. But the platform heels added at least another three inches to her height, which in my book put them in the Barbie shoe category.

But the fact that I looked like a *Glamour* "Don't" beside the two of them wasn't the reason I didn't want either of them to see me. The last thing I wanted was to have to explain why I was lurking outside one of the stores that had helped make the Drayton fortune.

I glanced around frantically, trying to find a place to hide. But short of ducking between a couple of SUVs and pretending I'd dropped my car keys, there was no way out.

I'd just resigned myself to confronting Darla and Nicole face-to-face when I heard Nicole cry, "Hey, look! It's Dr. Popper! Hi, Dr. Popper!"

I did my best to look surprised as I made a show of glancing in their direction. Nicole was wearing a big smile and waving as if the two of us were best friends.

"Nicole!" I exclaimed. "Wow! I never expected to run into you here. Oh, wait—your dad owns this store, doesn't he?"

"That's why we're here!" she replied. "I only have a half day of school today, so we're going to meet him for lun—"

Before she managed to get the word out, Darla grabbed her arm and pulled her forward with a jerking motion. Half-dragging her stepdaughter across the parking lot, she stomped over in my direction.

"He-e-ey!" Nicole complained. "That hurts! Darla, what do you think you're—"

"Quiet," Darla shot back. "Zip it, Nicole, or I'll tell your father about that little plastic bag full of

God knows what that I found hidden in your box of Tampax."

I did my best not to look shocked. Poor Nicole, I thought. There's obviously nothing that's off-limits where her stepmother's concerned.

"Hello, Mrs. Drayton," I said politely, forcing myself to smile.

"What are you doing here?" she demanded.

"I have quite a collection of pets," I replied cheerfully. "Two dogs, two cats, a blue-and-gold macaw, and a Jackson's chameleon. So I always seem to be running into a store to pick up something or other."

"Besides, she's a veterinarian," Nicole added, glaring at her stepmother. "Isn't that a good reason to shop at a pet store?"

"Speaking of animals," I said, focusing on the more congenial half of this pair, "have you had a chance to call that animal behaviorist, Nicole? I really think she could help you with Maggie."

Before she had a chance to answer, Darla stepped between us. Leaning forward so that her nose was about an inch from mine, she hissed, "Keep away from us. And that especially goes for Nicole."

Her antagonism caught me completely off guard. "But I was just trying to be helpful!" I protested. "I could see that you have problems with Maggie, and I thought—"

"I don't know what you want from us," she interrupted. "But I don't like you. If you come near me or any member of my family again, I'm going to call the police."

And have me arrested for recommending an animal

behaviorist without a license? I thought crossly. Come to think of it, I *do* have a license.

Nicole cast me a look of despair. *See what I have to put up with?* her expression said.

"There's no need to get upset," I told Darla, struggling to keep my voice steady. "Of course I'll respect your privacy. Nicole's too."

As they disappeared around the corner of the building, I realized I was shaking.

But the intense interaction I'd just had with the Wicked Witch of Walt Whitman Hills made me realize something: Nicole wasn't the only one who had to put up with Darla's bizarre behavior. So did Nicole's father.

Still, that realization didn't do much to make me feel sorry for him. Not when meeting the man and seeing his operation left me convinced that he was selling a lot more than birdseed—and that he could even have been responsible for getting Erin killed.

Chapter 13

"People go to the zoo and they like the lion because it's scary. And the bear because it's intense, but the monkey makes people laugh."

—Lorne Michaels

Friday morning, I once again found myself in the green room at Sunshine Multimedia's headquarters, waiting for Marlene to summon me to the *Pet People* set. A few prebroadcast butterflies wriggled around in my stomach. But it wasn't because I was imagining all the ways some cute animal appearing with me on the show might misbehave.

Instead, I was imagining all the ways the not-so-cute *human* on the schedule was likely to misbehave.

Stop worrying! I told myself. Marcus is a grown man. Surely he'll manage to conduct himself with dignity on your television show.

And then he sashayed in.

"Marcus?" I croaked.

I did a double take, hoping I wasn't really seeing what I thought I was seeing. I told myself I was probably just hallucinating, perhaps from having consumed too much caffeine. That had to be the explanation, since the figure standing in front of me couldn't possibly be real.

"Hey, Popper," the mirage replied breezily. "All set to make me a star?"

It was Marcus, all right. In the flesh. Unfortunately, said flesh happened to be covered with a jacket made from a fabric that was printed all over with animals. Large, colorful animals. So large and so colorful, in fact, that it looked as if he'd stolen the bedspread out of some poor toddler's room.

But that wasn't even the worst of it. The tie dangling from his neck was studded with lights. Tiny blinking lights that were probably powered by a battery hidden away somewhere in his Fruit of the Looms.

When I peered at it more closely, I saw that the tiny lights were actually the eyes of little doggies and pussycats that were printed on the necktie's fabric. They might have been cute if those glowing orbs in the middle of their faces didn't make them look like something Stephen King had dreamed up.

I suddenly had a few ideas about what I'd prefer to see around Marcus's neck.

"Uh, Marcus?" I said, trying not to let on that intense feelings of panic were threatening to overtake me. "You're not planning on wearing that jacket on the air, are you? And, uh, what's with the electrified tie?"

"What, this?" He glanced down at his chest. "Are

you kidding? This tie is great! And the lights will probably show up really well on camera."

No doubt, I thought grimly. "It's just that I try to maintain a certain level of ... shall we say, *professionalism* on the show."

Grinning, Marcus slung his arm around me and patted my shoulder. "Anybody ever tell you that you worry too much, Popper?"

I gritted my teeth, reminding myself that before I knew it, today's show would be over. I just had to get through it. In fact, it was kind of like enduring a root canal. Without any Novocaine.

Besides, I reminded myself, Marcus, his tie, and his Amazing Technicolor Dreamjacket still have to get past Patti. Surely the producer of an informational television program will have the clout required to prevent medical experts from coming on her show in costume.

A minute later, when she popped her head into the green room to let us know it was nearing showtime, I waited breathlessly for her to set some serious limits with Marcus.

"You're on in five," she told us. "You're Marcus Scruggs, right? Today's guest? Hey, cool tie!"

Dead man walking, I thought as I shuffled down the hall toward Studio A. I'm about to appear on television with a man who looks like a recent graduate of clown school.

Once we were in the studio, Marcus and I took our seats in front of the backdrop of stuffed animals. The sound guy barely had time to wire us up with microphones before Patti launched into her usual countdown. I took deep cleansing breaths, wondering why I'd never taken the time to learn yoga.

"Welcome to *Pet People,* the program for people who are passionate about their pets," I began as usual, trying not to get distracted by the tiny blinking lights next to me. "I'm Dr. Popper, your host. Today, we have a very special guest. Dr. Marcus Scruggs is a veterinarian here on Long Island. We're going to be discussing some issues that are bound to be on pet owners' minds. Dr. Scruggs, thank you for coming on the show."

"Are you kidding, Popper?" he replied with a leer. "I'd follow you to the ends of the earth."

I let out a nervous laugh, hoping that some really popular show was being aired at the same time as mine this morning so that only a handful of loyal viewers had tuned in. Viewers who were loyal enough not to care that the show's standards had unexpectedly plummeted to the bottom of the Grand Canyon.

Striving to hang on to whatever shreds of my dignity still remained, I adopted the most serious expression I could manage. "Tell me, Dr. Scruggs, how do you think technology has affected the field of veterinary medicine?"

"Interesting question," he observed, nodding. "But I'm surprised you want to talk about something as dry as technology when there's undoubtedly a much more pressing question you're dying to ask."

"What question is that?" I said, completely baffled.

"Where I got this fabulous necktie, of course!"

At that point, I wasn't sure who was the bigger

idiot, Marcus or the fool who had just walked right into his trap.

I cleared my throat. "Uh, actually, I wasn't going to ask you about that at all—"

"Believe me, you wouldn't be able to find such a distinctive, high-quality product just anywhere," Marcus continued. "But thanks to Blooming Tails, the gift shop at Innovative Pet Care, discriminating pet owners can have their animals examined *and* buy this tie along with hundreds of other unique pet-themed products in one convenient place!"

Instead of conducting an informative television show for concerned pet owners, I suddenly found myself smack in the middle of an infomercial. I glanced over in the direction of the blinking lights, intending to cast Marcus the dirtiest look I could muster. But I discovered that he wasn't even looking at me. He was staring straight into the camera.

"What is Innovative Pet Care, you ask?" he continued.

"I don't think anyone asked that," I corrected him. "In fact, I think we should get back to the topic of technology and how—"

"It's a veterinary clinic, centrally located in Woodview, that presents a brand-new concept in total pet care," he went on. "One that's completely innovative, just as the name promises. Working with two other dedicated veterinarians who are as talented as I am, I've created a clinic that has first-rate medical professionals, state-of-the-art equipment, and auxiliary services for every treatment imaginable, all under one roof. But we offer so much more!"

I checked the monitor and saw that the cameraman had zoomed in on Marcus. I had been left out of the picture, both literally and figuratively.

"We have hotel rooms, right on-site, that make it possible for pet owners to spend the night with their ailing loved one," Marcus informed whatever viewers hadn't already turned off their TVs. "We have a wine bar that serves twenty reds and fifteen whites by the glass. We also have a snack bar that whips up fruit smoothies, including Strawberry Mango, our smoothie of the month. But we certainly haven't forgotten our four-legged friends. Innovative Pet Care has a bakery on the premises that specializes in healthy, wholesome between-meal treats for dogs, cats, birds, and even reptiles."

Reptiles? I thought. Since when do lizards snack?

"Dr. Scruggs," I cut in, figuring my voice deserved a place on the show even if my face didn't, "this is all fascinating. But let's get back to the ways in which advanced medical technologies like sonograms and MRIs can be used in treating—"

"How about animal crackers in the shape of your favorite pet?" Not only did Marcus keep his eyes fixed on the camera, much to my horror he whipped out a cardboard box that looked a lot like the bright red one in which animal crackers for humans are sold. Only this one was much bigger, since it probably contained animal crackers for Great Danes. "At the Pawtisserie, we have croissants for French poodles, black-and-white cookies for Scotties and Westies, cat's tongue cookies for felines, and Napoleons for Chihuahuas. Cash, checks, money orders, and all major credit cards are accepted. And everything we sell is made with one hundred percent natural ingredients, all of them good for your pet."

Helplessly I glanced toward the cameraman, trying to will him to have the good sense to shift the focus away from my wayward guest. Instead, my eyes lit on Patti, who was standing right next to him. And she didn't look at all pleased.

"Dr. Scruggs," I tried again, this time letting my irritation show, "we really need to get back to the discussion at hand."

I might as well have been talking to one of the stuffed animals behind me.

"At Blooming Tails," Marcus went on, staring into the camera as intently as if it was a lover, "you'll find a truly unusual boutique packed with a wide range of hand-selected items that every pet owner will want to stock up on. For example, check out this little gem." He reached into his pocket and pulled out the same flashy dog collar he'd shown me before, the pink suede one decorated with real diamonds.

I glanced at Patti and saw that her mouth had dropped open. And not in a good way.

And then a minor miracle occurred. I discovered a way out. The red light was blinking on the telephone in front of me, the one I used to answer questions from viewers who called in. Maybe I wasn't having any luck saving the show, but hopefully someone out there in TV land could.

"We have a caller!" I exclaimed, pressing the speakerphone button. "Hello! Thank you for calling *Pet People*!"

"Hi, Dr. Popper?" the female caller began hesitantly. "This is Jane from Eastbury."

"Hello, Jane. We're on the air. How can I help you and your pet?"

"Actually, my question is for your guest," Jane from Eastbury said. "Dr. Scruggs, does that collar come in purple? I mean, the pink is cute and everything, but my cockapoo's favorite color is purple."

By the time the show ended, it was all I could do to keep myself from strangling Marcus with his ridiculous tie. Either that or pouring water on him so that there'd be a short in his shorts.

But I didn't have a chance, since he immediately sprang out of his chair and made a beeline for the best-looking female in the room, who happened to be the show's production assistant, Marlene. Besides, Patti the Producer was marching toward me. And for the first time since I'd met her, she looked mad. Really, really mad.

"Jessie," she hissed, "what on earth was *that*?"

I shrank away from her like a kid who's just been called into the principal's office. *That*, I thought, is a stellar example of what's generally known as bad judgment.

• • •

"Tell me again why we're spending our Friday night having dinner with Suzanne and some stranger instead of eating Chinese food and watching a video," Nick said that evening as he and I pulled up in front of Kieran's residence.

"Because Suzanne is a good friend and we're both

anxious to get to know the new man in her life," I replied.

I made a point of leaving out the part about the new dog in her life. Even though I was primarily here to make firsthand observations about the dynamics of a threesome that Suzanne claimed was troublesome, I didn't see any reason to have my opinion colored by someone else's. Especially someone of the male variety, since it was possible he wouldn't be sympathetic to my role of undercover relationship counselor.

As I climbed out of Nick's black Maxima, I studied the modest-size tract house that looked as if it had been designed by an architect who had stolen the blueprints for Levittown. Actually, the tiny, one-story house on an equally compact piece of land looked pretty nice for a bachelor pad. Or at least my preconceived notion of a bachelor pad, which I had to admit had been formed primarily by movies like *Animal House*. The lawn was mowed and the shrubs running along the front of the house were neatly trimmed. White impatiens lined the walkway. True, they were still in the plastic pots they'd originally come in, with the white price tags in full view. But that didn't keep them from making the front yard look pretty.

The house was also well cared for. It looked as if it had been repainted recently—not only the white shingles, but also the dark blue shutters. Between the cheerful little touches Kieran had added and the fact that it was well maintained, it had a homey, welcoming feel.

In fact, as Nick and I strolled up the front walk arm

in arm, I was psyched for a really pleasant evening of good friends, good food, and good conversation.

So I was taken aback when I saw how our hostess for the evening looked when she opened the door.

"H-hello, Jessie. Hi, Nick." Suzanne's cheeks were flushed and she'd screwed up her face in a way that meant she was on the verge of tears.

I glanced at Nick. He already looked ready to bolt. I grasped his arm more tightly.

"Hi, Suzanne!" I greeted her brightly. Of course I wondered what was wrong. It was just that I wasn't going to start off the evening by giving Suzanne a chance to tell me.

Instead, I thrust the bakery box that contained our contribution to the evening's meal at her and announced, "We brought dessert."

"Thanks," she said morosely. With a loud sigh, she added, "You might as well come in."

As Nick and I stepped into the hallway, I noticed that there was a big red blotch on Suzanne's snow-white shirt. Frankly, I thought the shirt would have been pretty unflattering even without the stain, given the fact that it was made of clingy fabric that emphasized every twist and turn of her complicated silhouette.

"Suzanne," I said softly, not sure if this was going to turn out to be one of those occasions when honesty was not the best policy, "I think you may have, uh, spilled something on your shirt."

"It was Skittles's fault!" she shot back in a hoarse stage whisper. "*She* did it, not me!"

I blinked. Kieran's canine partner was undoubtedly

smart, but I doubted that even a well-trained German shepherd of her caliber possessed that much fashion sense.

Nick, clever man that he is, took this as his cue. "I'll go find Kieran and introduce myself," he said, dashing away before I had a chance to grab him.

"Suzanne, I really don't see how a dog could do something that vengeful—"

"This is my favorite shirt!" she wailed, her lower lip puckering into a pout. "I absolutely adore it! It's Dolce & Gabbana. I paid a fortune for it!"

Yet you got such a small amount of fabric, I thought.

"I guess Skittles decided it was a little too sexy," she continued, her tone bitter. "I'd barely had it on for five minutes before she poured merlot all over it."

Somehow, I couldn't picture a German shepherd—even one capable of sniffing out and chasing down perpetrators—picking up a glass of red wine and flinging it at her rival for Officer Hottie's affections. While Skittles probably possessed the smarts, I didn't think she had the required paw-eye coordination.

"I guess I'm missing something," I confessed. "Like how a dog could possibly manage to pour wine on someone's shirt."

"Oh, she didn't do it directly," Suzanne replied tartly. "She's much too clever for that. She waited until I was pouring myself a glass. As soon as it was full, she hurled herself against me. Of course, she knew full well that would cause me to spill it all over myself!"

"I see." Even though I did my best to sound sympathetic, I still thought Suzanne was overdoing it in the accusation department. Especially since she was attributing such evil actions to a creature whose idea of a good time was sniffing another dog's butt.

"I'm telling you, Jessie, she hates me!" Suzanne whined. "She's doing everything she can to drive me away!"

I opened my mouth, prepared to try to convince her that she was reading way too much into Skittles's behavior. But before I'd uttered a single word of my logical, carefully thought out argument, I snapped it shut again. I could see there was no point in trying to change her mind.

"I'd put cold water on that stain if I were you," I advised. "That'll probably take it right out."

"You think?" Suzanne's expression softened for the first time since I'd walked in the door. "Thanks, Jess!" She turned and dashed through a door I assumed led to the bathroom, no doubt to try some emergency stain removal.

It's going to be a long night, I thought with a deep sigh.

I ambled toward the kitchen, where I could hear Nick and Kieran engaged in an enthusiastic discussion about the respective pennant potential of the Mets and the Yankees this season. When I reached the doorway, I saw that Nick was perched on a stool with a bottle of beer in his hand. Kieran was standing at the counter, emptying a box of sesame crackers onto a plate. Skittles stood at his side. In fact, she was practically glommed on to his left leg, as if somehow the Velcro on the pockets of his cargo pants had gotten stuck in her fur.

As I was about to step into the room, she let out a low growl.

"Quiet!" Kieran commanded. Glancing at me sheepishly, he said, "Sorry about that, Jessie. I don't know what's gotten into her lately."

"You mean she's become nervous around strangers?" I asked.

"That's the funny thing," he replied, frowning. "Only around female strangers. And it only happens when we're at home. Whenever she's on the job, she's her usual self."

Aha, I thought. So maybe there is some basis for Suzanne's complaints about the other female in Kieran's life.

I edged my way around the kitchen, giving Skittles wide berth. Even though I'm comfortable around dogs—even king-size ones with king-size teeth—I also have a healthy respect for the damage they can do if they feel threatened. Once I made it over to Nick's corner of the room, I plunked down on a stool next to him.

"Can I get you something to drink, Jessie?" Kieran offered. "Soda, beer, wine—"

"Wine sounds great."

"Red or white?"

"White," I replied quickly, glancing down at my shirt. "Definitely white."

While Kieran and Nick dissected New York's two baseball teams, I worked on my wine and marveled over how much the male half of the species' endless fascination with ball playing resembles terriers' passion for the very same activity. A few minutes later,

Suzanne appeared in the doorway. Instead of an unattractive red wine stain, her blouse was covered with an even less attractive wet spot.

I wasn't the only one who noticed her entrance. Another growl emerged from Skittles. Actually, this time around it was more like a snarl.

"Quiet, Skittles!" Kieran barked. "Honestly, I don't know what's gotten into her."

Skittles stopped growling, all right. But as Suzanne took a step into the room, the powerful German shepherd stepped directly in her path, as if to block her.

Kieran didn't notice. He was too busy reliving the 1969 World Series, when Tom Seaver went 25–7 with a 2.21 ERA and 208 strikeouts. This was apparently a good thing.

From across the room, Suzanne cast me a look of desperation. *See?* she seemed to be saying. *I told you so.*

True, it looked bad. But I still wasn't entirely convinced that Skittles wasn't simply reacting to having a stranger—any stranger—in the house. Or that something hadn't happened to her on the job that was affecting her behavior at home.

Or that she wasn't just being a dog and we humans were reading all kinds of motives into her behavior.

Kieran finally seemed to have noticed that his ladylove—the human one, that is—had entered the room. "What are you drinking?" he asked Suzanne as he emptied a can of mixed nuts into a wooden bowl.

"I think I'll stick with water," she answered quickly. Kieran suddenly seemed strangely interested in the beverage issue. "I thought you were drinking red wine."

"I was," she replied, "but, uh, I don't want it to go to my head."

Or her skirt, I thought ruefully.

"Why don't we go into the living room?" Kieran suggested once we all had a glass in our hand. "We'll be more comfortable in there."

The four of us paraded into the next room, carrying our drinks. After Kieran arranged the snacks he'd prepared on the coffee table, he sat on the couch. Suzanne plopped down next to him.

Skittles immediately jumped up onto the cushions, wedging her sleek butt between the two of them. As she did, the water in Suzanne's glass went flying, landing all over her pale pink skirt.

"Eeek!" she cried, jumping up. As she did, she bumped against the coffee table, knocking over the bowl of nuts and sending almonds and cashews flying all over the carpet.

"Down, Skittles!" Kieran commanded sharply. Skittles reluctantly crawled off the couch, then glared at him.

So did Suzanne. "My whole outfit is ruined!" she shrieked.

"They're just clothes," Kieran replied. Frowning, he added, "I don't know what's going on with Skittles. I'm really worried about her." He reached down to scratch the fur on the dog's neck. In a soft, concerned voice, he asked, "Are you all right, Skittles? Huh? Is my best girl doing okay?"

I couldn't tell if the look Skittles cast Suzanne was

one of triumph or disdain. But I could see for myself that my friend was absolutely right. She really was caught in a love triangle.

And the fact that one of the three members happened to have four legs didn't make it any easier. Especially since she was using every one of them to walk all over her rival.

Chapter 14

"Just 'cause you got the monkey off your back
doesn't mean the circus has left town."

—George Carlin

B y Saturday morning, I'd forgotten all about the
trials and tribulations of Suzanne's love life. I
was too focused on the fact that I had an entire
day with no responsibilities ahead of me—that is,
aside from acting surprised at my unsurprising wedding shower that night.

That meant I finally had a chance to do more research. I hadn't stopped hoping that somehow I'd be
able to use the Internet to make some progress in deciphering the writing on Erin's cocktail napkin.

Right after breakfast was the ideal time. Nick and I
lingered on the patio, each of us hunched over our
laptops as we sipped coffee and basked in the warmth
of the perfect June day.

I began by opening Google and typing in the keywords *100* and *brown* once again. Only, this time, I added the words *Long Island*.

The screen that appeared was completely different from the one that had come up the last time. There was no mention of any Christmas lights, leather recliners, or baby-proof electrical outlet covers.

Instead, the first listing was for Norfolk Self-Storage, located at 100 Brown Street in Bellpoint Beach.

"Oh, my God," I breathed. "Nick, you're not going to believe what I just found."

He looked up from his computer screen and blinked. "Something good, I hope."

"Something important," I replied. "Anyway, I think it is. You know the words *100 brown BB plus*?"

"Of course. From the cocktail napkin."

"I'm pretty sure they refer to a self-storage facility I just found. There's a place called Norfolk Self-Storage located at 100 Brown Street. And it's in Bellpoint Beach."

Nick came over to check my screen. " 'Your Best Bet on Long Island,' " he read aloud. " 'Clean! Private! Secure!' Jess, I think you hit the jackpot. That conversation you had with Drayton at his store makes it pretty clear the guy is involved in the illegal animal trade. And that means a self-storage unit could come in pretty handy."

"Exactly what I was thinking," I agreed. "It would be a great place for him to stash the animals he's selling—the ones he doesn't want every Tom, Dick, and Harry to know about."

"If he is hiding something illegal," Nick mused as

he sat back down, "it's possible that even his business partner doesn't know what he's up to."

"Good point," I said thoughtfully. "If Drayton had a storage facility that Ben knew nothing about, that would help exonerate him, wouldn't it?"

It wasn't until that point that I realized just how badly I wanted to prove that Ben wasn't doing anything illegal. I especially wanted him to be innocent of Erin's murder.

"Speaking of Donald Drayton," Nick remarked, "I was just doing a little research on him myself, like you asked me to."

"Have you found out something?" My heartbeat had already kicked up a notch.

"Here's the thing," he said, frowning, "Donald Drayton doesn't appear to be that wealthy."

"But I saw for myself—"

"At least in legitimate terms. I'm talking about his company. All those Pet Empawrium stores are doing well, but not that well. The venture is pretty new, after all. Besides, there's only so much money to be made selling pet supplies."

"Maybe he has family money," I ventured. "Or maybe his wife does."

"Not that I can see," Nick replied, peering at the screen of his laptop. "At least not if you believe his tax returns. I'm usually pretty good at locating hidden assets and even unreported income. When I was a private investigator, I had my share of clients who were getting divorced and wanted to find out how much money their spouses *really* had. In fact, it became kind of a specialty. But this guy looks like he's barely getting by—at least on paper."

Trips to exotic places, a luxurious lifestyle with no legitimate income to support it, an expensive trophy wife, and on top of all that, a casual offer of a gorilla or an endangered snail... The more I learned about Donald Drayton, the more convinced I became that he really was involved in the illegal animal trade.

Anxious to learn more, I Googled the keywords *animal, trade,* and *illegal,* then hit Enter.

"Wow, where should I start?" I mumbled when a long and varied list of websites came up.

I clicked on the first one, the website of a well-known newspaper, and started to read about the billions of dollars that change hands around the world each year as a result of the illegal wildlife trade, estimated to be second only to the illegal trade of narcotics.

It is estimated that approximately seventy percent of these animals are endangered species. Others are threatened species, and the illegal activity contributes to their demise. Some are sold as pets, while others, particularly mammals, are frequently used for meat. Some animals are used for traditional medicines. For example, the horns from African and Asian rhinos are said to cure fever, the musk of the Siberian musk deer is used to treat heart disease, and the bile of Asiatic black bears supposedly helps arthritis. Still other animals are considered trophies.

Things are even grimmer than I imagined, I thought.

I moved on to another website, one that belonged to an animal conservation organization that focused on primates. I was greeted by a montage of photographs of grinning baby chimpanzees, powerful gorillas, and intelligent-looking baboons. While the primates in the photos were enough to make anybody smile, the text below was anything but uplifting.

While laws in nine states make keeping primates as pets illegal, there are currently no federal laws that regulate ownership. An estimated fifteen thousand primates are currently kept as pets in private homes in the United States. While the Center for Disease Control has prohibited importing them as pets since 1975, people have simply bred them from primates that were already in this country. Despite the difficulty of meeting the complex needs of primates, especially their social and emotional needs, anyone can buy lemurs, gibbons, and other endangered primates for as little as $2,000. The fact that others can be sold for $50,000 induces primate traders to persist despite all the negative factors, including the detrimental effects on the animals.

I skimmed the rest, then returned to the Google page and clicked on one more website.

Wild animals are meant to live in the wild, not in captivity as pets. Their owners can rarely provide them with the diet and the level or type of exercise they need to flourish, especially since there is usually no choice but to keep them in cages—the equivalent of being imprisoned. In addition, animals require an appropriate social system. Without the chance to live normally among other members of their species, they often become bored and lonely, suffering detrimental mental and emotional effects.

It can also be difficult to find a veterinarian who is able to treat exotic pets, especially if it is an illegal animal. If the animal bites someone or proves to be a nuisance in some other way, such as noise, it will invariably be confiscated. If the animals escape, they are rarely able to survive.

Animal diseases transferred to humans are another problem. In fact, zoonotic diseases account for three quarters of all infectious threats that are currently emerging. Of the six diseases the Center for Disease Control views as the top threats to national security, five are zoonotic.

I realized that my heart had started to pound violently and that my stomach was so tense that I actually felt sick. That didn't stop me from clicking on to one more website, especially since I hoped that this one would provide some good news.

Attempts at Regulating the International Animal Trade

The Convention on International Trade in Endangered Species of Wild Fauna and Flora (CITES), also known as the Washington Convention, is an international agreement between governments that was put in place during the 1970s. CITES regulates and in some instances restricts trading in certain animals either because they are endangered or threatened or because they present the possibility of becoming an invasive species—that is, a species that is not native to a particular ecosystem and which is likely to harm human health or cause economic or environmental harm.

Created by representatives of 80 governments, today 172 nations have agreed to participate voluntarily. CITES currently protects approximately 5,000 animal species and 28,000 plant species from overexploitation through international trade. Animals include such groups as primates, cetaceans (whales, dolphins, and porpoises), sea turtles, and parrots. Plants include corals, cacti, and orchids.

I was so absorbed in what I was reading that I didn't even notice that Nick was staring at me until he said, "Jessie? Are you okay?"

I glanced up, startled. In a hoarse voice, I asked him, "Did you know you can buy a tiger over the Internet?"

Before he had a chance to reply, I continued, "Listen to this. 'Over a three-month period of monitoring the Internet, our organization found thousands of endangered animals, as well as animal products, for sale on the Web. They included a tiger priced at seventy thousand dollars and so-called medicines whose ingredients included parts from leopards, elephants, and rhinoceros. During one particular week alone, we discovered that more than nine thousand were being sold, either through chat rooms or websites specifically dedicated to the animal trade.' "

Pausing to look up at him, I said, "No wonder the illegal animal trade has grown into a multibillion-dollar industry. Apparently it's second only to the international drug trade."

"Wow," Nick said. "I'd heard about it, of course, but I had no idea it was operating on such a huge scale."

"Me either."

Still, while I hadn't known much about the details, I knew the cost it extracted on individual animals, the ecology of their natural habitats, and even the people who insisted on acquiring monkeys or lions or tarantulas because they thought the animals were cute or that owning one made them cool.

I'd also known that there was plenty of money to be made by dealing in exotic animals. Especially the illegal ones.

What I didn't know was whether Donald Drayton really was subsidizing his expensive lifestyle by doing something so contemptible. But I'd never been more determined to find out.

• • •

The Web research I'd just done on the illegal animal trade not only made me anxious to find out for sure what Donald Drayton was up to, it had also inflamed me. I couldn't seem to stop myself from feeling as if I'd gulped down a two-liter bottle of coffee—which made it hard to put everything I'd learned into some cohesive form.

Yet I knew I had to pull myself together. Tonight was the wedding shower that was being held in my honor. The one Suzanne had ordered me to act surprised about.

Nick and I had arranged to go out for dinner while she set everything up in Betty's living room. I was supposed to appear at the front door promptly at eight o'clock—without Nick, since this was girls only.

As I sashayed toward the front door of the Big

House, I made a point of adopting a casual pace. For some reason, I couldn't help throwing in a swagger that made me look like an extra in a Western.

I even hummed a little as I turned the key in the front door. Not that I'd ever hummed before in my life. Of course, I don't usually enter the house through the front door either. Not when the back door, the one that opened onto the kitchen, was so much closer to where I parked. Still, if I was going to do my best to convince all my breathlessly expectant guests that I was completely shocked over finding a full-fledged wedding shower taking place in Betty's living room, I figured I might as well go all the way.

I'd barely stepped into the foyer before a loud chorus of "Surprise!" surrounded me. Even though I'd known it was coming, somehow the sudden burst of noise still managed to make me leap about four feet into the air.

"Oh, my God!" I cried, clutching my heart with both hands. Instead of playing a cowboy, I seemed to have segued into the role of damsel in distress.

"What is all this?" I squealed. "A wedding shower? For *me*? I don't believe it!"

Glancing around, I saw that all my friends were there. All my female friends anyway. They stood crowded together in front of Betty's grand piano, their faces lit up with glee. The sight made me glad I'd knocked myself out playing the part of guest of honor on the verge of having a heart attack.

Even Max and Lou were there, although thank goodness Suzanne hadn't insisted upon dressing them up in tuxedos, the way Betty had at her wedding. This was one time I had no desire to be upstaged by my incredibly cute dogs.

My cats either. Fortunately, Tinkerbell, who deserved some kind of cuteness award even on her worst Bad Fur Day, was hanging out with the rest of the girls, no doubt enjoying all the excitement. I noticed that Cat had hidden under the piano bench, but even she couldn't resist looking on. What female can resist a wedding shower?

"You guys! Who put you up to this?" I demanded. As if I didn't know.

Predictably, Suzanne stepped out of the crowd. For the occasion, she had donned a minidress so tiny I suspected she'd filched one of Betty's place mats.

"Surprise, Jessie!" she exclaimed. "You had no idea, right?"

"None whatsoever!" I only hoped that none of the party guests had plans to torture me to make sure I was telling the truth.

Now that I'd had a chance to look around a little more, I saw that Suzanne really had done a fabulous job. She'd strung pink and white crepe-paper streamers across the ceiling, prom style. From the point at which they crossed in the middle of the room, a cascade of pink and white balloons bobbed happily. The decorations would have looked like somebody had planned a sweet sixteen party if it wasn't for the white crepe-paper wedding bells. Another clue was the white veil that somebody had plopped on the marble bust of Socrates on a Greek column in the corner of the room.

The large rectangular cake on the dining room

table could also have passed for a sixteen-year-old girl's high-carb fantasy, since it was thickly iced with white frosting and smothered with pink sugar roses. But someone, probably Suzanne, had drawn a few wedding bells with pink icing, although from where I was standing they looked kind of like amoebas.

Suzanne had also arranged all the gifts on the coffee table, small ones in front, big ones in back. Not the most original arrangement, but it showed that at least she'd put some thought into it.

"You did an amazing job," I told her sincerely. "Thank you so much."

"Enough with the empty praise," she whispered, scowling. "I have something really important to discuss with you. In the kitchen. *Now!*"

Turning to the crowd of guests and smiling, she said, "I'm just going to steal away our bride-to-be for two minutes. We have some important details to discuss in the other room."

With that, she grabbed me by the arm and dragged me away.

I had a feeling that the "really important" something had to do with her, not me. So I wasn't surprised when she closed the kitchen door behind us, whirled around to face me, and announced, "We broke up."

"Why?" I was truly surprised. "You're crazy about Kieran! And he's clearly crazy about you!"

"Why do you think?" she shot back. "It's because of *her!*"

"Kieran's been seeing someone else?" I asked, bewildered.

"Of course not!" Suzanne shot back. "It's not

another woman that's the problem. It's that...that animal!"

It took me a few seconds to realize that the animal she was referring to really was an animal—rather than another person. An obnoxious future mother-in-law, for example.

"You broke up with Kieran because of his *dog*?" I cried.

"Skittles is not just any dog," she snapped. "You saw that for yourself last night, didn't you? That beast refuses to accept me. She hates me!"

I had to admit that Suzanne had a point. Kieran and Skittles were extremely close. But that didn't mean there wasn't room in his heart for a female of the human variety.

"Isn't there some way you can win her over?" I asked. "Everybody has their price. Maybe Skittles's is filet mignon."

"Kieran only allows her to eat the official state trooper diet," she replied bitterly. "The one for dogs, I mean."

"Then how about taking her on an outing?" I suggested. After all, if Skittles had been a jealous stepchild, Suzanne could build goodwill by taking her to the zoo or Chuck E. Cheese's or someplace easy like that. Of course, when it came to winning over a German shepherd, I couldn't think of anyplace appropriate. A park? A beach? A beer garden?

"Kieran doesn't allow other people to socialize with Skittles," Suzanne said. "It's against police regulations."

I'm no psychologist, but I was starting to see that

there was more to this love triangle than simply the tension between Suzanne and her four-legged rival. Kieran was also playing a major role in this ongoing conflict.

"Suzanne," I said gently, "I'm getting the feeling that it's not only Skittles you're angry with. I think you might also be a little P.O.ed at Kieran."

"That's ridiculous!" she shot back. "Like you said, I'm absolutely crazy about the man! It's that stupid dog who's the problem! If it wasn't for her, things between us would be perfect!"

O-kay, I thought. Short of Dr. Phil miraculously making an appearance at this particular moment, I don't see that I'm going to get very far with this.

"I'm really sorry," I told her sincerely. "But we'd better get back. There's a roomful of people waiting for the festivities to begin."

I was actually relieved that I had someplace else I was supposed to be, even though what stretched ahead of me was a long evening of oohing and aahing over salad tongs and silver candy dishes. Sure enough, I'd barely had a chance to sit down before somebody called out, "Jessie, open your presents!"

Suzanne, who'd already made the transition from spurned lover to hostess, clapped her hands for attention. "Okay, people!" she commanded. "Let's all sit in a circle. Jessie's going to open her gifts."

I guess I shouldn't have been surprised that she pushed her way through the crowd so she could take the seat next to mine. It also happened to put her closest to the presents.

"Okay, we'll start with this small one," she announced. She picked up a small box wrapped in paper printed with yellow-and-white daisies.

As I reached for it, however, she pulled it away, then ripped off the card taped to the top. "This is from Amy," she read. "Amy, raise your hand in case anybody here doesn't know you. Everybody, Jessie and I both know Amy from college. We were all at Bryn Mawr together." Turning to me, she said, "Okay, Jessie. You can open it now."

I opened my mouth to protest that my shower was beginning to feel like a gym class with a particularly sadistic gym teacher. But I didn't want to offend her, even if the woman was coping with her heartbreak by acting like the dictator of a police state.

So I dutifully tore off the paper, murmuring, "Now, what could this be?"

I opened the lid and thrashed through a wad of yellow tissue paper. Not surprisingly, the rustling sound brought Max over. He raised himself by placing his two soft white paws on my knee and sticking his wet nose into the box. No doubt he hoped that the gift-giver had thoughtfully tucked in a little something for him. A Milk-Bone, perhaps, or maybe a new plastic friend for his beloved pink poodle.

Instead, I pulled out a silver picture frame.

"Isn't this pretty!" I exclaimed. "Thank you, Amy. I love it!"

"You're welcome, Jess," she said happily. "I thought it would be perfect for a picture of you and Nick."

"Right," Suzanne commented loudly enough for everyone to hear. "So when the two of you break up, you'll be able to look back on the good times."

A heavy silence fell over the room. In fact, it was as if a cloud of noxious gas had sneaked in under a crack in the door.

And then someone laughed. "As if that would ever happen," one of the other guests said. "I never saw any two people as much in love as Jessie and Nick!"

"Here, here," someone else agreed.

I cast them both a grateful look.

"How about another gift?" I asked. "This is fun!"

Suzanne reached for a long thin box, this one robin's egg blue. "This one's from me," she announced. "Open it next."

"It's heavy," I observed as I pulled at the tape, trying not to hit my helper Max in the nose. "What could this be—oh, look! A marble rolling pin! I love it!"

"Good," Suzanne replied. "I figured it would come in handy during your first fight."

"Why don't we open some wine?" I suggested, thinking that maybe a drunken stupor would shut Suzanne up.

"I have something even better!" she cried, her mood instantly improving. "Champagne. Lots of it. After all, special occasions like this one demand a little bubbly!"

Anything, I thought. As long as it has the power to alter Suzanne's mood.

Within seconds, Suzanne had whipped out a tray of crystal champagne glasses that had probably been looted from one of Betty's china cabinets.

"Let's do this the right way," she insisted. Carefully she arranged the glasses so there was one on top, two in the next tier, and so on. When she was done, she poured champagne into the top one, filling it so that it spilled over the sides to fill the two below. I had to admit, it was pretty cool.

Festive too. I hoped the champagne fountain would shift the mood.

"I propose a toast," Suzanne cried after the glasses had been passed around. She stepped into the middle of the room and held hers high in the air.

We all raised our glasses.

"To the bride and groom," she continued. "Jessie, who's been one of my closest friends since our days together at college, and Nick, the man who sooner or later is going to break Jessie's heart!"

"Suzanne!" I exclaimed. By that point, I was practically ready to deck her.

What else could possibly go wrong with an occasion that was supposed to be happy? I thought crossly, downing the champagne in a few quick gulps.

But before I'd had a chance to even contemplate a possible answer to that question, the silence that had once again fallen over the room was interrupted by the sound of screaming.

"Is that what I think it is?" someone asked.

"It sounds like someone screaming," somebody else added.

"It sounds like *Sunny* screaming," I cried, dropping my glass onto the carpet and dashing toward the front door.

Chapter 15

"A person who misses a chance and the monkey who misses its branch can't be saved."

—Indian proverb

As I sprinted across Betty's lawn, I glanced over my shoulder and saw that Suzanne was a few steps behind me. The other guests stood clustered in the doorway, looking confused.

"Somebody call 911!" I shouted.

"I've got my cell phone right here!" somebody yelled back.

When I reached the cottage, I found the front door wide open. Even though it would have been smart to proceed with caution, for some reason having Suzanne along made me brave. I rushed inside, meanwhile taking a mental inventory of the contents of my living room and trying to decide what I could use as a weapon.

Frankly, I didn't know what I expected to find. But it certainly wasn't Sunny standing by herself in the middle of the room. From what I could tell, she didn't appear to be in any danger.

That didn't keep me from grabbing the umbrella leaning against the wall. Maybe it wasn't the most threatening object in the world, but I wasn't in a position to be picky.

"Sunny, are you all right?" I demanded, clasping the umbrella tightly.

"What happened?" Suzanne cried at the same time.

"I'm fine," Sunny replied breathlessly. "Jessie, somebody broke in. Whoever was in here climbed out the bedroom window when they heard me come in. I don't know why, but I just started screaming."

Now that I'd seen that Sunny was safe, I calmed down enough to look around. The entire room was in chaos. The intruder had slashed two throw pillows on the couch, including the one that had recently become Cat's favorite lounging spot. Clumps of orange foam rubber spilled over the cushions and onto the floor. Lamps were knocked over, books were pulled from shelves, and the contents of a twenty-pound bag of dry dog food had been dumped in front of the TV.

At first I thought the birdseed strewn under Prometheus's cage was one more act of vandalism. But then I realized that the perpetrator was probably Prometheus himself. For some reason he found it endlessly amusing to use his powerful beak to wrestle with his plastic dish until he managed to turn it upside down.

Still, the state of the room made my chest tighten. "Oh, my," I breathed.

Sunny's face crumpled. "It gets worse," she said miserably. "Look behind you."

Suzanne and I swiveled around in unison. We both gasped when we saw that scrawled in red on the blank wall next to the front door were the letters *MYOB*.

Mind your own business.

The champagne I'd gulped down suddenly felt as if it was burning a hole in my stomach.

The feeling wasn't helped by Suzanne shrilly demanding, "Is that *blood*?"

Even though the room was swirling around me, I forced myself to step over to examine the big red letters up close. "I'm pretty sure it's paint," I said, only slightly relieved. "But I bet it's supposed to look like blood."

I turned back to Sunny. "You said the intruder disappeared out the bedroom window?"

She nodded. "I heard a thump when I came in. It sounded like it was coming from the bedroom, and when I went in, the window was wide open." She swallowed hard, as if her mouth was dry. "I'm positive I left it closed. There are no screens on that window, and I've got a thing about bugs."

I wrapped both arms around my waist. Even though it was June, I suddenly felt chilled.

"Maybe you'd better go back to the beginning," I suggested, doing my best to sound matter-of-fact.

"Okay." Sunny took a deep breath. "I went out with some friends tonight. A guy a bunch of us know just started a garage band a few months ago, and they got their first gig at a club in Port Townsend. But I came home pretty early, right after their first set. I just wasn't into the kind of music the band that came on after them was playing, and I didn't want to hang out because—"

"Sunny?" Suzanne interrupted. "What happened when you came home?"

"Oh. Right. Okay, so when I got here, I noticed that the front door was open. Not a lot, just a couple of inches. At first I wondered if maybe I'd left in such a hurry that I hadn't closed it all the way and the wind had blown it open. But I knew that couldn't be what happened. I always make sure I shut the door behind me on the way out, and since this isn't my place, I've been even more careful than usual."

She paused to take a breath. "Anyway, I was afraid something might be wrong, but I figured I'd better check. And wham! As soon as I walked in, not only was I instantly hit with the fact that the place had been vandalized; I also heard a noise in the bedroom. Like I said, it sounded like a thump. The kind of thump a person would make by bumping into a piece of furniture or knocking against the wall.

"I figured it had to be whoever had done all this damage. So I grabbed a knife from the kitchen drawer and ran into the bedroom. I didn't think I'd have the guts to use it, but I figured it wouldn't hurt to look scary. It turned out it didn't matter, since by the time I got there, all I saw was the open window. I looked out, but nobody was there. Not even any footprints in the dirt. At least, not that I could see."

She looked at me expectantly. "Jessie, do you have any idea what's going on?"

I did, but I wasn't ready to talk about it. Instead, I

stepped over to Prometheus's cage. He'd helped me out in a situation like this once before, and even though it was a long shot, I hoped he'd be able to do it again.

"Prometheus?" I asked him. "Did you see what happened? Who came in here? Can you tell me anything about what you saw?"

"*Awk,* Prometheus loves apple," he cawed. "Happy birthday to you."

So much for that strategy. With a frustrated sigh, I went into the bedroom. Sunny and Suzanne trailed after me.

"I didn't touch the window, in case the intruder left fingerprints," Sunny said anxiously.

"It's great that you're being so responsible," I assured her distractedly. At the moment, I was focused on trying to figure out exactly what the intruder had been trying to accomplish inside my cottage. Aside from giving my living room a makeover, that is.

As I headed toward the bedroom, I suddenly experienced a sinking feeling.

The cocktail napkin. The one with the mysterious scribblings that Kimberly was convinced had something to do with her sister's murder.

I dashed to my dresser and with trembling hands wrenched open the top drawer. Then blinked. There was the napkin, still safe in its Ziploc bag. Next to it was my jewelry box, my passport, and even the small pile of cash I keep on hand for emergencies. They seemed untouched too.

"What's that?" Sunny asked, pointing at the napkin.

I opened my mouth to tell her the whole story. But

I snapped it shut when I realized that at the moment I simply didn't have the energy. "Nothing. Just some doodles drawn by somebody I know."

She leaned over to study the napkin, her forehead furrowed. "That's a relief. For a minute there I thought that whoever broke in left behind that picture of a skull and crossbones."

Her words sent a jolt of electricity shooting through me. "Skull and crossbones?" I said. My mouth had become uncomfortably dry.

"Ye-a-ah," she replied uncertainly. "That *is* what that's supposed to be, isn't it?"

As I studied the napkin for what must have been the hundredth time, I realized she was right. That was exactly what the shaky drawing of Erin's was supposed to be.

All along I'd assumed that it was a weird take on a smiley face. But now I could see that the reason the circle was misshapen was that the indentation at the bottom was supposed to indicate the jawline. And the two lines I'd presumed formed an X were meant to signify two crossed bones.

Before I had a chance to tell Sunny how brilliant she was, Suzanne asked, "Was anything taken, Jessie?"

"It doesn't look like it," I replied, sticking the napkin back into the drawer with all my other valuables and quickly checking the other drawers, the closet, and the space under the bed.

In fact, not only did it look as if the intruder hadn't taken anything; it appeared that he or she hadn't been looking for anything in particular, including the cocktail napkin. And it wasn't simply a case of running out of time, given the fact that all the obvious hiding places, like the dresser drawers and closets, looked untouched.

Suzanne frowned. "So it wasn't a burglary," she said, drawing the same conclusion. "It looks like whoever broke in just wanted to scare you. And it was you they were sending a message to, right? I mean, you're the one who lives here. Most people would have no idea that Sunny was staying in the cottage for now."

My thoughts exactly, I thought grimly.

In fact, I knew precisely what the intruder was trying to tell me, thanks to the bloodlike paint on the wall. And I got the feeling that whoever had gone to all this trouble to send me that message wasn't kidding around.

• • •

As I expected, the police who arrived in response to the 911 call couldn't do much. I filed a report about the break-in, but since nothing had been stolen, no significant damage had been done, and the graffiti on the wall hadn't been either obscene or particularly threatening, the uniformed officer who showed up at my door didn't seem too alarmed.

"Probably an ex-boyfriend," he concluded with a smirk as he sashayed out the door. "Don't worry. He'll get over you as soon as he hooks up with somebody new."

Ordinarily, his lack of concern about both the crime and the victim would have gotten my dander up. But my expectations had been low from the start.

I knew that if anyone was going to figure out who

had decorated my walls with a warning spelled out in blood-red letters, it would have to be me.

Which meant there was no time to lose before I turned to the next item on my to-do list. And that was following up on the information I'd gotten while sneaking around the back office at the Pet Empawrium.

First thing on Monday, after enlisting Sunny to shuffle around my morning appointments, I climbed into my clinic-on-wheels and headed toward the home of Louis Santoro, whose address I had memorized during my spying spree at Pet Empawrium.

I had to find out once and for all if my suspicions about Donald Drayton's real line of business were correct.

Finding Lloyd Cove, one of Long Island's most exclusive communities, was no trouble. Located on a peninsula that jutted into the Long Island Sound, just north of Earlington, the strictly residential area was dotted with huge estates, most overlooking the water. They were the kind of residences that came equipped with their own swimming pools, guesthouses, and in some cases, helicopter pads.

However, finding the Santoro residence was a different story, mainly because Hillsboro Drive didn't appear on my map. The only reason I eventually found it was that I veered onto a side street to turn around and happened to notice the street sign.

This is a man who really values privacy, I concluded as I drove down what looked like a thoroughfare but which I soon realized was a long driveway.

When I reached the end, I stopped dead in my tracks. Or was stopped dead in my tracks, to be more accurate. As the old saying goes, I'd hit a brick wall. A real brick wall.

A high one too. Probably twelve or fifteen feet high—certainly tall enough to keep anyone from seeing what was on the property.

But that was just the beginning of a security system that looked as if it had been engineered by the same folks who designed San Quentin. Only this one looked as if it had been devised to keep people out, rather than in.

Okay, so the place doesn't exactly scream welcome, I thought, surveying the wall and noting that it stretched as far as I could see. But there has to be a way to get inside. Without a helicopter, that is.

I finally located the entrance after driving along the brick wall for a quarter of a mile. But the iron gate that separated me from the driveway wasn't very encouraging. For one thing, it was almost as high as the brick wall. For another, it had metal spikes running along the top that looked as if they meant business.

It was also secured with a lock that was practically the size of a small refrigerator.

The good news was that there was a buzzer set into a metal plate along the edge of the wall, as well as a speaker that appeared to be part of an intercom system.

Here goes, I thought, driving up alongside it.

I lowered my window and pressed the buzzer. I'd barely gotten my arm back in the car before a gruff voice demanded, "Yeah, can I help you?"

Interestingly, the owner of that voice didn't sound the least bit eager to be helpful. But in the most confident voice I could muster, I replied, "I'm here to see Mr. Santoro. Donald Drayton sent me."

Silence. My heart pounded so loudly that I suspected the faceless individual at the other end of the intercom system could hear it. I wished I'd thought of turning on the radio and playing a song with an unusually loud drumbeat.

"Drive in," the voice finally said.

As the gate slowly opened, I wasn't sure if having been invited onto Louis Santoro's property was a good thing or a bad thing. But one thing I *was* sure of was that getting through the next few minutes was going to demand some first-rate acting on my part. And that included pretending to be cool, calm, and collected.

I took a deep breath, jutted my chin in the air, and drove in. I just hoped this little adventure of mine wouldn't turn out to be something I'd end up regretting.

I covered a fairly large stretch of property before Santoro's house even came into view. It looked like a museum, thanks to its size, the numerous steps leading to the front door, and the abundant use of marble in places where more economy-minded homeowners might have used more ordinary materials, such as slate, concrete, or aluminum siding. There was also plenty of statuary in front, leading me to wonder if Santoro and Drayton used the same landscaper.

As I walked up the steps toward the front entrance, clutching the handle of a black bag with a few medical instruments in it, I hoped the person who answered the door would be a housekeeper. Some nice older woman who would take pity on me—or at least wouldn't be packing heat in her apron pocket. That was certainly preferable to confronting the owner of the ragged voice that had beckoned me inside. It was a voice I imagined belonged to a beefy guy with no neck and the IQ of a kumquat. Then again, I've seen a lot of Scorsese movies.

So I was somewhat relieved that the man who answered was surprisingly ordinary. He wasn't much taller than I was, but he probably weighed close to twice as much. His pink knit shirt, embroidered with an energetic-looking polo player, stretched over a middle-age paunch that demanded he wear his khaki pants almost as low as a rapper's. The pinkish skin of his pudgy nose and cheeks matched the top of his head, which peeked out from what remained of his strands of dark hair.

My relief faded as he stood in silence for what seemed like a very long time, looking me up and down.

"Drayton sent you?" he finally growled.

I recognized the voice as the one that had floated through the intercom. Much to my surprise, the man actually possessed a neck.

"Of course," I replied, acting annoyed over his apparent confusion. "You make it sound as if you weren't expecting me."

"Should I have been?" he asked curtly.

I sighed, meanwhile waving my hand in a gesture of frustration. "I guess there's been some kind of miscommunication. My name is Dr. Popper. I'm a veterinarian." I gestured toward my van to substantiate my claim. "I'm here to do a routine checkup of your...a routine checkup."

The man, who by now I figured had to be Louis Santoro, eyed me suspiciously. "I didn't make an appointment."

"Maybe somebody else in the household did," I suggested. "Your wife, perhaps."

"She's not home right now," he said, still guarded.

I frowned, still pretending to be annoyed. "Look, all I know is that I got a call from someone in Donald Drayton's office giving me your address and telling me to come today at ten o'clock." Checking my watch, I added, "Actually, I'm a few minutes early."

"Donald set this up?" he asked, furrowing his brow. "I don't remember him saying anything about that. Unless it has something to do with the new delivery."

"Exactly," I said. "It's standard practice whenever there's a new delivery. Maybe that's why Don forgot to mention it."

Santoro frowned. "It didn't used to be."

"It is now."

Please don't call him to check, I thought, suddenly on the verge of panic. Something told me that getting out of this place could turn out to be as difficult as getting in.

Instead, he shrugged, and opened the door to let me in. "In that case, let's just get this out of the way."

As I stepped inside, I didn't know whether the feeling that swept over me was delight or dread. Anxious to believe it was the former, I told myself that no matter what I found, I wouldn't be in any danger. At least not if I managed to act as if nothing I found on this side of the wall surprised me in the least.

I followed Santoro through one cavernous room after another. If Donald Drayton's house was an American version of Buckingham Palace, this place was Versailles. The decor embraced ornately carved tables and chairs, gaudy chandeliers, and hand-painted murals that recaptured the glory days of the Roman Empire. I suspected that this man's cable TV service didn't include the Home and Garden channel.

Yet I forgot all about Louis Santoro's bad taste the moment I stepped outside.

His backyard was filled with exotic animals. The first one I spotted was a peacock wandering around the immense property. Behind a chain-link fence in the corner was a pair of ostriches. Other birds were housed in tall, circular cages. I wasn't much of an ornithologist, so I couldn't identify them. But I noted that most had gorgeous plumage or other distinctive physical characteristics, such as unusual beaks or colorful crests that made them intriguing to watch.

But Santoro collected more than birds. An ocelot paced back and forth in a cage, while a chimpanzee, also behind bars, gazed out at me mournfully. He reminded me of a prisoner who had never figured out what crime he'd committed. Other cages contained additional primates. I recognized some from my trip to the zoo, including the gold lion tamarins with their fiery red-orange fur and the tiny pygmy marmosets.

It took every last ounce of control I possessed not to react.

I cleared my throat, hoping Santoro would assume

that allergies, not emotion, were responsible for my sudden bout of congestion. Then again, he didn't seem the least bit interested in me.

"So which one's the latest delivery?" I asked, sounding as matter-of-fact as I could.

"This one, over here." He walked me over to one of the cages. Held captive inside was a squirrel monkey, huddled in the back corner.

At least I thought it was a squirrel monkey. It was hard to be sure, since the poor creature looked so different from the squirrel monkeys I'd seen at the zoo. Those had been full of energy, happily swinging from vines and chasing around like maniacs. This little guy, however, looked too terrified to move.

"I'll just leave you to do whatever you gotta do," Santoro said breezily. "You can get to your van from here, so there's no reason to come back into the house." Suddenly looking nervous, he added, "There's no extra charge for this, right?"

"It's part of the deal," I assured him.

As I watched him walk back into the house, I fussed with the stethoscope and the few other basic tools of the trade I'd brought along for show. I had no intention of going anywhere near that unfortunate little monkey. For one thing, I know my way around primates about as well as I know my way around motorcycles. I hadn't opted to take any courses in exotic animal medicine in school, and I simply didn't feel qualified.

Besides, I had no way of knowing if this monkey was diseased. It was also likely that he'd make a run for it the moment I opened the door of his cage—or do his best to tell me how he felt about his situation . . . with his sharp little teeth.

Instead, once I was sure Santoro was out of sight and out of earshot, I leaned over so I was as close to the monkey as possible. Blinking away the tears stinging my eyes, I whispered, "Don't worry, little one. We'll find a way to get you out of here."

• • •

I couldn't wait to get away from Louis Santoro's compound, which seemed as creepy and depraved as the island of Dr. Moreau. But that didn't mean I wasn't geared up to make another stop, one that I knew might take me out of the flame and into the fire.

I had to confront Ben.

Now that I knew the truth about his business partner, I needed to find out if he was involved too. It was difficult to believe, since like me, he was a veterinarian. He had spent four years at college and another four in vet school, preparing to spend his life taking care of animals. That meant improving their lives, not harming them.

Then again, people changed. Especially when money was involved.

My blood was close to the boiling point as I pulled up in front of Ben's house. I slammed the door of my van so forcefully that I swear the plastic flowers on the porch quivered.

But as I marched toward the front door, I realized I had to calm down. Confronting Ben while I was in such an enraged state wasn't exactly the best way of fostering honest communication. So before ringing the doorbell, I took a few breaths, meanwhile reminding myself that I was doing this for Erin.

"Jessie?" Ben said as he opened the door. "What are you doing here?"

His eyes looked clouded. I couldn't tell if it was because he was simply surprised to see me—or if he'd been hoping that I'd leave him alone.

"Ben," I said evenly, "there's something I need to talk to you about. Something kind of . . . sensitive."

All the blood drained from his face. "Something about Erin?"

"No. At least not directly." I hesitated. "Can I come in?"

"Uh, sure." He moved aside, but his face still reflected uncertainty.

I waited until we were sitting in the living room before I began. Once we'd both settled in the exact same spots we'd been in the last time we'd spoken, I said, "I actually wanted to talk to you about your business partner."

"Donald?" he asked, sounding confused.

I nodded. "Ben, how much do you know about him?"

He sat up a little straighter and squared his shoulders. "I know that Donald works hard and that he's committed to making our stores a success. I also know that he's always been fair with me. In fact, I feel pretty damn lucky to have gone into business with him. I mean, look at this place, Jessie. It's a palace. Do you think I could have gotten any of this without a shrewd, knowledgeable guy like Donald working with me?"

I felt as if I was treading in dangerous waters here.

"Okay, so the two of you have done well in the pet store business. But what about any other ... business endeavors he might be involved in?"

"I'm afraid I'm not following."

I studied him carefully, trying to figure out how much he knew. And trying to decide just how honest to be with him.

After all, I was well aware that he and I were alone in the house—and that he might have already committed one murder. And he could have killed his wife precisely because she'd confronted him with the exact same information I was now planning to confront him with.

I leaned forward and pinned him in my gaze. "Ben," I said in a soft, gentle voice, "you and I went to vet school together. We both spent four years of our lives learning how to care for animals. I have to believe that anybody who worked that hard has to be truly committed to looking out for their welfare.

"Donald Drayton, on the other hand, is a businessman," I continued. "His perspective is completely different from yours and mine. I don't know him personally, but I'm sure he views what you're doing in an entirely different way. I can't imagine that he—"

"You know, don't you," Ben said flatly. It was a statement, not a question.

"I don't actually know anything," I replied. I was trying to keep myself from falling into a trap. Especially one I'd created myself.

"But you have your suspicions." An odd smile played at his lips. "I can't imagine what you must think of me, Jessie. At the very least, I'm sure you feel

I'm not the same person I was when we knew each other at vet school."

His comment startled me—and not only because my impression of him back then had been that he was a shallow, if likeable, party boy. And given what his former friend Jack Krieger had told me about him cheating on the pharmacology final in order to graduate, I now thought even less of who he'd been in vet school.

I certainly wasn't about to admit that now though.

"Ben, people don't change," I insisted. "Maybe some things about them do, but fundamentally, they stay the same. At least that's what I believe."

I wanted to appeal to the good in him, or at least the part of him that wanted to appear to be good.

"I haven't done anything wrong," he said in a hoarse voice, breaking eye contact and instead staring off into space. "At least, not directly. All I did was provide them with the best medical care I could. Sometimes they contracted diseases I couldn't identify. And sometimes I didn't have access to the right drugs. They don't all make it, but damn it, I do my best."

I remained silent. I wanted him to go on—even though his words were making my temples throb and my stomach wrench.

"Donald's been doing it for years," he continued in the same dull voice. "He started long before I came on the scene. That was after I met him at a dinner the chamber of commerce held so local business people could meet each other. I went alone, since Erin had to work late at the zoo that night. Don and I happened to sit at the same table, and when he found out that I was a veterinarian, he seemed really interested. He told me he was thinking of opening a chain of pet stores, but that he was looking for a partner who knew something about animals.

"What happened next was kind of strange. It was almost like he started cultivating me. Working on me, you know? Like, he kept inviting me to play golf and he wouldn't take no for an answer. He even had Erin and me over to his house for dinner a few times. She couldn't stand his wife, of course. She thought she was a complete airhead. In fact, she used to refer to her as Silicon Barbie.

"But I was flattered. I could see how high on the hog the guy was living. The idea that he wanted somebody like me to go into business with him totally impressed me. He didn't even expect me to put that much money in, at least compared to what he was investing.

"In fact, Donald didn't seem to expect much from me at all. He kept saying that he thought that having a veterinarian as a business partner would lend credibility to the venture. That the banks would like it, the customers would trust us, that kind of thing."

He paused to take a deep breath. "Honestly, Jess," he said, finally looking me in the eye, "it wasn't until I'd signed on the dotted line and was already committed that I found out what was really going on."

"And what exactly is that?" I asked quietly.

"Donald Drayton deals in illegal animals," Ben replied, sounding pained. "The pet stores are just a cover for what he really does. He smuggles them in from Africa and Southeast Asia and anyplace else with animals that there's a market for. Sometimes he sells them to people he finds through our stores, but he has plenty of other ways of finding buyers.

"As for the real reason he wanted me as his business partner, I didn't find that out until after I was too far in to get out. That was when he told me the real reason he'd worked so hard to get me involved—he'd been looking for a way to keep sick animals who arrive in this country from dying." Smiling coldly, he added, " 'Cutting his losses' is the way he phrased it."

I didn't react, since I didn't want him to see how horrified I was by what he was telling me. "What about Erin?" I asked. "What did she—"

"Nothing!" he cried. "Erin had absolutely nothing to do with any of this. She didn't even know about it. I swear, Jessie. I did everything I could to keep the truth from her. And I know for sure that she never found out."

Shaking his head, he gasped, "It would have killed her."

Maybe, I thought, still watching him closely and wondering whether he was sincere or just putting on a performance. Or perhaps something went wrong and she did find out—and *that* was what killed her.

Suddenly Ben's entire demeanor changed. The muscles of his face tightened as, in a hard voice, he said, "Now that you know about this, you can't tell anybody."

I just looked at him, thinking, How can I *not* tell? Do you really think I could live with the knowledge that someone I know is involved in activities that are so deplorable, not to mention illegal?

Of course I was going to turn Donald Drayton in, even though I swore up and down that I had no intention of doing so. Ben too.

But not yet. First, I had to find out if when Erin was in the same position I was in now, one of them had decided that she, too, needed to remain silent.

Chapter 16

"The surest way to make a monkey of a man is to quote him."

—Robert Benchley

A s I snuggled with Nick on Betty's comfortable couch that night, I was glad this was one time he'd agreed to help me with a murder investigation. But while the research he'd done on Donald Drayton's finances had been valuable, it was nothing compared to having him as a sounding board.

Even if he wasn't exactly pleased when I told him I'd taken a field trip to Louis Santoro's compound.

"Jessie, I thought you promised you wouldn't do anything dangerous!" he exclaimed.

"I was never in danger," I assured him. "Santoro was completely convinced that I work for Drayton."

Just like Ben Chandler, I thought grimly.

"Besides," I went on, "now I'm certain about a really important piece of the puzzle. I know for sure that Donald Drayton is involved in the illegal animal trade. If Erin found out, that could have been the reason she was murdered. Somebody, probably Drayton, wanted to keep her quiet."

"So he's your number one suspect?" Nick asked.

"He's certainly high on the list," I replied. "But it's also possible that her husband killed her for the very same reason."

I had to admit that Ben had sounded sincere when he'd told me that Donald had talked him into going into business with him without being honest about what his business really was. He'd also sounded pretty convincing when he'd insisted that Erin never found out anything about it.

But that could have just meant he was a good actor.

"I have to consider Ben a suspect," I continued. "If Erin discovered the truth about their business—which seems highly likely given the notes on that cocktail napkin—the possibility of her going to the police would have been just as threatening to Ben as it was to Drayton."

"Good-bye swimming pool and Sub-Zero freezer," Nick muttered. "Hello jail cell with the bed attached to the wall. For a lot of people, that would be a good enough reason to kill."

"But then there's Dr. Zacarias," I noted. "As far as I know, she doesn't have anything to do with the illegal animal trade. In fact, she's dedicated her life to animal conservation. But that doesn't mean she's above acting in a less than ethical manner when it comes to furthering her own career. At least, if I believe what Walter told me, not to mention what I observed for myself. From the things she said about Erin, it's hard to believe we were talking about the same person."

Thoughtfully, I added, "I also know that Dr. Zacarias was at that fund-raiser. She told me she helped plan it, that it was a huge success."

"In other words, she might not have been smuggling animals, but there are plenty of other things she could be guilty of," Nick commented. "And if Erin found out she was doing something she wasn't supposed to be doing, that could have given Dr. Zacarias a reason to kill her."

"Right." I sighed. "Then there's Walter. Not only was he part of a love triangle, he might also have believed Erin was pregnant. His role as the jealous lover could certainly have motivated him to kill her."

"He's also someone we know is comfortable around scorpions," Nick added. "I'd say that earns him an especially high spot on your list of suspects."

He was silent for what seemed like a very long time. By the tension in his forehead, I knew the wheels in his head were turning.

"What about someone who doesn't have such an obvious motive?" he finally asked.

"Like who?"

"I was thinking of Erin's sister."

"I thought of her too," I said. "She seems more distraught than anybody about Erin's death. But it has occurred to me that it could simply be an act. For all I know, she could have come to me with those notes from the fund-raiser as a way of getting me to look closely at everyone but her. She might have worried that Erin told me more over the phone than I'd let on."

"A good reason for her to go out of her way to throw you off," Nick mused.

Now it was my turn to remain silent for a long time. But the wheels inside my head were turning as hard as Nick's had.

"I can't help thinking that Walter knows more than he's telling me," I finally said. "Nick, I'm positive that he was lying about being at that fund-raising event. At first, I wasn't convinced that the notes Erin made on the cocktail napkin that night had anything to do with her murder. But now that I know what most of her scribblings meant, I'm convinced that something happened at that dinner. Maybe even something important enough to get her killed."

But aside from Dr. Zacarias, Walter was the only other person I knew who'd been there. And of the two of them, he was the only one who'd been willing to talk to me.

Which meant he was not only on my list of suspects, he was also on my list of last resorts.

• • •

I made a point of going to Walter's house the very next day. This time, when he opened his front door and saw me standing there, he didn't look the least bit surprised.

"Come on in, Jessie," he said with resignation.

"Walter, I need your help," I began, launching into my pitch as soon as I sat down on the dusty brown couch. "You strike me as the one person who knows more about what was going on with Erin right before she was murdered than anyone else—including her own husband."

Since I'd clearly gotten his attention, I paused long enough to take a deep breath. "The more people I talk to and the more questions I ask," I continued, "the more I keep coming back to that fund-raiser. I have to know what went on that night. I believe something significant happened—something that's the key to Erin's murderer."

I stared at him beseechingly, wondering what else I could say that would motivate him to tell me what he knew.

Instead, he sank into the soft cushions of the couch beside me and buried his face in his hands. "I was afraid it would come to this," he said softly.

"Walter," I said firmly, "tell me."

When he finally looked up, he shook his head slowly. "It all started a few months ago, when I was working at the zoo. I was there to make their computer systems work better. That meant looking through all their files to figure out what belonged where. That's when I found out that Annalise Zacarias really is as unethical as people say."

The room suddenly felt strangely warm—and the air so thick, I could hardly breathe. "What did you find?"

"That the good doctor was skimming money from the funds she was raising for the zoo," he replied bitterly.

I gasped. "Are you sure?"

"Completely sure. She kept two sets of books, the official set and the one that showed what was really going on." With a cold laugh, he added, "At least she was putting the money she stole to good use. From what I could tell, it looked as if she was funneling it into her research."

"Why didn't you report her to the police?" I demanded. "Or at least to someone at the zoo?"

"I was going to," he replied. "And looking back, I realize that's exactly what I should have done." He swallowed hard. "Instead, I made the biggest mistake of my life. I followed my first impulse, which was to tell Erin what I'd uncovered."

"Why was telling Erin a mistake?" I asked, puzzled.

Walter remained silent for a few seconds. "Because," he finally said, "I believe it's the fact that Erin knew that prompted Annalise Zacarias to kill her."

"Dr. Zacarias murdered Erin?"

"I'm certain of it," Walter replied in a dull voice. "It all makes perfect sense."

"But if you already knew about what she was doing, why weren't you in danger as well?"

He smiled coldly. "You didn't hear Erin go on and on about Zacarias the way I did. The woman was jealous of Erin from day one. She could see for herself how smart Erin was. Talented, too, not to mention accomplished. Erin was also young, with a great future ahead of her. Zacarias's career was on the decline, and it killed her to be around someone whose future was as bright as Erin's."

"Okay," I said slowly. "So what you're saying is that from the start, Dr. Zacarias was looking for a way to discredit Erin."

"Exactly." He hesitated before asking, "Did you bring that copy of the cocktail napkin you showed me last time?"

"I have it right here." I pulled it out of my purse and handed it to him.

"I wasn't being truthful when I acted as if I'd never seen this before," he admitted as he unfolded the single sheet of paper. "I was there when Erin wrote it."

"So you *do* know what it means." My mouth had become so dry it was difficult to get the words out.

"I'm afraid so." Pointing to the only line I had yet to decipher, he said, "See what this says, over here?"

"Sure," I replied. "That's the letter A, the number two, and then the letters R and X."

"That's not a two," Walter corrected me. "That's a Z. Now do you understand?"

"AZ," I read aloud. I could feel the tumblers in my brain moving into place. My voice a whisper, I said, "Annalise Zacarias."

"You got it."

"But what does the RX mean?" I asked. Maybe it all made sense to Walter, but it remained a mystery to me.

"*RX* is often used as shorthand for *research*," Walter explained. "In other words, these four letters that Erin wrote mean 'Annalise Zacarias's research.' And what follows is supposed to be a skull and cross-bones."

A skull and crossbones. Exactly what Sunny's take on the crude drawing had been.

I frowned. "Does that mean that Dr. Zacarias's research is dangerous?"

"It means that what Zacarias found out while she was doing research is dangerous."

I was still confused. "Dangerous to Erin?"

Walter must have noticed the perplexed look on my face because he sighed. "I think I'd better go back to the beginning."

He took a deep breath as if he found what he was about to tell me upsetting.

"The night of the fund-raiser, I went along to keep Erin company. We certainly didn't want people to know we were seeing each other, but she had an extra ticket and there was no way she was going to bring Ben. By that point, the two of them were barely on speaking terms. Anyway, she didn't think it would be much fun to go alone, and everyone knew that she and I had been working together. In the end, she decided it would seem harmless enough.

"And it turned out she was right. Erin and me showing up together wasn't the problem; the problem was what went on that night between Zacarias and Erin."

"What happened?"

"Zacarias got Erin alone, and once they were out of earshot, she told Erin that while she was in Africa, doing her usual thing at her research center, she got into a conversation with some of the locals about the poaching problem." He paused. "The name Donald Drayton came up."

I drew in my breath sharply. "So Dr. Zacarias knew that Erin's husband and his business partner were involved in the illegal animal trade."

"That's right. Apparently she'd overheard Erin talking about her husband's new chain of pet stores, and in the course of the conversation Erin mentioned that Donald Drayton was Ben's business partner. For some reason, Zacarias had remembered his name, so when she heard it again, a lightbulb went off.

"After she came back to the United States, she'd done some investigating. That's how she came up with the address of one of the places where Drayton stores animals he's had smuggled in to fill orders he's gotten from his customers."

"The self-storage facility in Bellpoint Beach," I whispered.

"Exactly. Zacarias told Erin that was the only address she was certain of, but that she knew there were others. That's the meaning of the plus sign Erin wrote over here."

"So it was Dr. Zacarias who told Erin the truth about the business Ben was running with Drayton," I said, thinking aloud.

"Yup. And I'm sure she told her about it with a real sense of triumph. Having the ammunition she needed to discredit Erin probably meant more to Zacarias than the fact that she could have gone to any one of these organizations listed on this napkin to turn in both Donald Drayton and Ben Chandler."

With a bitter laugh, Walter added, "Zacarias may love animals, but she loves herself even more. And she suddenly had Erin—who she saw as the competition— exactly where she wanted her."

"How did Erin respond when Dr. Zacarias confronted her with all this?" I asked.

Walter's face clouded. "That's the part that fills me

with regret. Over having told Erin what I knew about Zacarias, I mean."

I blinked as a few more tumblers turned. "Are you saying that Erin told Dr. Zacarias that she *knew* she was stealing from the zoo?"

He nodded. "Of course, Zacarias denied it at first. And when Erin said she'd found out from me, Zacarias just laughed and said that no one would believe either of us.

"But then Erin told her that I'd printed out copies of both sets of financial records as proof of her financial finagling. Zacarias knew she was cornered. Still, at that point, the two of them had struck a sort of balance. They each had something on the other. Erin knew Zacarias was stealing from the zoo and Zacarias knew Erin's husband was a criminal."

I was silent for a few seconds as I tried to digest everything Walter was telling me. "It sounds as if Erin told you everything that happened that night," I finally commented, "practically word for word."

Walter nodded. "I ran into her in the hallway right outside the room where she and Zacarias had their confrontation. From the look on her face, I knew immediately that something terrible had happened. We sneaked outside where no one could hear us and she told me all about it.

"Then we heard the speeches starting. We didn't want anyone to notice our absence, so we hurried back to the dining room. But believe me, what Erin had just learned was still very much on her mind. So while some muckety-muck from the zoo was making a speech, Erin grabbed a paper napkin and wrote down those notes you showed me."

Pointing to the different lines on the page, he said, "She wrote down the address of the self-storage facility—see, 100 Brown Street in Bellpoint Beach—because she wanted to make sure she didn't forget it. She also jotted down the initials of some of the largest and most active animal conservation organizations because she wanted to find out more about what she now knew her husband was involved in."

"She must have been devastated," I said. "I realize that she and Ben weren't getting along that well, and that it was at least partly due to his absorption with his newfound wealth. But I can't imagine how she must have felt when she found out the real source of all that money!"

"She was beside herself," Walter replied. "In a way, she was dying to turn him in herself because she was so outraged. But she not only had some sense of loyalty to the man she'd been married to for ten years, she also realized how badly it would compromise her goal of promoting animal conservation. Especially since Zacarias was clearly determined to use it against her in every way possible."

"But Erin must have known that sooner or later Dr. Zacarias would go public with what she knew."

"Of course she did. She understood that even though she and Zacarias were on even ground, at some point Zacarias would realize how precarious her situation was. She had to have figured out that Erin was completely devoted to animals and that it was only a question of time before she went to the authorities. In fact, Erin was on the verge of doing exactly that when Zacarias killed her."

"So Dr. Zacarias had to have known that Erin was about to turn in her own husband," I said.

"She must have figured it out somehow," Walter agreed.

"Which means she also understood that once Erin had no more reason to fear Dr. Zacarias's retribution, she was likely to turn her in as well," I mused.

"That's what I believe," Walter replied. "And I've given this a lot of thought. In fact, it's pretty much all I've been able to think about since Erin was murdered."

His voice grew hoarse as he added, "As soon as I heard, I knew exactly who the guilty party was. I also knew that I was partly to blame. If I'd done things differently, Erin would still be alive."

• • •

No matter how hard I tried to convince Walter that he was in no way responsible for Erin's death, I couldn't stop him from feeling guilty. The fact that he had such strong feelings for her made the whole situation even more tragic.

He seemed so sure that Annalise Zacarias had killed Erin that it was hard not to be equally convinced. I really believed what I'd said about him being the person who was closest to Erin during the last weeks of her life. And, I mused, working at the zoo meant that Zacarias had access to all sorts of exotic animals, not just the primates in her department. I wondered if the New York Zoo housed a yellow fat tail scorpion—maybe it was worth giving Forrester a call to see if he knew. Yet, even still, I couldn't prove who had ultimately killed Erin. The only thing for certain was that Erin knew her husband and his business partner were involved in illegal animal smuggling, which meant that there was a good possibility she had confronted one or both of them, and either Ben Chandler or Donald Drayton had murdered her.

It seemed so obvious that Erin's death was related to the smuggling operation, and I had proof of that now that Walter had deciphered her scribblings on the cocktail napkin. Maybe I should just turn it over to the police and let them sort out which of the participants was the murderer.

I was wryly contemplating the possibility of Falcone taking any evidence I presented seriously when I turned my van off Minnesauke Lane. As I trundled down the long driveway, I nearly collided with a taxi that was on its way out, a reminder that Betty and Winston were coming home today. My first impulse was to rush over to welcome them back. Instead, I decided to give them some space. From Betty's distraught e-mails, it sounded as if the newlyweds had had enough company lately.

Besides, I was anxious to get settled back in my cottage. While Betty's mansion had been wonderfully luxurious, I was glad that I was moving back home. My little house could definitely be described as humble, but it was mine, all mine. I was eager to unpack Nick's and my belongings, which we'd lugged back to our place early that morning. I was also anxious to see my animals, who were happily ensconced back in the cottage.

I was putting the last pair of jeans into a drawer when I heard a soft knock. Suspecting that it was finally time for a homecoming celebration, I raced to the front door and flung it open.

"Welcome home!" I cried, throwing my arms around Betty. "I'm so happy to see you!"

"I'm happy to see you too," Betty exclaimed, returning the hug. "I want to hear all about everything that went on while I was away!"

"But you're the one who was off on an adventure," I replied. "Come in. I'll make us some tea."

"I'd love some tea. Goodness, I missed you." Bending down to pet the canine contingent of my entourage, both of whom were giving her a real hero's welcome, she burbled, "I missed *all* of you!"

Betty looked surprisingly relaxed, not to mention quite content. Somehow, the way she was glowing didn't quite fit with the distressed tone of her e-mails. I decided she was simply a better sport than I was. After all, I'd run into a similar situation myself when Nick's parents had moved in with us for a few days, taking over our bedroom while we camped out on the lumpy fold-out couch.

"I'm sorry your honeymoon was such a disaster," I said as I joined her on the couch. I set down a tray with the makings of an impromptu tea party. In my case, that meant two cups of water boiled in the microwave, a couple of store-brand teabags, and a handful of the cookies I'd found stashed in my freezer.

"Actually," Betty replied, her blue eyes twinkling,

"it turned out quite well. Winston and I finally came up with the perfect solution to our house full of unwanted houseguests."

"What did you do?" I asked, widening my eyes.

She smiled impishly. "We sneaked out of the villa one day and did some poking around town. We found a charming little *pensione* just a few miles away and booked a room on the top floor with a balcony and a fabulous view. A very *private* room. Then we went home, packed our things, and left his children a note—one that didn't include our new address."

"Good for you!" I cried.

So maybe there really is such a thing as happily ever after, I mused. At least where Betty and Winston are concerned.

My stomach tightened as I wondered if Nick and I could manage to pull off such a happy ending.

• • •

I was still pondering that question after Betty went home to unpack. Given the fact that I would be walking down the aisle in less than two weeks, I knew my answer should be a resounding "Yes!"

I nursed my third cup of tea, meanwhile trying to ignore the mild anxiety that continued to grip me. Watching Lou play his new game was a pretty good distraction. I only hoped he'd be able to keep himself occupied for a while, since I wasn't in the mood for crawling around on the floor.

But it wasn't long before he began making little barking sounds, looking up at me pleadingly every now and then.

"Please, Lou," I begged. "Not now."

Pleas for mercy were clearly not part of his working vocabulary. Instead of taking pity on me, he let out a whimper, an annoying, high-pitched sound that made me glad I was no longer living in close proximity to Betty's collection of fine crystal.

"Lou-ou-ou," I whined, "will you please stop doing that? I'm not in the mood for playing fetch right now. Not when I'm the one who's expected to do the fetching!"

He just stared at me woefully with his big brown eyes.

"Oh, all right," I finally agreed with a sigh. "But just this once, okay? I'm not going to do this over and over again."

With an exasperated sigh, I got down on the floor in front of the couch, then lay flat on my stomach and stretched my arm under the couch. Naturally, the tennis ball wasn't within easy reach. Oh, no, that would have been too easy.

So I flattened myself even further, putting my cheek on the floor so I could peer underneath. I spotted the tennis ball, all right. But as I pulled it out and passed it on to my excited Dalmatian, I saw that tennis balls weren't the only things Lou had gotten into the habit of pushing under the couch.

An interesting array of artifacts was tucked away near the wall, all of them coated with clumps of dust. I cupped my hand and pulled out the whole collection at once. A bottle cap, a quarter, a half-eaten cookie that had probably fallen onto the floor unnoticed, a piece of paper that looked like the corner of a take-out menu...

There was something else as well. Something I didn't recognize right away.

It looked like a piece of clear plastic that had chipped off a larger piece. Embedded inside was a thin strip of metal that had been crafted into a specific shape. It looked like a company logo.

It wasn't until I studied it closely in the bright light that I realized what it was. Or at least what I *thought* it was.

My heart thumped loudly in my chest as I grabbed my laptop, typed eight letters into Google, and clicked on the first website that came up. I held my breath as I waited for the page to load.

Seconds later, an insignia filled the screen, one that the plastic shard in my hand could have fit into like the piece of a puzzle. Right below it were the words *Maserati: Excellence Through Passion.*

Chapter 17

"By trying often the monkey learns to jump from the tree."

—African proverb

I put down my laptop and picked up my second favorite technological advancement. Nick answered my call on the first ring.

"Jess?" he answered anxiously, no doubt having spotted my name on his caller ID. "What's going on?"

"You'll never guess what I found under the couch just now!"

"Let me see," he replied dryly. "More dust than the archeologists found in King Tut's tomb?"

"Nick, this is serious. I'll give you a clue: It's something Lou must have pushed under there with his nose."

"Okay, then how about . . . a tennis ball?"

"How about something that the person who broke into my cottage Saturday night dropped without realizing it?" I said impatiently.

"Seriously?" His attitude had gone from saucy to serious in record time. "What did you find?"

"A piece of a key chain," I replied. "From a Maserati."

I must admit, I found his silence most rewarding.

"Do you realize what it means?" I cried. "It's concrete evidence that Donald Drayton is the person who broke into the cottage! He's the only suspect on my list who owns a Maserati. It must have fallen out of his pocket that night. It's the only possible explanation…which means he's got to be the murderer. It was obvious from the start that whoever broke in was trying to scare me. Maybe he even planned to kill me. But the fact that the man was inside my house tells me how desperate he is not to let anyone find out about his despicable sideline that pays for his exorbitantly priced boy toys."

"It does make sense," Nick agreed.

"Nick, when I saw Walter today, he told me that Erin found out the truth about Drayton's business from Dr. Zacarias at the fund-raiser that night." I went on excitedly, "Zacarias also told her where Drayton was keeping the animals he was smuggling in illegally. That's why Erin wrote down the address of that self-storage facility in Bellpoint Beach."

"Those self-storage places do offer total privacy," Nick said thoughtfully. "Most of the time, only the renters have keys."

"Especially the units that are set up like rows of garages," I added. "They allow people to come and go at any hour of the day or night without anybody to let them in. According to Norfolk Self-Storage's website, it's even climate-controlled. That would be critical for keeping the animals alive until Drayton could deliver them to his buyers and collect his hefty payments."

"It does sound logical, but you still can't be completely sure," Nick warned. "We have to consider the possibility that Dr. Zacarias was wrong about what that self-storage facility is used for. It's possible that Ben and Donald simply keep some of the products they sell in their stores there. Maybe they ran out of room in their main warehouse—or maybe they maintain satellite storage facilities that are located close to each store. There could be lots of explanations."

"True," I agreed. "Which is why I intend to find out."

This time, I got the feeling Nick's silence wasn't a sign that he was impressed. This one meant he was nervous.

"Jessie," he said slowly, "you made me a promise. You swore that even though you were investigating Erin's murder, you wouldn't do anything dangerous."

"I won't."

"Oh, really?" he replied. "Let me be clear about this. You plan to sneak into a place where you think illegal activity is going on—probably at night, since it'll be easier to stay hidden when it's dark. And you'll probably go there alone. Unarmed, too, even though you don't know karate or any other form of self-defense that would help keep you safe. So would you mind telling me how you intend to make sure you're not going to get hurt?"

"Don't worry," I assured him, my tone reflecting

my complete confidence in my plan. "I've already got that all figured out."

• • •

Just as I'd promised Nick, the next thing I did was make another phone call, a crucial step designed to guarantee my safety during my clandestine visit to 100 Brown Street. Once that was done, I focused on preparing for a stakeout, methodically carrying out every task on my mental checklist. I made sure the gas tank in my VW was full and charged my cell phone battery. Then I changed into a black shirt and pants and grabbed a dark knitted hat that looked roomy enough to tuck in all my hair. The last step was gathering a flashlight, a digital camera, a bottle of water, and—just in case—snacks for energy.

Since it was June, it seemed to take forever for the sky to darken. After looking out the window several hundred times, I finally decided it was time to set out.

As I drove east on the Long Island Expressway, I warned myself that the trip would probably turn out to be a fool's errand—with me playing the role of fool. Chances were good that I wouldn't see anything. In fact, I'd probably just sit in an empty parking lot for hours, wolfing down the granola bars I'd brought just so I'd have something to do. For all I knew, I'd even been wrong about *100 Brown BB* being shorthand for the address of a self-storage facility.

Even though my rationalizations all made perfect sense, for some reason the butterflies in my stomach weren't buying any of it.

In fact, my heart was fluttering and my stomach

was in knots as I drove through the main entrance of Norfolk Self-Storage. Roughly a dozen single-story cinder-block buildings lined the property. Every one had large doors that opened from the bottom up, giving each row the look of a twenty-car garage.

There didn't appear to be much action at any of them. Not at nine-thirty at night, which even under the best of circumstances wasn't exactly the ideal time to retrieve the family's lawn furniture or store a box of photos from Mother's Day. The fact that the only illumination came from the few feeble bulbs that dotted each building and the streetlights that popped up here and there along the perimeter of the parking lot made putting things in or taking things out even less convenient.

Of course, that also made it the perfect time for people who didn't want to call attention to their comings and goings.

Given the fact that no other cars were around, I realized I would be wise to hide mine. After a quick drive around the parking lot, I ascertained that the only place to hide a shiny red VW was behind the two tremendous Dumpsters in the back corner.

The good news was that there was just enough space for me to wedge my car in between the green metal containers and the stockade fence that protruded from the stubby growth of weeds edging the property. The bad news was that someone seemed to have disposed of something extremely malodorous inside one of the Dumpsters, an item that had probably smelled bad enough when it was originally dumped there but now, hours or days later, had reached new heights of stinkyness.

There was more bad news. While the Dumpsters hid my car, they also kept me from seeing anything. Which meant I had no choice but to tuck my hair into the hat and climb out of my car through an eight-inch opening. That was all I could manage, thanks to steel's unwillingness to yield. I positioned myself between the green metal of the Dumpster and the red metal of my car, a spot that afforded me a decent view of the storage facility's entrance.

I watched and waited, quickly learning that there's a good reason why most people don't wear wool hats in June. Or crouch for long periods of time. Especially near large quantities of fermenting garbage.

Note to self, I thought grimly. From now on, avoid choosing Dumpsters as hiding places.

It didn't take me long to figure out that lurking in the dark was also incredibly boring. I couldn't even turn on my car radio, since the whole point of being there was to remain undiscovered. Besides, I wanted to be sure I could hear any unusual sounds—for example, the sound of someone sneaking up on me.

After nearly an hour of entertaining myself by trying to remember every word of anything I'd ever memorized in my life—including the preamble of the United States Constitution, Lincoln's Gettysburg Address, and the Robert Frost poem "Stopping by Woods on a Snowy Evening"—I was beginning to wonder if it was time to pack up and go home. I knew that meant coming back for more of the same the following night. But at the moment, the prospect of cool sheets and a warm boyfriend sounded pretty darned alluring.

In fact, I was just about to give up when the yellow-ish beams of a pair of headlights suddenly lit up the night. Someone was driving into the parking lot.

My heart began to pound as I saw it was a truck. Not a big truck, but one big enough to carry, oh, say, cages or tanks filled with animals. Including illegal ones.

It was also unmarked.

There are a hundred reasons why that truck could be here, I reminded myself. You don't even know if it's going to stop in front of the unit that Donald Drayton rents—that is, assuming Drayton really *does* rent space here, and...

I hadn't even had a chance to spell out all the reasons why I may have been wasting my time by coming all this way, not to mention getting sore leg muscles and probably destroying my sense of smell, when the truck pulled up to the row of storage units one up from where I was crouching.

Which meant it was time for me to come out of hiding.

Thank goodness I was dressed in black, I thought. My heart began to beat even faster as I contemplated sprinting away from my secure spot behind the Dumpster—kind of my second home by this point—and finding someplace new, like a doorway or at least a shadowy corner.

I stood up and jiggled around for a couple of seconds, trying to work the kinks out of my muscles. As I did, I struggled to spot a new post, wishing that last year's Christmas list had included a pair of night-vision goggles. Even though nothing very promising jumped out at me, I realized that I could at least move to the edge of the building where the truck had stopped.

Making the short trip was pretty easy, since it basically required nothing more than sprinting from one side of the asphalt strip to the other. By the time I did, the truck had backed up in front of the door of Unit 59, which meant its occupants were getting ready to either load or unload. I crouched down again, telling myself to be glad that at least this time the air smelled just fine. Besides, my new hangout on the side of the long building, near the front, gave me an excellent view.

Whoever's inside that truck might be here to stock up on big bags of dog food—or birdseed, I reminded myself as I watched two brawny men climb out of the cabin and open up the back of the vehicle. Not to mention a million other things that someone might be inclined to stow in a self-storage facility.

I watched the men head toward the door of the unit. One of them pulled a folded piece of paper out of his jeans pocket and checked it in the dim light.

"Okay, we're gonna have to do this by the numbers," he said in a gruff voice colored by a thick Brooklyn accent. "Unless you can pick out a—what's this say, a giant African snail?"

The other man snorted. "Yeah, like who'd want somethin' like that around the house?"

"I dunno," the first man replied. "Maybe they taste good."

Guffawing loudly over their clever repartee, they unlocked the door, opened it by pushing it upward, hit a light switch on the wall, and disappeared inside the storage unit.

I was right! I thought excitedly. This *is* where Drayton stores part of his inventory—inventory that consists of illegal animals.

Now I need a way to prove it.

I told myself that all I had to do was convince the cops that Unit 59 at Norfolk Self-Storage was worth investigating so that they'd obtain a search warrant and see for themselves what was stored inside. Then, all they'd have to do was get hold of the rental agreement. I would bet anything that either Drayton himself or someone who worked for him had signed it.

The next step, identifying Drayton as Erin's murderer, was a little trickier. But that was where the break-in at my cottage—and the calling card he'd left behind—would come in handy.

The good news was that I was finished here. All I had to do was get myself out without being spotted.

I was looking back at the Dumpster longingly, wondering if I should make a mad dash toward it or simply wait until the men were gone, when I heard their voices once again. Peering around the side of the building, I saw that one of them was hauling a large wooden crate. The other was carrying a glass tank.

"Creepy, huh?" the man who'd been in charge of the list commented. "I like the cute fuzzy ones much better."

"Yeah, except the ones with the teeth," his buddy

replied as they stashed their first load in back of the truck.

"Hey, Paul, y'ready for a cigarette break?" the list-checker asked.

"Good idea, Fred, but we better do that outside," Paul replied. "We don't want to smoke around all the nice little animals, do we?"

"Right," Fred replied. "I'd hate to have to tell the boss that we damaged the merchandise."

Just a minute or so earlier, I'd been ready to hightail it out of there. But I realized that I'd just been presented with a golden opportunity. Not only had I been given the chance to see for myself exactly what was inside Unit 59, I could photograph it with the digital camera I'd brought along, which would provide me with exactly what I needed to interest the police.

Still hiding at the side of the building, I waited and watched. The men flicked off the light inside the storage area, then took a little stroll as they lit up—fortunately, in the opposite direction. Once they stopped and were standing with their backs to me, I stole through the shadows, toward the gaping door.

Let's hear it for rubber soles, I thought as I ducked inside the storage facility, relieved that I'd managed to make tracks without making a sound.

Even in the dim light from the street lamps outside, I could see that the storage unit was filled with wooden crates that were identical to the one I'd just seen the two men load onto the truck. Each one was stenciled with a number in black, which I figured was how Paul and his sidekick, Fred, were able to locate the specimens on their list.

Since I wanted to get out of there as fast as I could, I decided to focus on taking the photos I needed. I quickly flipped open the lid of the first crate in my path, snapped on my flashlight, and directed the beam toward the bottom. What I saw was what looked like a bunch of rubber hoses that someone hadn't bothered to coil up very neatly.

"Argh!" I cried as I realized I was staring at a cluster of snakes, their writhing bodies intertwined.

I've always been embarrassed by my horror of snakes, even though it's out of my control. After all, animals are my business, not to mention my life. But this wasn't the time to consider whether I should have chosen a different career path. Not with Paul and Fred's cigarettes getting shorter and shorter with each passing second.

I pulled my camera out of my pocket, no easy feat given the way my hands were shaking. I'd barely had a chance to think about how I was going to deal with the flash when I heard footsteps.

"Great," I muttered under my breath.

I switched off the flashlight, only vaguely aware that I'd broken into a cold sweat. Those footsteps certainly didn't sound as if they belonged to the two burly guys sharing a Marlboro moment. They were much lighter. Faster too.

But that didn't exactly make the arrival of someone else on the scene good news.

I was still agonizing over who they might belong to when I noticed they'd stopped. Instead, I heard a loud grating sound, then a thump.

It had suddenly gotten strangely dark.

Glancing up, I saw that the reason was that someone had closed the door of the storage unit.

I was trapped.

My stomach instantly knotted and I couldn't swallow. I knew I had no time to lose. I grabbed my cell phone out of my pocket, hit a few buttons, and dropped it back where it came from.

Even though I was gripped with fear, the feeling was nothing compared to how I felt when a shadow in front of me moved. Which meant that whoever had locked me in here had locked himself in with me.

Drayton? I thought, panicking. Does he know I'm here?

I'd barely formed the question in my mind when I heard a cold, metallic click. One that sounded like the cocking of a gun.

Apparently he does, I thought.

I instinctively turned in an attempt to get away. As I did, I bumped into the wooden crate, knocking it to the floor.

At that moment, an overhead light switched on. I glanced up, expecting to see Donald Drayton standing a few feet away, holding a gun.

Instead, I found myself looking at Darla Drayton holding a gun.

"*Darla?*" I cried, unable to conceal my astonishment.

"That's right," she replied. "Turns out there's a lot more to me than good looks!"

I could see her eyes flashing angrily behind thick smears of blue eye shadow and long, spiky eyelashes. The heels on her black shoes were equally spiky, so high and so pointed they could have been used to build the railroad. A slinky blue wrap dress clung to her curves, both the real ones and the biologically engineered ones. The latter were further emphasized by the deeply cut V-shaped neckline.

My mind raced as I tried to come up with a way of removing myself from her line of fire—literally. The obvious way to escape was to distract her long enough to run. But I didn't have a lot of options in the distracting department. I wished I had the nerve to pick up one of the writhing snakes beside me and hurl it at her. But as much as I hate to admit it, I couldn't bring myself to do it—even though at the moment overcoming my fear of snakes appeared to be a matter of life or death.

Fortunately, these vipers had some plans of their own. Plans that apparently consisted of trying to make a quick getaway.

One of them—the longest, thickest, creepiest one—suddenly began slithering toward the door. It was probably only a coincidence that Darla Drayton happened to be standing directly in his path, but I wasn't about to complain.

"Oooh," she cried, stepping away as quickly as her expensive stiletto heels would allow. "I hate snakes! Snakeskin is an entirely different matter, of course, but—hey! Where do you think you're going?"

I'd turned ever so slightly, figuring that I'd take my chances by flinging myself behind some crates and trying to make my way toward the door. I just assumed she was as deathly afraid of snakes as I am.

But not only did Darla not share my ophidiophobia; she was apparently one fashion plate who was as sharp as plate glass. She'd noticed that I was about to copy the snake by breaking for freedom, and she clearly wasn't about to let that happen.

She took a step closer to me, which also put the gun she had pointed at me a step closer. That made it pretty close. Too close.

Since Plan A—escape—didn't seem to be working, I decided to try Plan B: divert her attention. I figured that if I could get her talking, she might become distracted enough that I'd spot a way to revert to Plan A, and escape. Even if that didn't quite work, I could still buy myself some time.

"It looks like you've got me cornered," I said, hoping that would turn out to be a good conversation starter.

She tossed her head triumphantly. "I'm not the bimbo everything thinks I am."

"I never thought that!"

"Sure you did. Everybody does, just the way they all assume I married Donny for his money."

Right on both counts, I thought. But this wasn't exactly the best time to play True Confessions.

"Actually, I'd say you're a pretty smart cookie," I told her. "So smart that you managed to kill Erin Walsh without anybody figuring it out."

"I had no choice!" Darla insisted. "If she'd gone to the police, she would have ruined everything!" She laughed bitterly. "Do you believe that when my wimp of a husband realized she knew what was going on, he was ready to skip the country? Either that or hire the best damn defense attorney he could find to try to get him out of it.

"But I knew better than to leave our fate up to some stupid lawyer. And I certainly didn't want to go live in some dumb country full of foreigners. My house is here, my friends are here ... for heaven's sake, all the best shopping is here!

"Don't you see?" she continued, her voice becoming more and more high-pitched. "Everything was at risk! Do you really think that the reason I had these boobs installed and haven't let myself eat more than twenty-five grams of carbs a day for more than two years is for my health? No way! I did it all so I could land myself a rich husband. And it worked! I wasn't about to give all that up for a life of disgrace. The last thing I wanted was to see myself on the eleven o'clock news. Not when those TV cameras make everybody look at least ten pounds heavier!"

"Of course you didn't want that!" I cried, doing my best to sound sympathetic. "And the plan you hatched was brilliant."

She screwed up her face, as if she was thinking really, really hard. "It was, wasn't it?" she finally said, her scowl melting into a smile.

"But how did you find out that Erin knew about Donny's, uh, sideline? And how did you ever manage to commit the perfect crime?"

"It's a long story," she warned.

"That's okay," I assured her. "I've got time." At least I hoped I did.

"Let's see." She took a deep breath, rolling her eyes upward as if trying to cheat off a crib sheet that she'd craftily hidden on the ceiling. "About three weeks ago, back when I thought everything was moving along as smooth as always, I stopped over at Ben and Erin's to drop off something for Donny. A bunch of papers that had something to do with the store." She sniffed impatiently. "Do I look like a UPS delivery guy?"

Not unless they've started arming them, I thought.

"Anyway," she continued, "when I got to the house, I rang the bell a bunch of times, but nobody answered. I wasn't about to make a *second* trip all the way to Bay Village, so I walked around back to see if there was somebody in the kitchen who could let me in. Erin was outside on the deck, talking on her cell phone.

"I stood there for a few seconds, just minding my own business, waiting for her to get off her frigging phone. I guess she didn't realize I was there though. And I figured maybe that wasn't such a bad thing, since while I was waiting, I could overhear what she was saying. And it didn't take me long to realize it was pretty interesting stuff.

"She was talking to somebody named Walter, and from what she said, I knew she'd figured out what Donny's real business was. She told this Walter guy she was about to go to the authorities and spill her guts—and that she didn't care what happened to Ben as a result.

"Well, as soon as I heard that, of course I knew I had to do something about it. I also knew I had to do it fast, since she sounded like she meant business. So I got her to invite Donny and me over to their house for dinner a couple of nights later. And I made a point of bringing a little something with me besides a nice French cabernet—a fat yellow scorpion, or whatever that disgusting creature is called."

"They're so dangerous!" I interjected, trying to sound impressed. "How did you manage to handle it?"

"I carried it around in this darling patent-leather clutch bag with a fourteen-carat gold clasp," she informed me. "Kate Spade. It's the kind of purse that goes with everything.

"Anyway," she continued, "before we sat down to dinner, I told Erin I had to go to the little girls' room."

I was horrified by the thought that one of my favorite ploys had been used by such a despicable creature.

"But instead of going to that horribly decorated dungeon of a bathroom—have you seen it? It's done in black and silver, like what were they thinking?—I sneaked into the master bedroom," Darla went on. "Inside the closet, I found this ratty raincoat that Erin's always wearing. Not only is it so last year, it's actually fraying around the sleeves. Personally, I wouldn't be caught dead in something like that."

I thought of the sorry state of my underwear. I hoped I wasn't about to be caught dead in it.

"I wasn't sure if it was the best place to put my fat yellow friend," Darla said breezily, "but before I had a chance to look for something else, I heard Erin coming. So I just slipped it into the pocket. Frankly, I was glad to be rid of the thing, since it totally gave me the creeps.

"When Erin showed up about two seconds later, I

pretended I'd gotten lost. I even made a joke about how big her house was. I said it was almost as big as ours. She didn't laugh. But aside from the fact that she never appreciated how clever I am, it didn't take me long to realize that she figured out that something funny was going on, because as soon as the four of us sat down to dinner, she started talking about you, of all people."

"Me?" I squawked.

"That's right," Darla insisted. "Before she'd even served that yucky cold potato soup that everybody pretends is such a big deal, she started yapping away about her old pal Jessie Popper. She said that she'd heard that somebody Ben and her had gone to vet school with—that's you—had done this really amazing job of investigating a few murders. She said it was something you'd done on your own, for fun or something. She kept saying you were really good at it too. That absolutely nothing gets past you. From the way she was talking—and the funny looks she kept giving me—I knew she knew that I knew what she knew." She stopped and scrunched up her face. "Did you follow that?"

"As a matter of fact, I did," I told her.

"After all that, of course I was anxious to know if the yellow scorpion had worked its magic and gotten rid of that busybody. I couldn't resist finding out. So the next morning, I got up really early to do a stakeout. That's what they call it when you sit outside somebody's house to see if they're wearing a completely out-of-style raincoat with a poison scorpion in the pocket, right?"

"I believe that's the correct term," I said, even though my mouth was dry.

"I got there early, because I knew she had a long commute and so she probably left the house before the sun comes up. I didn't have to wait long before I saw her come out of the house. She was wearing the raincoat, all right. She was also talking on her cell phone, which made me kind of nervous. I mean, I couldn't imagine who she'd be calling at that hour."

Me, I thought grimly.

"But she got in the car and started driving, acting as if nothing was wrong even though there was this thing in her coat pocket. So naturally I followed her. Everything seemed normal, until she'd driven a few miles. All of a sudden, she started driving erotically."

"Uh, I think you mean erratically," I corrected her.

"Isn't that what I said?" she asked, looking surprised. "Anyway, I figured the reason she was driving crazy was that the scorpion was biting her over and over again."

Stinging her, I thought. But I figured I'd already corrected the woman who was holding a gun on me enough times.

"Finally, when we'd reached Pohasset, she turned down a residential street, probably to keep from having an accident. She stopped the car practically in the middle of the road. I hoped that meant she'd finally bit the dust. You know, that the scorpion's poison had killed her. Instead, when I got out of my car to check, she was still alive. In fact, she was staring right at me."

Darla sighed. "At that point, I realized that the stupid scorpion was useless. It's like the old saying goes, if you want something done right, you gotta do it yourself." With a shrug, Darla added, "So I opened the car door and strangled her to death.

"It was still pretty early, so nobody was around. I just got back in my car and drove away." Smiling proudly, she said, "How's that? Like you said, I committed the perfect crime, didn't I?"

"You certainly did," I replied mechanically. "You're an absolute genius."

"You know it. I don't think the cops are ever going to figure it out. Donny can keep his profitable little business going, and I can keep on enjoying those profits. And in just a few more years, that annoying daughter of his will be going off to college."

With a little shrug, she concluded, "Which is why I have to take you out of the picture."

"But this has nothing to do with me!" I insisted. "It's not as if I'm going to tell anybody."

Darla snorted. "Yeah, right. Like I trust you. Remember, Erin told me herself how you go around solving crimes all the time. The last thing I need is you turning me in for killing her—and turning in Donny for importing a few animals that some tree-huggers put on some stupid list."

"I have no intention of doing that," I insisted. "You have my word." Once again I took a step forward, figuring that gaining even a few feet would at least get me that much closer to the door.

"Hold on there!" she cried, pointing the gun at me with renewed fervor.

"You're not really going to shoot me, are you?" I

tried to sound friendly, as well as a little surprised. After all, we'd been having such a nice little chat.

"I have to," she replied. "You know too much." She thought for a few seconds, then added, "In fact, you know everything."

Right, I thought. Because you just told me.

I did some quick thinking. "I understand completely, Darla. But you're too smart to shoot me in here, right?"

My question clearly caught her off guard. She lowered the gun an inch or so, which I took as a sign that she was weakening. "Why wouldn't I?"

"First of all, because those two guys outside will know exactly what happened."

"I can trust Paul and Fred," she said. But the way her voice wavered told me she wasn't quite sure how much. "Besides, I sent them away. I told them to get us all coffee. Decaf, since it's so late."

"That was clever," I said. "But you'll still have a major problem: a body to dispose of." *My* body, I thought, trying not to dwell on the image of me lying among the crates. *And* the snakes. "You'll also have bloodstains and . . . and fingerprints and other kinds of evidence, all in this enclosed space."

The way her face clouded told me that what I was saying made sense to her.

"You'd be much better off doing it outside," I told her. "In fact, I know the perfect spot."

I felt as if I was trying to come up with the best place for my pal Darla and me to go shoe shopping.

"There are a couple of huge Dumpsters outside," I went on. "They're in the back corner of the parking lot." I wondered if I should add that one of them was really smelly, then figured she wouldn't necessarily see that as a plus. "The Dumpster company will probably be picking them up soon, which means everything inside them will just vanish, never to be seen again."

"I see your point," she said.

At least *something's* going right for me, I thought.

She pondered my idea for a few seconds, then took a step sideways and hit a big plastic button on the wall. The garage door immediately started to open.

"Okay," she said, gesturing toward the opening with her gun. "Outside. And no screaming."

"There's no one around to hear me anyway," I pointed out as I headed outside.

"I almost forgot—put your hands on your head!" she demanded.

I complied, fully aware that Darla was just a few steps behind me. So was her gun.

And then, as I was just a couple of feet away from the doorway, I heard a familiar voice command, "Go get 'er!"

It was followed by the most beautiful sound in the world.

A snarl.

Not Darla's either. This snarl was much deeper and more heartfelt than even a woman with a chest made of silicon would be capable of producing. In fact, it was a sound that could only be made by a muscular German shepherd who's really ticked off.

I watched Skittles leap out of the darkness, thrust her mighty paws against Darla's balloonlike chest, and clamp her powerful jaws around the very arm the woman was using to fend the animal off.

Darla let out a shriek as she tumbled to the ground, causing her wraparound dress to unwrap in a most unladylike manner. As she fell, she let go of the gun, which slid a good five or six feet across the ground.

I glanced up and saw Trooper Kieran O'Malley standing over Darla, holding a gun of his own.

"Skittles, heel!" Kieran commanded, his voice almost as deep as Skittles's growl.

The dog released Darla's arm from its jaws, then dutifully retreated to her master's side.

"Watch!" Kieran commanded.

Skittles dropped her butt to the floor and sat perfectly still, her steely gaze fixed on the woman sprawled across the ground. As for Darla, she lay pretty still herself. Her eye makeup had smeared, making her look like a raccoon with a serious hangover. Her pantyhose had a huge rip at the knee, and the spiky heel on one of her shoes had broken off.

At the moment, the trophy wife didn't exactly look like anything anyone would want to put on display.

With Skittles still looking on, her muscles tensed in case she was once again called into action, Kieran snapped a pair of handcuffs on Darla. I studied her for a few seconds, trying to imagine how she would look in an orange jumpsuit.

As Kieran helped her up off the ground, I breathlessly exclaimed, "Talk about perfect timing! Another few seconds and—well, I'm not even going to think about it."

He nodded. "I was parked down the street, just like

we planned, when your cell phone number showed up on my caller ID. Even though I knew it was your call for help, it still took me a couple of minutes to figure out where you were. This place is huge. You have Skittles to thank for that."

"I can't thank either of you enough," I told him sincerely. "I owe you. You, too, Skittles."

"Glad we could help—although I'm kind of curious about what you were doing all alone at a deserted storage facility this late at night."

"I promise to tell you the whole story," I said. "How about coming over to dinner at my place? Skittles is invited too."

"That sounds great. And, uh, maybe you could invite Suzanne over too." Kieran's tone was casual, but I could see the anxious look in his eyes. "Speaking of Suzanne, I don't suppose you've talked to her lately, have you?"

Before I had a chance to answer, he mumbled, "I sure miss her."

"I have a feeling she might be willing to give you a second chance," I said.

Glancing at his partner, who had just saved my life, I added, "I think she'll be willing to give Skittles another chance too."

Chapter 18

"Man, as we know him, is a poor creature; he is halfway between an ape and a god and he is travelling in the right direction."

—Dean Inge

There's nothing like a June wedding," Betty said with a wistful sigh, pulling back the cream-colored lace curtain and gazing outside.

I joined her at the window, carefully lifting the skirt of my long white dress as I crossed the room. Three floors below, on the green velvet lawn, a dozen rows of folding chairs fanned out from a wooden archway. The graceful structure was draped with gauzy white fabric and festooned with colorful wildflowers. Off to one side stood a large white tent that shielded the round tables draped in white linen, the stack of presents, and the three-tiered cake from the late-afternoon sun. I had to admit that while Dorothy wasn't likely to be named Mother-in-Law of the Year anytime soon, she'd done a great job as a wedding planner.

The guests who had already arrived wandered

around the estate, no doubt oohing and aahing over the gardens and grounds surrounding the charming house that 150 years earlier had been home to a prosperous sea captain. A couple of months earlier, when I'd come out to Long Island's North Fork to decide whether or not this site would make a good spot for my wedding, I'd done some serious oohing and aahing myself.

I'd known immediately that this was where I wanted my wedding to take place. The fact that it was available on such short notice sealed the deal.

At the moment, however, I wished I were anywhere but here. My stomach was in knots and my head buzzed as if I'd chugged half a gallon of espresso for breakfast.

Relax! I scolded myself. Of course you're nervous. This is a big day. One of the biggest, right up there with graduating from college and vet school, buying my clinic-on-wheels, letting Suzanne talk me into a bikini wax...

Fortunately, Betty chose that moment to take my hand and give it a squeeze. "It's going to be a perfect day, Jessica," she said. "You couldn't have asked for better weather."

"As long as those rain clouds don't come back," Dorothy grumbled. "When I woke up this morning and looked out the window, I figured we'd all end up wearing waterproof ponchos at the ceremony."

The woman who was about to become my mother-in-law peered over her shoulder at the free-standing Victorian mirror in the corner and frowned. "Does this dress make my rear end look big?"

Your rear end *is* big, I thought. And that awful blue-gray dress—which gives new meaning to the word *matronly*—doesn't do a thing to hide it.

But I had a feeling she wasn't looking for an honest answer.

"You look lovely, Dorothy," I told her. "You, too, Betty."

At least the second part wasn't a lie. While I'd half-expected Betty to show up for my wedding dressed in some flamboyant outfit—one with feathers, perhaps, or a dress that incorporated several different colors of the rainbow—she looked positively regal in her pale yellow silk dress with a matching jacket. It was the perfect ensemble for a maid of honor.

"You look nice, too, Jessie," Dorothy said begrudgingly. "In fact, you actually look pretty!"

"You mean she looks even prettier than usual," Betty corrected her, smiling. "Dorothy is right, Jessica. You're positively radiant."

Panic will do that to a person, I thought. Flushed cheeks, bright eyes, that special glow that can only come from an overabundance of adrenaline coursing through one's veins . . .

Yet once I finally dared to check the mirror, I saw that she was right. I did look nice, whatever the reason. Of course, the fact that Suzanne had spent the entire morning working on me didn't hurt. She'd twisted my hair into an elaborate up-do, leaving a few loose strands to frame my face. She'd done an expert job with makeup, too, the result being that I didn't look as if I was wearing any. I looked like my regular self, only better.

As for my dress, it was nothing short of fabulous. Gabriella Bertucci, one of Long Island's premier fashion designers, had created an empire-style dress that was simple yet amazingly flattering. The ivory silk was just creamy enough to keep me from looking like the mansion's resident ghost. Since I'm not the veil type, I'd opted to wear a cluster of white flowers in my hair.

Betty came up behind me and gazed at my reflection. Sighing, she said, "I wish your parents were here to see you."

"*You're* here," I replied, turning around to give her a hug.

The tender moment was interrupted by Suzanne barging into the room, huffing and puffing from having just dashed up two flights of stairs without stopping. In high heels, no less.

"I hope we're running on schedule," she declared, standing in the doorway as she struggled to catch her breath. "If not, we're going to have a lot of unhappy campers to deal with. Do you believe this crowd has already gone through more than half the champagne?"

"I told you we should wait until after the ceremony to open the champagne," Dorothy said with a haughty toss of her head.

"Nonsense," Suzanne insisted. She stalked across the room, placed her hands on her hips, and stood nose to nose with Dorothy. "Some of these people just drove for three hours to get here. What kind of hostess doesn't offer her guests something to drink the moment they show up?"

Dorothy didn't even flinch. "It didn't have to be

champagne," she sniffed. "What's wrong with lemon-ade?"

"You've obviously never driven on the Long Island Expressway in weekend traffic," Suzanne replied, glowering.

"I certainly have," Dorothy retorted. "Even though I don't live on Long Island any more, I'm certainly aware of—"

"Ladies!" Betty cried. "We're putting on a wedding here, not a boxing match!"

Dorothy and Suzanne both looked surprised by Betty's outburst. But I noticed that neither of them looked contrite, since each one was completely convinced she was right.

"I'm glad we're putting all that champagne to good use," I said. I realized I was taking a risk by siding with my bridesmaid, but I wanted to do my best to make sure no one at my wedding suffered any bodily harm. "It was very generous of Winston to provide it. And Suzanne, I really appreciate you making my guests feel welcome."

Suzanne cast Dorothy a look of triumph, then said, "It's Kieran you should thank. He's been doing a fabulous job of greeting everyone." Smiling dreamily, she added, "And he looks absolutely amazing. I thought he broke the cuteness barrier in that state trooper's uniform of his, but wait 'til you see him all dressed up in a suit and tie."

"I'm surprised Skittles let him out of her sight long enough for her to come to my wedding," I joked.

"Don't you dare say anything bad about Skittles!"

Suzanne shot back. "That darling dog saved your life!"

True, I thought. But don't I deserve at least a little credit for having had the foresight to arrange for a German shepherd with teeth the size of the Wicked Wolf's and training the caliber of a U.S. Marine's to be in the right place at the right time?

Still, I couldn't have been more pleased that Suzanne and Skittles had finally become friends. In fact, ever since Skittles had come through during my late-night adventure at the self-storage facility, not only with saving my life but also helping put Erin's killer behind bars, Suzanne couldn't do enough for her.

And Skittles felt the same way. In response to Suzanne's change of heart, Skittles had become equally protective of Kieran and Suzanne. Equally adoring too.

In fact, I would have invited Skittles to my wedding if I hadn't decided to limit the four-legged guest list to my own two canines. I was still shell-shocked by Frederick's Dr. Jekyll and Mr. Hyde routine on *Pet People*. At least Max and Lou had already proven themselves, at Betty and Winston's wedding. Besides, Sunny had agreed to keep an eye on them during the ceremony, and even as capable as she'd proven to be, I didn't want to give her more than she could handle.

I froze at the sound of the string quartet, which Nick and I had agreed would serve as a signal to our guests that it was time to be seated. Once that had been accomplished, the musicians had been instructed to launch into "Here Comes the Bride," which Nick had insisted had to be playing when he stood in front with the judge and watched his future wife walk down the aisle.

"It's time," Betty said, her voice a near-whisper.

As if I didn't know, I thought, gulping loudly.

At that moment, the butterflies that had been caged inside my stomach ever since I'd opened my eyes that morning began kicking up their heels.

You can do this, a voice inside my head insisted.

No, I can't! another voice shot back.

Yes, you can, the first voice repeated, more firmly this time.

The argument would have continued if it hadn't been for a sudden push from behind. Whether the hand that made firm contact with my back belonged to Betty, Dorothy, or Suzanne, I couldn't tell. But my feet started moving, an automatic response to the not-so-subtle reminder that I hadn't come all this way simply to model this gorgeous dress.

Over the next few minutes, I was so dazed that I felt as if I was dreaming. I was vaguely aware of descending two flights of stairs, with Betty and Suzanne fussing around me. They seemed afraid that I'd either trip on my dress or tear the hem.

The next thing I knew, I found myself walking down the aisle one step at a time behind Betty and Suzanne, my bridesmaids. As I did, I was struck by the similarities between a wedding and a funeral. They were both somber ceremonies with slow processions, an abundance of flowers, and ponderous music, performed in front of a crowd of well-wishers dressed in their finest clothes....

Stop! I commanded myself. You're thinking too hard. The time for debate is over. Let it go!

I forced myself to focus on Nick, who was standing at the other end of the aisle, between Winston, who was his best man, and the judge. He was wearing a tuxedo, a white boutonniere, and the biggest grin I'd ever seen.

There's Nick, I told myself, taking deep breaths. You like Nick, right? You love Nick, in fact. And that's all this is about. Demonstrating your commitment to this wonderful man.

I was suddenly having trouble breathing.

The dress is too tight, I told myself. I shouldn't have eaten such a big breakfast.

I remembered that I hadn't eaten breakfast at all.

There's not enough air in here, I thought.

Then I realized I was outdoors, with a blue sky up above and green grass beneath my feet.

By that point, I'd made it all the way to the other end of the aisle. I could feel the eyes of all my guests boring into me. Then there were Nick's eyes. True, they were warm and filled with love, but they were still fixed on me in a way I found most unnerving.

"We are gathered here today..." the judge began.

I didn't hear what he said afterward. The swishing sound that echoed through my head was much too loud. In fact, I fell into a stupor that came pretty darned close to an out-of-body experience.

I didn't snap back into the moment until I heard the judge say, "Do you, Jessica, take this man, Nicholas Burby, to be your lawfully wedded husband, to have and to hold, in sickness and in health..."

The entire planet seemed to be spinning. The planet *is* spinning, I told myself. It does that. It rotates on its axis. That's what makes day and night...or maybe that's what makes summer and winter...

Even my most basic science knowledge was eluding me.

"For better or for worse, to love and to cherish..."

The people in charge should really slow this planet down, I thought. For goodness sake, somebody's going to get hurt!

Glancing around, I saw that Betty was frowning with concern. Suzanne, meanwhile, looked as if she was about to hurt me.

Desperately I turned to Nick. He was still watching me, although at the moment, he looked pretty confused.

"...'Til death do you part?"

The judge's words cut through the swishing sound in my head with such clarity that even I couldn't block them out.

Say "I do!" I ordered myself. Say it! Just *say* it!

"Jessica?" the judge prompted.

I still wasn't sure whether I was capable of speech. But I opened my mouth, hoping for the best.

Acknowledgments

Writing this book afforded me the privilege of learning from helpful experts in a number of fields. I would like to thank Chief Technical Sergeant Timothy L. Fischer, Canine Coordinator for the New York State Police, and Dr. Roger D. Farley, Professor Emeritus, Department of Biology, University of California, Riverside, for sharing their knowledge with me.

I would also like to thank Dr. Marc A. Franz, Dr. Jennifer Mignone, Wendy Niceberg, and the entire staff of the Woodbury Animal Hospital in Woodbury, Long Island: Kim Marino, Lisa Rivera, Sharon Harker, Denise Spielman, and Diana Weiss.

And thanks to Patricia C. Wright, Professor of Anthropology at Stony Brook University and Executive Director of the Institute for the Conservation of Tropical Environments, and her students Brienne Giordano and Domonique DeLeo; Cheryl Maude, Bridget, and Toby; Lisa Pulitzer; and as always, Faith and Caitlin.

About the Author

CYNTHIA BAXTER is a native of Long Island, New York. She currently resides on the North Shore, where she is at work on the next *Reigning Cats & Dogs* mystery, which Bantam will publish in 2009. She is also the author of *Murder Packs a Suitcase*, the first mystery in a new series, on sale in November 2008. Visit her website at www.cynthiabaxter.com.

Read on for an exclusive sneak peek
at *two*
new mysteries by

Cynthia Baxter:

MURDER PACKS A SUITCASE
The First in a Brand-new Series!
On sale in November 2008

&

A New *Reigning Cats & Dogs* Mystery
On sale in Summer 2009

MURDER PACKS A SUITCASE

CYNTHIA BAXTER

author of the *Reigning Cats & Dogs Mystery series*

FLORIDA

MURDER PACKS A SUITCASE
The First in a Brand-new Series!
On sale in November 2008

After an entire afternoon of Courtney's chattiness, Mallory welcomed the silence of her hotel room. The Florida Tourism Board reception wasn't scheduled to start for a couple of hours, so she filled up nine pages with notes on the *Titanic,* then took her time showering and blow-drying her hair.

At twenty minutes to seven, she slipped into a black halter-top dress splashed with red flowers. She smiled as she remembered what David said the last time he'd seen her in it: that it made her look like one of those women in the L'Oréal ads who claimed, "I'm worth it." Then she slipped on a pair of strappy red sandals with heels that were much higher than she was used to. When she'd spotted them at Macy's, she hadn't been able to resist trying them on. When she saw how long they made her legs look, she'd had no choice but to whip out her charge card.

The final touch was makeup. She put on more than she'd bothered with in months, with the exception of her interview at *The Good Life*. It was hard to believe that it was only days earlier that she'd ridden up the elevator with butterflies in her stomach. Now here she was, standing in front of the bathroom mirror more than a thousand miles from home, agonizing over which pair of earrings looked better, the white pearls or the red chandeliers.

And enjoying every minute of the trip. In fact, she suddenly stopped what she was doing simply to marvel over how much fun she was having. And fun was something that had been in short supply since David's accident.

She understood that she'd needed time to mourn. That in fact she was still mourning. Yet she was dealing with even more than grief. She also had to cope with the feeling that everyone she loved was deserting her.

It was something that dated back before David's death. She'd spent so many years catering to the needs of her family that once they vanished, one by one, she had found herself floundering for a new way to define herself. When Amanda went off to college, she felt as if a part of her body had been cut off. But she still had David and Jordan with her at the dinner table every night. Then, when Jordan was only weeks away from going off to college, David was suddenly gone, too.

Even her son's return only a few weeks after leaving for school hadn't helped the aching in her heart. True, he was living in her house again. But he didn't belong there. He was just stopping in while he decided where to go next, like someone who was idling in a No Parking zone.

The result was a feeling of emptiness that never quite went away. At least until now. Before coming on this trip, Mallory had been afraid that being thrust into a new and unfamiliar situation would cause her to lose whatever sense of balance she still clung to. Instead, she abruptly found herself being forced to play a completely different role. And her personal life didn't matter one bit. Whether or not her children were at home, whether or not she had a husband . . . in this context, none of it was the least bit relevant. All that mattered was what Wade and Annabelle and Courtney and the others could see: that she was a travel writer working for a well-respected publication, here to do a job.

The question that kept nagging at her was whether or not she could rise to the occasion. Yet here she was, doing exactly that. She was holding her own in a situation that a lot of people would find downright intimidating. She wasn't surprised that she was managing to handle herself just fine. What did surprise her was the ease with which the old Mallory was resurfacing, pushing aside the timid, uncertain Mallory who had appeared from nowhere when David died.

Still marveling over the attractive, self-confident woman staring back at her in the mirror, she decided that tonight she would quietly celebrate her unexpected return to her old self. Surely a reception in a big, flashy hotel would include champagne or some other appropriately festive drink. She vowed to make a toast to the return of Mallory Marlowe, a woman who only hours before a virtual stranger had characterized as "spunky."

The Bali Ballroom, Mallory discovered as she teetered inside on her red high heels, had the same faux-Polynesian decor as the lobby. The walls were covered with coarse straw mats that she assumed were supposed to look as if they'd been woven in huts made of the same material. More artifacts from the South Seas dotted the walls, the usual assortment of tiki gods, masks, and weaponry. But the centerpiece was the ceiling-high waterfall, which splashed over fake rocks and then spilled into a dark pool that was surrounded by a low stone wall.

There were also signs of the festivities to come. A long table along one wall was lined with empty chafing dishes, and a small bar was tucked into one corner. Clustered around it were small round tables covered in fabric that looked very much like the bedspread in her hotel room.

As she headed in that direction, she stumbled. "Klutz," she muttered, assuming her ineptness with impractical shoes was to blame. But when she glanced down, she saw that she'd tripped on a spear.

She automatically leaned over and picked it up, figuring there was no reason for anyone else to trip on it. Besides, she'd spent half a lifetime cleaning up after other people, moving Jordan's gargantuan sneakers out of the hallway and Amanda's heavy textbooks off the dining room table.

Once she was holding it in her hands, she saw that it was made of metal, unlike the wooden spears the natives of the South Sea islands undoubtedly used to kill one another. She also noticed that it was discolored at the end. It looked as if it had been dipped in something red. Dark red.

But before she had a chance to examine it any further, the sound of a human voice—a very perturbed human voice—prompted her to turn around.

"Oh, my God. Will you *look* at those horrendous tablecloths? Whatever possessed them to use those ancient things?"

Desmond Farnaby stood in the doorway, his hands on his hips. "If I told them once, I told them a thousand times. You can't—oh, hello, Mallory."

"Hello, Desmond." Holding out the spear, she said, "It looks like this fell off the wall. You might want to—"

"Oh, my God!" he screeched, this time with considerably more vehemence. "Oh, my *God*!"

Mallory just stared at him, puzzled over what indecent thing any tablecloth could possibly have done that would cause the hotel's general manager's hands to fly to his cheeks like the child star in *Home Alone*. But something about the look of shock on his face told her it was something a lot worse than outdated fabric.

She followed his gaze to the waterfall. It was only then that she noticed something unusual protruding out of the little pond surrounding it. Something large. Something oddly shaped. Something brightly colored.

Mallory's forehead tensed as she tried to make sense of what she was looking at. And then, in a flash, she realized that Phil Diamond was floating facedown in the pool of water.

And from where she stood, he looked very, very dead.

To read more about travel-writer-turned-sleuth Mallory Marlowe, pick up your copy of Cynthia Baxter's Murder Packs a Suitcase, *on sale in November 2008. Includes Mallory's travel tips and reviews of real Florida attractions!*

A New *Reigning Cats & Dogs* Mystery
On sale in Summer 2009

"The greatest fear dogs know
is the fear that you will not come back
when you go out the door without them."
—Stanley Coren, dog psychologist

Every woman expects her wedding day to be something out of a dream. So how could I ever have anticipated that mine would turn out to be a total nightmare?

It all went as planned until I found myself standing in front of the judge. I could feel the eyes of more than a hundred guests who looked on eagerly, perching on the edges of the seats that fanned out from the wooden archway curving above my fiancé, Nick, and me.

And I pretty much appeared to be a typical bride. I wore a beautiful ivory-silk dress, and my straight, dark-blond hair had been twisted into an updo that made me more glamorous than I'd ever looked my life. With both hands, I clutched a bouquet of delicate white roses.

At the moment, I desperately hoped they hid the fact that my hands were trembling.

The reason I was having so much trouble keeping my severe case of nerves from showing was that I was still wondering if I was ever going to manage to say those fateful, life-changing words: *I do*.

As I opened my mouth, doing my best to force myself to get those two syllables out, the peaceful scene was shattered by a woman's piercing scream.

"A-a-a-ah!"

Instantly, everyone froze.

Nick turned to me, wearing a puzzled look. "Jess?" he asked questioningly.

I didn't have time to be offended that he apparently assumed the desperate cry for help was mine. The shriek sounded as if it had come from inside the three-story Victorian that was the centerpiece of the estate on Long Island's east end. A hundred fifty years earlier it had been the home of a prosperous sea captain, and just for today, it was all mine.

Maybe it's because I'm a veterinarian who's used to handling emergencies, but before I had a chance to mentally form the phrase "ruining your own wedding," I whirled around, hiked up my long skirt, and raced back down the aisle toward the house. I was only vaguely aware of the chaos erupting around me as guests rose from their seats, glancing around with worried looks.

"A-a-a-ah!" we all heard again, the horrible cry cutting through the warm June day like a bolt of lightning. "No! *No!*"

The second scream assured me I was doing the right thing. So did the fact that the groom was right behind me, racing toward the house so speedily that his tuxedo could have been made of spandex.

"It's coming from the house," I yelled to Nick over my shoulder.

"It sounds like somewhere on the first floor," he added breathlessly.

Even though I was wearing cream-colored heels, I managed to reach the front door just seconds after Nick. The two of us rushed inside, exchanging a look of concern over the unmistakable sounds of gasps and sobs.

"The kitchen!" I cried, sprinting down the hall.

I wondered if I'd be able to move faster if I kicked off my silly Barbie shoes, now that I was dealing with polished hardwood floors instead of the velvety-green grass on the back lawn. But I didn't want to waste any time. Instead, I skidded around the corner toward the kitchen doorway, not knowing what I'd find.

But I certainly didn't expect it to be a man lying completely still on the tile floor of the immense kitchen with what looked like an extremely sharp knife sticking out of his chest. And from the pallor of his skin and the dullness of his eyes, it looked as if he was dead.

I blinked. The man wasn't anyone I recognized. He didn't appear to be part of the catering staff; in fact, from the way he was dressed—a blue-and-white-striped seersucker suit, a lemon-yellow necktie, and white patent-leather loafers—I concluded that he had to be a guest. But he certainly wasn't anyone I'd told my future mother-in-law, Dorothy, to add to the list of invitees.

"Do you know who he is?" I asked Nick, my voice a near whisper.

He shook his head. "I never saw this man before in my life."

It was only at that point that I realized someone else was in the room. I studied the young woman cowering a few feet away from Nick and me, the expression on her face one of complete shock. Her shiny black hair was pulled back into a neat ponytail, and she was dressed like a penguin, leading me to the conclusion that unlike the man on the floor, she did work for the caterer.

I also assumed she was the screamer.

"What happened?" I asked her.

"I—I don't know!" She gasped. "I went downstairs to the wine cellar for about ten minutes. I guess I was the only person in the house, since it looks as if everybody else sneaked outside to watch the ceremony. We're not supposed to, but whenever it's time for the bride and groom to say 'I do,' we can't help it. Anyway, when I came upstairs just now, this is what I found!"

She paused to take a deep breath, then asked, "Do you think he's dead?"

"It looks that way," I replied gently.

Her expression still stricken, she pulled a cell phone out of the pocket of the tailored black pants she wore under a crisp white apron emblazoned with the caterer's logo. As she punched in three numbers, she stepped away to a back corner of the kitchen. That left Nick and me with the unfortunate dead man.

"Who *is* he?" I asked, my head spinning as I tried to make sense out of what I was seeing. "I don't think he's affiliated with the estate, since when I booked it someone would have mentioned that he'd—"

I never finished my sentence because I'd just become aware of the sound of rubbery heels, the kind that are attached to practical shoes, squishing against the tile floor behind us.

Which meant my mother-in-law had joined us.

"What's going on in here?" Dorothy Burby demanded. Smoothing the fabric of the drab, ill-fitting blue-gray dress she'd chosen to wear on this lovely June day on which her son was getting married, she added, "For goodness' sake, Jessica, you can't just leave your guests sitting out there in the hot sun! This is supposed to be a wedding, so I don't understand why—"

She gasped, then slapped her hands against her cheeks.

"Good heavens!" she cried. "What happened to Cousin Nathaniel?"

"Cousin Nathaniel?" Nick and I repeated in unison.

"That's right." Dorothy fumbled inside the oversized black purse cutting into her shoulder and pulled out a pair of what I assumed were reading glasses. She planted them at the end of her nose, then leaned over the poor man's body and peered closely at his face.

"That's Cousin Nathaniel, all right," she declared. Sighing loudly, she said, "I'm the one who invited him. I had to. He's family."

"You mean I'm related to this guy?" Nick asked, amazed.

"Of course." Dorothy sniffed. "He's Ruthie's son. You know, Gladys's sister's boy."

From the confused look on Nick's face, he didn't know any more about who Ruthie or Gladys was than he did about the man I'd just started thinking of as "poor Cousin Nathaniel."

"But I never expected that he'd actually show up," Dorothy added.

I bet he wishes he hadn't, I thought grimly.

It was at that point that I realized it would have been more appropriate for me to use the past tense when referring to poor Cousin Nathaniel.

"I'll be darned," Dorothy went on, shaking her head in wonderment. "He looks good. I mean, better than I would have expected. I haven't seen him in—I don't even know how long it's been. But it's so like Ruthie's family to ruin somebody's wedding. I bet the cheap so-and-so didn't even bother to bring a present!"

The fact that this particular guest might not have increased my ever-growing collection of small appliances even further didn't seem to matter much, given the fact that he wouldn't even be around to eat a piece of wedding cake.

Actually, thinking about my wedding suddenly seemed selfish. There were too many other questions to ask right now. But before I had a chance to ask even one of them, people began rushing at us from all directions. The rest of the catering staff crowded into the room first. Only seconds afterward the guests began streaming inside, their furrowed foreheads and clouded eyes completely out of sync with the bright flowered sundresses and pastel-colored sport shirts they wore.

I was about to tell them all to calm down and to back away from what I was beginning to realize was a crime scene when Dorothy grabbed my arm. She yanked me over to a granite counter covered with silver trays with tiny quiches and scallops wrapped in bacon.

"Will you look at this?' she hissed in my ear. "It started already, and the cops haven't even gotten here yet!"

"*What* started already?" I asked. Not only was I completely bewildered, I could practically feel a black-and-blue mark forming where Dorothy's fingers were clamped around my flesh.

"The—the chaos, of course!" she sputtered. "The craziness. And the newspapers and TV stations haven't even gotten wind of this yet!"

"I can imagine how you must feel," I said sympathetically. "Losing a relative in such a horrible way, even though it sounds as if you hardly knew him—"

"I was thinking of how bad this looks," she interrupted. "I mean, what kind of people have murders going on in their own families? Certainly not respectable people!"

I was dumbfounded. But when it came to dealing with the mother of the man I love, I always trod carefully.

"I can see why you're upset," I said.

"Of course I'm upset!" she spat back. "This is completely unacceptable, and I want it to go away as quickly as possible. And as *quietly* as possible. Which is why you have to do something about this, Jessica."

"*Me?*" I squawked. "What do you want *me* to do?"

"Find out who did this disgusting thing, of course!"

"Excuse me?"

"Solve the murder!" Dorothy insisted shrilly. "Find out who killed poor Cousin Nathaniel as fast as you can so we can all move on! That *is* what you do, isn't it? When you're not doing that—that *job* of yours, riding around in that ridiculous bus treating cats and dogs and Lord only knows what else. Solving crimes is your hobby, isn't it? You do it the way some people do needlepoint or—or collect porcelain dolls or Wedgwood."

It was hard to imagine putting solving murders and displaying dolls in the same category. Then again, this wasn't the first time Dorothy and I failed to see things in the same way.

"Solving homicide cases is the police department's job," I pointed out.

"Hmph!" With a toss of her head, she said, "Who knows how competent *they* are?"

"It's true that in the past, I've gotten involved in solving a few crimes." I was doing my best to remain calm—and diplomatic. "But it's not exactly what you'd call a hobby. In fact, it's—"

"Yes, but it's something you're good at, isn't it?" she persisted. "You have, shall we say, a knack for it. The way *I* happen to be good with people."

I wasn't going to touch *that* one with a ten-foot pole.

"I understand that you're upset," I said, trying a different tack. "And of course you're concerned. Anyone would be. But that doesn't mean—"

"Jessica, I've made up my mind," Dorothy said firmly. "You're going to solve this crime. After all, what else do you have to do with all your free time?"